Z

Ambiguous
Love

2023

Keep watch for more erotic novels from Z.M. Alcock, cumming soon...

Dedication

With this book, I am first and foremost going to thank my team. I never could have gotten to where I am today without the hard work and dedication I received from the various members assisting me on this endeavor. First off; Jeanie Creech at Creech Enterprises. Without her guiding hand, my work would have gone nowhere. Secondly, Mindful Virtual Assistance both Mikayla and Erin, I so appreciated your patience with me as well as your diligence. Kimberly Sue Iverson, your kindness and willingness to help was so refreshing and did not go unappreciated. Lastly to my family and friends, who kept me motivated and supported me through the whole process, a big and heartfelt, Thank you.

Author Forward

February 16, 2023

    So . . . I wrote this book on a whim. I had no plans for it, no idea where it would lead. I left it up to my dreams to decide and then allowed my fingers to translate it onto paper so I could share it with the world. If it seems a little amateur, that is entirely because it is. This is my first ever attempt at writing aside from projects in grade school. I had a passion as a kid for writing, and let life get in my way. I am now in the process of rediscovering myself and releasing the creative side of me I left forgotten for so many years. I hope to inspire others to do the same.

    Your life is your own story, write it how you want it.

Ambiguous
Love

| Chapter 1 |

Tree after tree whipped by, all a perpetual blur. I barely noticed the opposing traffic zooming past. I was on autopilot. I did this quite often whilst driving, as much as I hate to admit it. I got lost in my thoughts and zone out almost completely. I hadn't committed any violations that I had been made aware of. I considered myself a fairly safe driver, no tickets, no warnings, and no accidents thus far in my 16 years of driving. Those were the things I told myself, trying to rule out my guilt for not being able to just focus on the road. Long, daunting drives were just so dull and mindless.

On this particular cruise, I was headed to Kelowna, one of the neighboring larger cities to my hometown of Salmon Arm. I was enroute to pick up a girlfriend from the airport. Erika, my best friend, had been traveling abroad for the past year. I had regretfully not accompanied her due to my loathsome and unrelenting commitment to my responsibilities at home. Work, bills, family, etc.

I had three kids, an estranged husband, soon to be divorced. I worked as a nurse at the local hospital and just couldn't fathom leaving my kids for that long, or my job. It was one thing to take maternity leave for a year, but completely another to leave and go around the world. I'd worked hard to gain my seniority and earn my position; I wasn't about to give that up, even if it meant finally getting to see the world. I knew how completely insane that likely sounded to most people.

I groaned as I palmed my forehead and ran my fingers back through my dark auburn hair. Why? Why do I do these things to myself? Give up amazing opportunities just to live a droll and average life? Maybe had I considered it more, I could have convinced my ex to allow the kids to come with me? I chortled beneath my breath. Who was I kidding? Like THAT would ever happen!

My ex was a control freak. He didn't have a spontaneous bone in his body. He had to have a plan laid out and discussed for every moment of every day. The very thought of me pitching the idea of taking even one of our children, let alone all three, on an uncharted adventure, would literally make his skin crawl. A smirk crossed my lips. I did gather some sick satisfaction from the thought of it. I always found it absurd that the very idea of me or the kids having any sort of real freedom brought him such discomfort. He never appeared to be an insecure man, quite the latter actually. He seemed almost vain.

I saw Chad check out his appearance in any reflection he could find. I also noticed the vast number of flirtatious eyes he gave to other women and even my co-workers, or there were even the plenty of times I'd caught him manicuring himself to perfection over the years. I had so many hints right from the beginning that this man wasn't right for me, and yet I ignored them all. I had this notion, this deep seeded need for my first to be my last. That happily ever after bit, like in all the childhood fairytales.

I'd grown up on a farm. To me, a man should be hard working, always have an inch of dirt embedded under his nails, and a layer of dried sweat on his brow. But I knew times had changed; things were less laborsome these days and more technical. A man rarely got his hands dirty anymore unless he happened to be one of the few that landed a job in one of the labor fields.

Chad was not one of those men. Obviously, he was good looking, that was what initially attracted me to him. He had a great smile, and I had a weakness for nice smiles. He had tan skin, chestnut hair, gray eyes, a muscular physique. He could also be quite charming, and his height made most women gaga. He was the epitome of that tall, dark and handsome character you find in most romantic novels.

Chad had originally caught my eye in high school. He was a year older than me, but we hung out in the same crowd. I was more the tom boy type and he was the popular one. It took us a while to actually connect with one another, just due to the fact that our personalities were so different. He dated a lot! Whereas I didn't date really at all. If I dated, it was more like holding a boy's hand for a day and then realizing we weren't compatible and breaking up the following day, or even the following period. Chad, on the other hand, made it his mission to "test drive" as many chicks as he could those first few years of high school, before they all realized he was just a player and lost interest. It was just by fluke that Chad and I ended up together.

As I stated before, we were complete opposites, but we had a few similar friends, and over time we became friends ourselves. Chad made me discover my girlier side. I pushed him to be nicer and more respectable to girls. I didn't put up with his bullshit and called him out when he was being a douche. We, in that sense, made a good match and had a lot of fun together. We remained together the remainder of high school.

I lost my virginity to him a day before my eighteenth birthday, and we went to college together. I went to TRU for nursing, and he studied for a business degree and took coding classes. I barely understood the basics of computers, only enough to get me through day-to-day life and work. I never understood his talks about what projects he was working on, on the odd occasion when he wasn't partying. We both did our own things and then would meet up in the nights to be intimate and unwind. We had different dorms, but quite often still spent the night together. Two months before my graduation, I found out I was pregnant.

Looking back, I wished I'd done things differently, explored more, lived more. But then I wouldn't have my three reasons for living. My kids were my everything. Aeda 12, Austin 9 and Everley 5.

Aeda was my double for sure, but as most children are, she was definitely an upgrade from the original version. She was so mature and maternal, she doted on Everley as if she were her own. She had a great head on her shoulders, and I considered myself super blessed to have a kid as grounded and level headed as her.

Austin was quiet and thoughtful. He observed and took everything in, speculated his surroundings, and thoughtfully assessed before he said anything. His slender build was quite different from both mine and Chad's builds, but he shared his father's chestnut locks and gray eyes.

Everley was my little firecracker. She had my olive skin and pouty lips, but her big round doughy brown eyes were all her own. She could melt ice with those eyes, and she knew it! Her long lashes would bat at you, and you'd feel your anger ebb away. She had a way about her though. She was feisty and loved to argue sheepishly, catch you off guard and make you eat your words. Then she'd smile devilishly and cackle. Her temper could set you aflame if not extinguished quickly. She quite often got away with murder, and she was well aware of it and used it to her full advantage. I'm lucky she was as sweet as she was frisky though. Otherwise, I'd have been in far worse off shape than I was.

The five of us managed for quite a few years, but as time went on, the lack of understanding and lust between Chad and me, and the feelings of blame for stealing each other's youth, is what pulled us apart. It wasn't sexy coming home to the house destroyed and him glued to his computer screen, while the kids roared around. Aeda did her best to contain things, but Everley was a handful, and had enough energy for a preschool class of children. Austin would be so overstimulated he wouldn't want to sleep, and it was causing issues at school. I was working twelve hour shifts and wasn't getting any help at home. Chad left all the kids' stuff up to me, but then he also had to have a play by play of our daily activities. It was day in and day out, every week the same shit. I was stretched so thin, and my sanity was dwindling.

We had our last raging fight six months ago, and that was the one when I screamed, I wanted a divorce. Since then, there were many more arguments and full-fledged fights, name calling, caddy remarks and insults, all as out of earshot from the kids as possible. But I'm no dummy, I knew they knew and heard what was going on. I just hoped they could see things would eventually be better off, that we would all be happier. We broke the news to them together, and there were tears and anger. We both took some blame. I hated seeing their lives so disrupted by my decision. It was heart-wrenching.

I sighed and quickly glanced at the clock. I'd left early thinking I'd do some shopping prior to Erika's flight landing. I hadn't anticipated her flight being delayed by several hours. I'd gotten the text when I stopped for gas in Vernon. Erika apologetically explained that some bad weather had rolled in, and the airline decided it was best to wait it out. Oh well, I'd have a few more hours to kill. I rarely ever went shopping in Kelowna, so I was sure I could make a day of it.

Erika Crane was my very best friend. We met in grade-school and had been linked at the hip ever since. She was outspoken and fearless. I loved her bravery to say whatever she thought. We always had a good time together. We'd laugh and laugh, and not just normal playful laughter. I'm talking gut rolling with a side of drool laughter. The kind that makes your face hurt because you're smiling so hard and gasping for breaths between laughs. I'd missed her this past year.

I always wondered if she hadn't been gone, and I'd had my usual comic relief with our weekly vent sessions, if things between Chad and I would have been resolvable. Or at least maybe I wouldn't have snapped the way I had. I put my blinker on and changed lanes, buzzing past the exit for the airport. I had to get my mind off things and back on the road. Thinking about the "what ifs" and "maybes" wasn't helping matters.

Chad and I still had our irreconcilable differences, regardless of the surrounding factors and situations, his numerous affairs for one. Erika had been telling me for years, since even before Chad and I had started dating, that she wasn't a fan of his.

She had suppressed her looks of disapproval on our wedding day and had smiled for all our photos, but her eyes didn't have their usual joyful glow.

I knew she'd been waiting to tell me,

"I told you so!"

But she had been biting her tongue until she arrived back in Canada, and I was at least grateful for that. Erika had always wanted me to be a little wilder, like her, and she had always disapproved of Chad. She called him a womanizer, and a control freak. Took me until these past few years to see she was right all along.

I found his phone open one night and saw he had been texting a chick named Samantha. Those texts were a little more than friendly, to say the least.

When I called him out on it, he made it out as if she was texting him, he was innocent, and she had hunted him down. Of course, he did not realize that I had scrolled up through his messages as soon as they caught my attention.

I knew he had been the one to send the first unsolicited picture and asked her for some. They also went on to discuss the last time they *met up* and how he couldn't wait to be inside her again. There were many other messages and emails, very similar, to a handful of different women.

Ok, so there were A LOT more problems in our marriage than I had originally let on. Our marriage felt more like a fraud at this point, a waste of my years, with only three beautiful children to show for it.

I know I've painted my life as a horrible soap opera, but generally my life was quite dull and typical, just like me.

I stood about 5'4", average build, pear shaped like my mother before me, thick auburn hair with a bit of wave to it, hazel eyes that glinted green more often than not, olive skin, and pouty lips.

I was curvy, I definitely didn't lose all my added baby weight. I have stretch marks and the thirty-year sag that happens to tits naturally over time. Add breastfeeding three kids to the mix and you can paint your own image.

I was not ugly, but I'd never describe myself as good looking. As stated, I was completely average.

I used to constantly beat myself up, thinking I should have gone to the gym more, or I shouldn't have had that cake. But since I'd reached my thirty second year on this planet, I was in the mindset of just saying,

"Fuck it!" If I end up alone,

"Whatever."

I'd been basically abstinent for the past few years, sex deprived while my husband was either wanking off in the shower to God knows how many women. Or from what I'd seen in his texts, he'd likely been screwing all of them during all his "late work nights." I rolled my eyes and shook my head. I hoped Samantha, or whomever else he seduced, knew what she was in for.

Re-focusing on where I was headed, I decided instead of shopping, I'd actually like to hit up the beach. I'd been working so many night shifts; I hadn't gotten much sun as of late. I'd love to spend the day soaking in the rays and enjoying a swim! As much as I didn't want to go to the beach alone, I didn't see much other choice. I turned down Abbott Street towards Strathcona Beach Park.

Parking was congested, but I managed to find a stall eventually. I shimmied into the backseat and slipped on a bathing suit I brought just in case, a habit I picked up from Chad always insisting I pack ahead and plan everything precisely. In this case I was grateful for the pre-planning. I stuffed some cash in my bag and threw on my shades. My flip-flops slapped against the paved parking lot before I reached the sand and grass. I clicked the lock button on my key fob and stuffed that in my bag as well.

I purchased a cheap towel at a beachside vendor's stand and headed towards the rippling waters. Watching the sun glint off its reflective surface, it felt so welcoming. The warm breeze whistled through my hair and I took the opportunity to use it to lay my towel out pointing in the direction the wind was blowing. I used my bag to weigh it down, then I headed to the water's edge and dipped my toes in.

It was startling at first as it lapped at my feet, but I quickly adjusted and began wading in deeper until my thighs were submerged. I dove in, leaving the faint roar of traffic and people's distant voices behind.

The cold water hit my face and washed over my ears, drowning out the sounds and replacing them with the bubbling of the water's current. When I emerged, I was far out, and turning back, the people all looked so small, like ants bustling about.

Lying back and floating, I raised my chin to the sky and let the feeling of weightlessness take over. I closed my eyes and just breathed.

| Chapter 2 |

It was after lunch when I heard my phone buzz. I'd been lazing on the beach for almost two hours. Aeda was texting me asking where Everley's cleats were for soccer. I responded and decided it was likely time I headed back to possibly check out Costco. Getting dressed was much more of a task than suiting up was. I peeled off my damp suit, dusted the sand off my bits, then towel dried my hair and pulled my garments back on one by one until I was finally clothed again. I started driving, using my cell's GPS to guide me back as I wasn't overly familiar with the inner workings of Kelowna.

I absentmindedly forgot about the whole "hands free" rule of the road, when I heard a cop's siren and saw lights flashing in my rear view mirror.

"Shit!"

I hissed, and put my blinker on to pull over. I mumbled cuss words, and rummaged through my glove compartment, searching for my insurance papers. I found them under a stack of drive thru napkins I always stockpiled in case of emergencies. It's a mom thing. I heard the tap on the glass and I rolled my window down.

A hand extended through and I heard the usual commands.

"License and registration ma'am."

I hastily handed over my papers and dug out my license, handing over the tacky photo'd card. I still hadn't looked up. I just kept thinking,

There goes my clean driving record!

I wondered how much this was going to cost me when the cop said in his deep voice,

"Naomi? Naomi Wilkinson? As in Naomi Finstead?"

Puzzled, I looked up and pulled my shades down.

"Finstead is my maiden name, yes. How do you know tha...?"

I stopped as he pulled his rays down too.

"Oh my God, Dustin!"

Dustin Trail was yet another soul I attended high school with. He was actually pretty good buddies with Chad back in the day, until they had a big scuffle over something I wasn't aware of. He had moved a few weeks later after Chad and I started dating, and I hadn't seen him since.

He sure looked good now though! He stood approximately six foot two from what I estimated, his sandy blonde hair cropped short. A scruffy beard and piercing blue eyes peered down at me looking from my license photo and back at my face. His muscular build bulged in his crisply ironed uniform.

"Wow! Long time no see," he laughed.

"Yeah no doubt! How have you been? I mean you're a cop now, that's amazing!"

"Yep, been a cop now for a few years, I just made Sergeant, but we were short guys today so I stood in for traffic duty. I've been doing well though. Moved to Kelowna a few months ago, and just bought a place here. Things have been great!"

"That's so good to hear! I missed you! I never really got to say goodbye in high school before you moved away."

"Well, it all happened pretty fast and you were busy. Sorry, I never really said goodbye either under the circumstances...but hey, I'm here now and here you are!"

I was confused at his statement about *the circumstances*. I wasn't sure what he was referring to, but I decided best not to focus on that and chatted on.

"Yes, here we are! I actually live in Salmon Arm but came to pick up Erika from the airport. You remember Erika don't you, Erika Crane? Anyway, her flight got delayed so I thought I'd spend a few hours in town, kill some time!"

He nodded in response to my inquiry about Erika,

"Yeah, I remember Erika, how could I not. You two were always together! Do you have any idea when her flight gets in?"

"Unfortunately not. She just messaged me this morning letting me know it was being held up. I didn't imagine it would be more than a few hours, but she still hasn't told me she's left yet." I shrugged.

"I guess I should have waited to hear from her."

"Well, I only have a few hours left of my shift. It's a short day today for me. I don't suppose you'd want to kill some time with me and catch up, would you? I mean it's either that or I'm going to have to write you a ticket for distracted driving."

He winked and smirked at me, shifting his weight slightly and adjusting his finger on his belt loop.

I couldn't help but notice his gun...no, not his artillery gun...I meant his crotch. I wasn't sure if it was the way the seam of his pants laid, or just the way all his gear framed in that area, but holy hell. I swallowed and turned a little pink and quickly darted my eyes back up to his face.

"Um, I, uh" I stammered.

"I'm joking, Naomi, I'm not going to write you a ticket either way, but I'll give you a stern warning." He smiled.

"I would really like to grab a drink together or something though."

I relaxed a bit and returned the smile.

"I'd really like that too actually. What time were you thinking?"

He checked his watch and hummed.

"Can you meet me at say, three thirty? How about at O'Flannigan's Pub?"

I glanced at my phone that lay silent on the seat next to me.

"Umm, yeah ok. If I don't hear from Erika by then, for sure! But you'd better not write me a ticket for drinking and driving after!" We laughed.

"Three-thirty it is then. I'll see you there, Naomi!"

He did his subtle nod and then walked off back to his squad car. Meanwhile, I sunk back in my seat and breathed out hard, trying to ignore the butterflies in my stomach.

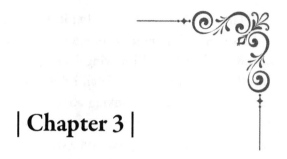

| Chapter 3 |

The next few hours crept by; it was harder to kill time than I thought. I impulsively bought a cute dress to wear, in the back of my mind full well knowing I bought it with the intention of meeting Dustin for drinks later. I didn't know why, but I felt both excited and panicked thinking about meeting up with him. I felt scatter-brained and in a fog. I kept having second thoughts as well. It had been forever since I went on a date, but no, this wasn't a date. I mean it was just two old friends catching up, having some drinks and bullshitting, right?

I couldn't answer my own question. I didn't know the first thing about interacting with the opposite sex in this day and age. I'd left all that knowledge far behind in high school when Chad and I first started dating and had never bothered to resurface it. No one wanted to date a woman as boring as I was, not to mention one that had three kids. And a guy as good looking and fit as Dustin? The idea was laughable really. I was not fat, but I was definitely not fit looking.

Childbearing had been rough on my body. My cesarean scar still ached periodically and had left that unattractive pooch of skin that hung over it. It was mortifying for me to think of any man, even my ex-husband, seeing me naked. Sex, on the rare occasion it happened, had to be performed strictly in the dark, just to save myself the shame of it.

I guess I just didn't want Dustin to see me as one of those classmates you bumped into at a reunion and thought,

"Dear lord, the years have been rough on them!" or *"Yikes, what happened to her!"*

I think that was my fear. I didn't want pity and I didn't want to feel any more ashamed than I already did. Erika always told me I was being unreasonable, or way too self-critical, but I couldn't help it! Those feelings didn't just ebb away; they'd gnaw at your very soul and darken even your brightest days. I knew thoughts like these had a negative effect on my marriage as well, I was not completely innocent in the grand scheme of things. I took a moment and glanced at the clock again, three ten flashed on the van's console. I figured I should likely get dressed.

I pulled out the little number I had purchased. It was a navy, almost black, dress that cut off just slightly above the knee. Its cap sleeves hung loosely around my shoulders. The sides ruched a bit, I liked that detail because I felt it hid my imperfections better. I ripped off the tag and slid myself between the seats into the back and began to undress.

I still hadn't heard from Erika; I didn't want to bombard her with messages and rack up her international phone charges. I had sent her one message telling her I'd made plans and to let me know as soon as she was able, what time to expect her. That was sent at approximately one in the afternoon. I still hadn't heard anything back.

I slid on the dress. The soft jersey fabric slipped easily over my bodice, and then I pulled it down over my butt and thighs.

I had a nice pair of leather strappy sandals in my trunk from an outing the kids and I had gone on the week prior. I'd just never removed them, but that oversight luckily paid off, saving myself wearing my flip flops into the pub.

I grabbed my light washed jean jacket and put that on as well to casual my look a bit and ran my fingers through my hair to brush it out as much as possible. I usually had my hair up, just a habit from having kids and working in the hospital so much, but today I had worn it down.

I pulled out a bit of makeup in my purse and tried to make myself a bit more presentable. I checked the time, *three twenty-two*.

Well, I thought looking in the mirror it's better than it was anyhow. I breathed out and shook my arms and shoulders trying to get rid of my nerves.

I jumped when I heard a vehicle door slam. A few spots down from me, I saw Dustin press the lock on his key fob. He still had the squad truck but had changed his attire.

He was sporting some jeans, a tighter relaxed fit that complimented his long muscular legs, and a plain white t-shirt.

He started walking towards my van as I hastily opened my door after scuttling back into my front seat.

"Hey there stranger!" I cooed casually, grabbing my wallet off the seat and shutting the door.

"Well don't you look nice!" His compliment caused me to go red hot. I couldn't help blushing. I just hoped he didn't pick up on the fact that it was on his account that I'd put some effort into my look for the evening.

"Thanks, I just had to change out of my beachwear. So, this is the place? Do you come here often?"

I scanned the old pub. It seemed quaint and I admired the aged wood trim of the building.

"Not too often." He laughed.

"But from time to time, if I want to enjoy a cold beer and maybe a meal, this is a decent spot as any!"

He opened the door for me and a blast of air-conditioned air hit us as we walked through.

The hostess grabbed two menus and greeted us with a smile,

"For two?"

"Yes, please."

Dustin and I spoke in unison as she guided us to a quiet water view table. We both ordered a water, and Dustin ordered a craft beer for himself and a gin and tonic for me before the hostess went to hand off to our waitress for the evening.

"So..." He began.

"What have you been up to all these years?"

Crap, I was really hoping to avoid the topic of my life and just focus on his. No one wants to start off any occasion talking about their mess of a situation. I tried to make light of it all.

"Oh not much really, nursing, three kids, living in Salmon Arm. Not a lot really, just making ends meet and making sure kids are happy."

I was hoping he'd allow me to brush off all the details but to my dismay he prodded.

"Three kids! Does that mean you're married then? Are you still with Chad?"

Ugh! That was a loaded question. I mean what should I even say? Just then the waitress, Erin, as she introduced herself, laid our drinks out in front of us, buying me some time.

We thanked her and said we'd let her know when we were ready to order more. Dustin then looked at me again, waiting for me to continue, once again prodding me with his eyes.

"Oh! Umm, well yes three kids, Aeda, Austin and Everley. They're Chad's kids, we were married, but as of six months ago, not so much anymore."

I took a long sip of my gin and tonic, pursing my lips awkwardly and then tried to interrupt the silence by asking him a question.

"How about you? Married? Kids? What's your deal, other than serving up justice on a daily basis?"

He held up his hand in a stop motion. The attempted diversion hadn't worked.

"Whoa, whoa, whoa! You separated six months ago? That's a lot for you to handle. You guys have been together a long time. How'd your kids handle it? That must be pretty rough on all of you?"

I squirmed and sucked in my breath. Opening up to people made me so uncomfortable, letting them see my vulnerability was unsettling, but I couldn't just leave him hanging, and his eyes were so kind and compelling.

"Well, I'd be lying if I said it hadn't been hard. There were always a lot of ups and downs like any marriage, but the cheating is where I drew the line, and that's that. The kids were super upset of course, and the whole rearranging our lives has been a challenge. I'm so proud of how they've handled it thus far, but my heart still breaks for them."

My gaze settled on the floor, and I took another long sip of my drink, savoring the piney taste and trying to focus on that instead of the tears that had started to swell in the corners of my eyes.

I hadn't talked one on one with anyone about all of the drama in my life. Erika had been gone, and I'm not what I would consider close enough to disclose to anyone else and trust it wouldn't reach the wrong ears.

At that moment Dustin reached his hand over and cupped my chin under his finger, nudging my gaze off the floor and up into his eyes.

"You're doing the best you can, and that makes you an awesome mom in my books. I know your kids know that. Don't fret, hold your head up high, and keep walking tall, you're doing great!"

He said it so effortlessly, he hadn't thought about what to say in an effort to console me. This was genuine, and that made it mean so much more.

Despite myself, a tear slid down my one cheek and landed on his forefinger. I gasped a bit and started apologizing profusely and wiping his hand with a nearby napkin.

He brushed off my efforts, lifting his hand and laughed a bit.

"Stop! You don't have to do that, Naomi, it's just a tear. It's ok to cry! I wish you'd just open up. Knowing you, you've probably been boxing this all up inside. You need to talk about it. You will feel better!"

I stopped, probably looking at him like a bewildered deer in headlights. How did he know? I swear he just read my mind. My expression must have said everything I was thinking in that moment as he chortled.

"I've known you since high school, and I paid a lot more attention than you think. Cop instincts I guess, picking up on details, reading expressions. We don't have to talk about it now. I'm just telling you, at some point you should, get it off your chest."

At that second, I swear I saw him glance at my breasts, but I thought it was probably just in reference. I ignored it and nodded my agreement, smiling a bit subdued.

"You're right. I will. Thank you. So? Are you going to tell me about your life now?"

He returned my smile, and that's where the conversation really began. Apparently, he was single, had moved from his previous station to Kelowna and had bought a place of his own.

He had been dating prior to moving, but his girlfriend, Angel, didn't want to relocate so they had parted on friendly terms.

He hoped to serve his years, put away extra for an early retirement, and then hopefully travel. I loved that he had a plan, and that he'd actually started putting it in motion already.

We talked for hours, and the waitress kept coming and re-filling our drinks. We ordered appys and tried to eat between stories and laughs, which proved to be more difficult than it sounds! I saw a flash and realized the manager had turned on their large lighted outdoor sign.

"Oh my God, what time is it?" I frantically started digging in my jacket that long before had been draped along the back side of my chair; rummaged through my pocket and grabbed my long-forgotten cell phone.

Dustin read the time off his watch before I had a chance to read my screen.

"It's eight thirty."

I panicked a little hearing the time and seeing unread messages displayed on my log as well as three missed calls. I went straight for the voicemails as they seemed to be a higher priority in my mind. I pressed *"1"* following the automated prompts and Erika's voice met my ears.

"Hey! Sorry about the wait, I hope you're not punishing me by ignoring my texts hahaha! Listen I'm really sorry they declared the storm is a hurricane and it had knocked out the cell tower here so I wasn't able to update you sooner. They've delayed the flight further and are putting us up in a hotel for the night until it dies down enough to attempt flying out! I don't want to be a pain but if you haven't bailed on me yet and went home, feel free to get yourself a hotel for the night, my treat and hopefully I'll be there in the morning!"

Phewf! I breathed out. I thought maybe I had left her stranded at the airport for hours. That was a relief, although I was still concerned about the hurricane she had been dealing with there.

I took a minute to hastily text her back and let her know I'd gotten her message and would for sure be having her reimburse me the room! I laughed to myself.

We had an ongoing thing where the other person always "owes" the other something. We used it as collateral, to get the other person to do what we wanted, etc.

Dustin must have read the look of relief on my face.

"Everything must be alright then?"

"Yes! There is a hurricane, but it's all good so far. Cell tower was out; that's why I hadn't heard from her in so long. She did offer to get me a hotel for the night, which is nice because I definitely won't be able to drive."

I shrugged goofily and we both laughed. I excused myself to the washroom and he did the same.

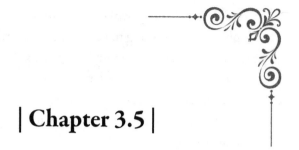

| Chapter 3.5 |

Bleep, Bleep, Bleep! I awoke to my alarm blaring at me from my nightstand. Squinting my eyes, not daring to believe it was time to get up yet. The red digital numbers glaring through the dark at me read *5:40AM*. I sighed my contempt and rubbed the sleep from my eyes, yawning simultaneously. Heaving myself off the mattress, I stretched and kneaded the floor with my toes as per a ritual of mine. I have many rituals.

I counted to seven and then flattened my feet on the floor and pushed myself into a standing position. I had gone to bed shirtless as always and in my black boxer briefs.

I rubbed my abdomen, still sore from last night's workout. I had literally made myself sick pumping iron and crunching my abs. I had recently been training for a promotion to Sergeant and had achieved it, but I wasn't about to let my physique slip at all. No, I needed to keep going, push my limits and work up to the next level, that's just how I roll.

I have always been a perfectionist in many ways, but only where I was concerned. I didn't much care what anyone else did, but I had to be immaculate.

My condo was always organized, neat, and dust free. Most food consumed was pristine in presentation, organic, non-GMO, lots of protein and vegetables. I did a workout first thing every morning, then would shower, get dressed and groomed, eat, and off to the station. I washed my vehicle almost daily and god forbid anyone that made a mess in it. I had a handheld vacuum and bin with cleaning supplies at the ready if they did. All of which I kept stowed in my trunk, just in case.

I didn't like to let on to people how orderly I liked things. I was sure for the most part they could tell, but definitely not to the full extent. I intended to keep it that way too.

I would describe myself as a pretty private person. Don't get me wrong, I could converse and socialize very well, but that's work. It was so much easier being alone, and that's how I preferred it.

Walking over to my closet, I grabbed my gray sweats off their appointed hanger and pulled them on as well as a pair of crisply ironed socks from my bureau drawer. Yes, I iron my socks.

Trodding down to my workout area, the dim rays of the light of dawn, finally starting to emerge from behind the hills, began to cast their still cool glow across the vinyl flooring. Sticking my feet into my eagerly awaiting runners and tying them, I thought of what workout I was aiming to fulfill today. Which areas of the body did I want to concentrate on?

As I had done abs last night, I figured I might as well make this one legs and arms. I grabbed my weighted vest and slipped it on then grabbed a 25lb dumbbell in each hand before stepping onto the treadmill for my warmup, a good 10km should be good.

The steam from the shower was so inviting, knowing how soothing the hot water would feel pelting down on my aching muscles. I clambered through the steam and into the blanket of heat awaiting me. It burned, but a good burn.

I allotted myself some time to let the water wash over me, closing my eyes, mentally preparing myself for the day before lathering up. I snatched my loofah off its hanger and squeezed some body wash onto it. The blue gel's aroma rose and invigorated my nostrils.

I began my usual washing regime; scrubbing every inch of my 6ft 2" frame, washing off the remaining sweat that lingered post workout.

When I felt clean enough, I turned off the taps and climbed out, toweling off quickly, and giving my sandy hair a shake.

I always wore casual attire to the station and from there changed into my crisp uniform. I had a few and rotated them through the dry cleaners after each time I wore them.

I walked up to my bathroom vanity and threw on my jeans and tee, ran a bit of gel in my hair and did a quick trim of my face scruff before opening up the mirror to retrieve my vitamins. I popped a handful in my mouth and took a long drink of cold water from the faucet to swallow them down before walking out to get breakfast.

My coffee maker was programmed to turn on at 6:40 and was ready and waiting for me. I poured the black seething hot liquid into a thermos for the drive to work and then went about blending myself a protein shake for breakfast.

My watch was laying in its appointed spot. I checked the hour, right on time as usual. I promptly went and brushed my teeth after swallowing the last gulp of my shake then applied some deodorant before heading to the door. My keys hung on their hook, and I slipped my leather-bound wallet in my back pocket before heading out the door.

Entering the change room at the station felt like entering the high school gym locker room, guys talking, showering, bull shitting, and the mixed smells of deodorant, BO, and leather polish.

Opening my locker, a couple of the guys broke their conversation briefly to greet me, and I returned the gesture before delving into getting geared up. I buttoned my shirt, strapped on my bullet proof vest, gun holster and badge.

My freshly polished boots caught the fluorescent lighting and its reflection shone bright against the faded cement flooring. I approved of my facade with a quick glance in the plastic mirror hanging in my locker, my sandy hair lifted just where I liked it, and my blue steely eyes popped against the blue of my uniform.

I slammed my locker door shut and turned to head to the armory, ready to load up. Grace, the armory attendant, signed out my guns for me, sliding them through the slot and handing me my ammo, every bullet accounted for.

Assignments were being handed out for the day up in the conference room, or the pig pen as it's often referred to. I detested the name, although I did see the irony. Constable Martens was hollering at each member, informing them of their duties.

"Cash, You're on highway patrol today. Jenkins, they need you baliffing today. Trail, you're on traffic patrol."

God damn it. My rank was above petty traffic duty.

"Sir, isn't there anyone else that can do traffic?" I attempted to protest.

"Trail, you know how short staffed we are. I know you've put in your time, but I need good men on the ground and that's you."

Constable Martens looked at me with pleading eyes, and I felt my objections resolve.

"Fine I'll step in for the rest of this week and next until Gibbons returns."

"Thatta boy! Knew I could count on you."

Martens clapped a thundering hand on my shoulder and treaded past me to grab his morning coffee and collect his pile of papers off the table. I exited, feeling a bit of resentment building. I loved my job, but I was just a bit tired of picking up the slack. Swallowing my animosity, I departed, forcing myself to be optimistic. At least I'd get to ride in my squad truck for the day.

My backside was sticking to the leather interior of my truck, the heat of the day causing a muggy sweltering environment in my cab. I had been tucked on a side road with my radar gun for a few hours now. Had issued four tickets and one warning. I was bored out of my mind.

My mind began to wander, and I thought back to a few weeks prior when an old high school acquaintance had messaged me wanting to make plans to meet up this week. A mutual friend had been brought up and my inner workings warmed.

Naomi Finstead... my high school crush. I was crazy about her. Unfortunately, she'd been my mate's girl. He was a bastard and was always cheating on her, although I'm certain she was unaware, as she remained loyal to him throughout, and as a result, I never got the chance to make my move.

I've had several relationships, some long term, over the course of years since high school, but in the back of my mind, I knew I still wanted a chance with Naomi.

I had felt like I'd met my soulmate. If only she knew. Or if only she could know how I felt for even a second, I'm sure she'd realize she felt the same. I knew, if I could ever have a chance with Naomi, she would undoubtedly feel the same. Maybe now was my chance.

I looked up the name, coordinated it to the plate number and scanned the area for the vehicle that matched the description. I even went as far as to call it out to dispatch. They alerted me that a similar vehicle to my description had been visualized down near the beach. I turned the key in my ignition and headed in that direction.

Pulling into the parking area, I scanned, watching for it. It took me a few passes before I located what I was looking for.

About a half hour passed, the heat of the day pounding down, sweat forming on my brow. I was lucky no calls came in during this time, and the end of my shift was drawing near.

I couldn't wait any longer, it was too damn hot. I started the engine again and cranked my A/C, my windows were all cracked, but that did nothing to alleviate the heat.

I wiped my brow again as sweat trickled down between my eyes. The cool air of the A/C finally kicked in as I gulped the last of my water. My sweat dried up as I was being pelted with the icy rush of air. That's when I saw the vehicle backing out.

Now I needed a reason...any excuse. I didn't have to think about it.

I saw the screen of a mobile device as the vehicle moved forward ready to turn into traffic, and that's when I made my move. I cranked my engine over, peeled out of my hideaway and flicked on my lights. Within seconds, the van pulled over.

"License and registration ma'am."

| Chapter 4 |

Exiting my stall, I began washing my hands. The sweet rose scented soap invigorated my nostrils. I breathed it in. Normally I would have called my kids to wish them a goodnight's sleep. But Chad said he didn't want me calling every night when they were at his place. I understood where he was coming from, his place, his time, but I still missed them.

I glanced up in the mirror and straightened my hair a bit. I really liked this dress! Normally I was not a confident shopper. I hated putting on anything new, for fear of how it might look on me. But pushing myself out of my comfort zone that afternoon, I did well. The dress hugged my curves in all the right areas and accentuated them. I felt more feminine, and it boosted my composure, as I usually looked and felt like a hot mess.

Drying off my hands, and disposing of my towelette in the garbage, I exited the bathroom, taking one last fleeting glance backwards, catching sight of my backside, looking rather, I dared say, *bodacious*. As I started walking back in the direction of our table, I noticed Dustin had gathered our belongings and was awaiting me at the hostess desk, so I veered to meet him there. He handed me my wallet and I clicked it open to retrieve my debit card and pay for my bill, but he placed his hand over top of it and said,

"It's all paid up, let's go."

My eyes opened wide and my bottom lip popped open, a little stunned I suppose. That bill couldn't have been too affordable after all the drinks I'd consumed as well as the appys we shared.

"You didn't have to do that." I half stammered walking out the door as he held it for me.

"I wanted to!" he replied curtly.

The cool dusk breeze felt so refreshing as it swirled around my ankles and up my legs.

We briskly walked towards our vehicles. I really didn't want to say goodbye. I'd had so much fun tonight, and the longing I'd felt earlier that day when admiring Dustin's physique was prominently growing into a series of nagging urges.

"So did you decide on a hotel?" He asked, whilst scanning the buildings surrounding us.

"No, I guess I was so busy talking with you I hadn't really stopped to give it much thought. Any recommendations?"

"The Cove is your closest bet and it's pretty nice; it's just down that way there, decently priced too."

"Ok, well sounds as good a place as any. Maybe that's where I'll head."

I gave a little shrug and started to click the unlock button on my fob.

I was trying to think of any reason to keep visiting. I didn't want it to be so obvious that I was clearly very attracted to him. I didn't think I could handle that kind of rejection, but I had genuinely and thoroughly enjoyed his company. Before I could speak, he broke the silence.

"How about you give them a call, see if any rooms are available. In the meantime, we could hang a little longer. It's not overly late."

I jumped eagerly at his suggestion.

"Yeah, ok that'd be great!" I exclaimed.

I got my phone out and after a quick Google, I had the number and dialed. Stepping away to ask their availability, I looked back and quietly observed him. His denim jeans hugged all the right places. His lean muscular frame propped against his truck; I couldn't help feeling between my legs clench with want....

"Yes, Visa please!" Snapping back to reality in order to give my info, I looked away. I didn't want to risk being distracted while giving the booking clerk my expiry date.

"There!" I snapped my phone shut and palmed it as I strode back over to Dustin's side.

The aroma of his cologne trailed on the wind, and I couldn't help but breathe in deep. He smelt amazing, like leather, sweat, and Old Spice.

"What should we do now?" I queried happily.

He looked coolly at me, holding my gaze. He licked his lips and said,

"Well I have a few ideas, one in particular." He gave me one last look up and down and then turned back towards his squad truck and opened both the front and back seat doors.

"Have you ever ridden in a cop's vehicle before?"

"No, never!" I liked where this was going, I had always wanted to check out the inside of one of their vehicles but never had the guts to ask.

I stepped forward to the door's entrance and he motioned me in and helped me climb inside. It was roomier than I anticipated. The black leather seats shimmered, and I sunk into the middle partition; lots of legroom. I inspected the black metal cage separating the front from the back and the shatter proof glass on the other side of it. It felt kind of eerie being in the back, but I was thrilled, nonetheless.

Dustin hopped in the seat beside me and pulled the door slightly closed after placing something over the inner workings of the latch.

"So we don't get locked in." He explained when he saw me watching. He watched me look around some more, seeing all the buttons through the glass as well, and answered all my questions about *bad guys*. He smiled, amused at my excitement from it all.

"You really like all this stuff, eh?" He questioned.

"Yes. I feel like a kid in elementary school on a field trip."

"Well, you don't look like a little girl." He said, looking me up and down once again.

I blushed feverishly. Did he mean that as a compliment? Or was that meant to point out my flaws? I didn't have time to ponder much. In that second, he moved so swiftly, and I heard a *click*.

Looking down at my wrist, he had handcuffed me. I was dumbstruck.

He obviously noticed my bewilderment, and instead of explaining to me, he wrapped his hands around my waist, which felt unusually tiny in his big hands. He lifted me up with ease and slung me over his lap. There I was perched, straddling this mortifyingly sexy man, handcuffed in a caged backseat. I had only ever fantasized about scenarios such as this before. Never had I dared dream it would come true!

"Holy shit...is this really happening?" I whispered.

"You bet your hot ass it is!" He whooped, as I lunged forward, locking my lips on his.

The faint taste of scotch and salt on his lips met my tastebuds, and I kissed him deeper and even more passionately. His hands ran up my thighs hiking up my short dress so the hem settled just on the bottom of my cheeks. I ripped off his shirt with my cuffed hands and then wrapped them around his neck like a bridle. I began kissing his neck, and he started pulling down his jeans, and simultaneously pulled down the top of my dress, exposing my breasts.

He buried his face in them, kissing them, my neck and rib cage, before frenching me deep once again.

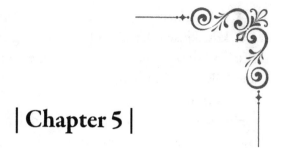

| Chapter 5 |

H is fingernails dug into my ass cheeks, and he groaned as I kissed his neck and ear lobes, sucking on them. I felt his hips thrust up in want, and I kissed him one more time, biting my lip seductively and whispered,

"I want you."

His eyes looked up into mine and I nodded encouragingly, showing my desire with my eyes and biting my lip even more provocatively. His fingers flew to his fly and he unbuttoned and hurriedly yanked his jeans the rest of the way down, all while still having me straddling him. His rock-hard cock sprung from his pants, veiny and plump.

My eyes bulged at the sight of it; it was a nice cock! His long shaft was almost the same delicious color as perfectly cooked pancakes. It was girthy and rigid and his tip throbbed and had beads of pre-cum, looking like delicious warm maple syrup drizzling over a stack of flapjacks, dripping, ready for me.

With an easy maneuver, he slid my panties to the side using his thumb, and with the other hand, bent and guided his dick to my eager slit. I held my breath and then gasped as he slid it in me.

It was much bigger than I'd ever had before and felt even larger than it already looked. Despite how wet I was with the excitement, his size did cause some friction, and it took a few gentle thrusts to get his full depth.

The second it all let go and he was able to get it all in, I moaned. The arch of his cock hit my g-spot effortlessly! I dug my nails into his back and began riding him. He gripped my waist and pubic bones, using them to direct my bouncing in the way that he liked best. I leaned back and his hand rose to the small of my back, and I rocked on his cock so he could watch his dick sliding in and out of me from the front. His many throaty groans showed his approval.

I was gushing wet, and my tits were bouncing. He didn't leave them neglected. He groped and squeezed them while simultaneously thumbing my clit as a skilled guitar player strums out an energetic solo. My pussy clenched around his shaft every time he'd lift his hips up into me by surprise, adding a few more centimeters of depth and he moaned in appreciation. It wasn't anything I did on purpose, it was just an automatic response to the pleasure I was being subjected to. So much pleasure.

Our bodies pounded into the seats, the truck shook with our rhythmic humping. He pulled my hair and spanked me hard, causing me to cry out and buck harder. Feeling his fat cock stretching me out. I did sensual circles, grinding down on him, making his shaft push on all my walls, forming them to his robust shape. I could feel *everything.* Every plump vein protruding from his hefty wood. Every curl of his dick skin with this motion of him pushing in and then pulling out. Every hook of his bulgy shroom caught on some ledge inside me right above my g-spot. It all shot nerve quaking tremors throughout my body, causing me to grind him harder and faster. The sound of our heavy breathing in unison and the fog forming on the windows added to my arousal. I wasn't missing a single detail of this erotic excursion.

My clit swelled under the humming of his thumb. The sound of my wet arousal sloshed with every plunge of his manhood into me. I bit my lip, I knew it was coming...

He must have sensed my closeness. He looked up at me and then pushed my thighs out even further, causing me to sink down on him balls deep. He then lifted up with his legs and held onto my ass and started wildly heaving into me.

I could feel that familiar tingling numbness starting in my toes and working its way up my legs. My eyes clouded, my pussy clenched again, and I saw stars. I couldn't help but scream my moans. They couldn't be contained! As I went off, I felt his dick swell up even more and then with a last wild jerk he let loose as well.

"Shhhiiitttt!"

He hissed in ecstasy. I was still clinging to his neck with my cuffed hands. I released his hair from the coils of my fingers. My body shivered as the last effects of my orgasm faded. We both collapsed into each other, panting and kissing.

Several moments passed before he finally broke the near silence.

"You have no idea, how long I have wanted to do that." He said, smiling and half laughing.

"Orgasm?" I asked teasingly.

"No, fuck you." He said directly.

He saw the stunned look on my face and responded.

"Naomi, I've been crazy about you since high school. How did you not know that? That's what mine and Chad's fight was about. He was being an ass and had been ... flirting with Jessica Horner."

By that, I knew he meant Chad had been fucking her behind my back, but Dustin was trying to save me the further humiliation by not disclosing that portion of things. He went on.

"I told him he didn't deserve you and fists flew. I moved away shortly after that when my dad transferred jobs. I had wanted to ask you out before Chad did. He found out I liked you and went behind my back and beat me to it. I never got the chance again."

"I...I never knew." I stammered.

Suddenly things from my past were all coming back into focus and making sense.

I unwrapped my arms from around his neck and he kindly un-cuffed me. I had to stifle yet another moan as I dismounted him and felt his still swollen cock gliding out of me.

"I think we made a bit of a mess in your squad truck."

We both laughed as we looked at the sticky mess left in his lap and between my thighs. My panties were soaked. I pulled them off and decided commando was probably a better option than "swampy" undergarments. I tried to tidy myself up as best I could, and he pulled his pants back up and put his shirt back on.

I couldn't read the room. Was this awkward now? Or just thoughtful?

We both walked back to the restaurant to clean up in the bathroom a little more and met each other just outside the front doors. It had seemed so brief, the whole experience, but looking at the time, it was eleven o'clock already. I was disappointed. That had been some of the best sex of my life up until this point, and it was likely just a one-night stand kind of deal. I began to thank him for the evening.

"Thank you so much for dinner, drinks, and your company. It was really great seeing you again, Dustin."

I couldn't even look up at him at this point. Maybe he just thought I was a common tramp. Reality had finally hit, and shame was settling in my conscience. It must have shown on my facial expression.

"Don't do that!" Dustin begged.

"I enjoyed my time with you too, and I don't want it to end. I'd like to see you again. This wasn't just a one-night thing for me, Naomi. Maybe we're both single now for a reason? I'd like to find out, if you're willing?"

I gazed at him, his cool blue eyes imploring me.

"Really?" I asked, unsure, my self-consciousness had returned full bore.

Deluded thoughts spun through my brain. If my ex-husband didn't even want me, why on earth would this chiseled, handsome near stranger want me? But I couldn't deny my inner urges. I knew I wanted to see him again, soon. Especially if it meant I'd get another ride like I'd just had. I decided to take my chances and push the envelope a bit.

"How about tonight?" I met his gaze and smiled out of the crook of my mouth.

His lip dropped in surprise and then lifted into a big goofy smile, which lifted my heart.

"Game on!" He agreed voluminously.

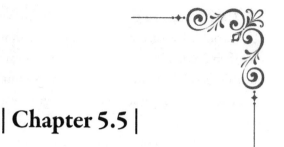

| Chapter 5.5 |

The evening had gone so well. We just *clicked*. Just as I knew we would. I wasn't sure what my next move should be. It wasn't too often I didn't know what I should do next when it came to a lady, but this wasn't just any lady. This was Naomi. The mere mention of her name caused my gut to churn in a good way. I think women often referred to the feeling as butterflies in their stomachs. Any opportunity to prolong the night, I was amply ready for.

"What should we do now?" She asked me, her big eyes round with hope.

I thought hard, licking my lips and said.

"Well I have a few ideas, one in particular."

I couldn't help but glance at her robust breasts surfacing at the top of her dress, but quickly looked away when I saw her eyes examining me.

A tour of my squad vehicle seemed like a reasonable option, although that wasn't exactly the idea I meant. Looking her up and down, taking in her shapely figure and then turning back towards my squad truck. I guided her to the doors.

"Have you ever ridden in a cop's vehicle before?".

"No, never!" Her excitement showed and I couldn't help but think, this was it, this was my chance!

Swinging both the front and rear doors open, I showed her the controls in front first, loving her genuine interest in my profession. Getting an idea, I stuffed a piece of strap tape in my pocket from my supplies while she explored all the buttons as well as my cuffs. We then perused to focus on the back of the vehicle, and I invited her to hop in with a simple gesture. She eagerly obliged and I held her hand to assist.

Noting my opportunity, I climbed in next to her and took the piece of tape from my pocket. Sticking it over the latch mechanisms. She paid it no heed, instead she continued to question me some more. It was adorable. The twinkle in her eyes and her bright heart melting smile lit up her face.

I couldn't help myself, being in such close proximity to her, my dream girl. I looked her top to bottom again, taking her all in. Her voluminous breasts, thick thighs and round ass. To me, she looked like a gourmet meal, and I...was ravenous.

I jumped to attention, making my move, not wanting to allow a second's hesitation to foil my plans. I pulled my cuffs from my pocket and planted them on her wrists with a *click*. She looked at me, her eyes bulging in question. But rather than take the time to explain, I grabbed her waist with my hands and spun her up and over my lap, perching her there, straddling me.

"Holy shit...is this really happening?" her tone of astonishment was notable.

"You bet your hot ass it is!"

My heart pounded as she bent down locking her supple lips on mine. The passion so strong between our kisses, the heat of her groins radiating outwards, my crotch and lap growing hot with want.

I was fast to rise to the occasion. I could feel my hard on chafing against my jeans, pressing so hard against the fabric. I gripped her thighs, rubbing my hands up them, sliding her dress up to her ass. Her hands suddenly clawed at my shirt, ripping it off me in her haste and wrapping her cuffed hands around the back of my neck, kissing down my nape then the sides.

Her tousled auburn hair flitted past my nose. The rose scent of her hair enveloped me, invigorating my sex drive. I started reefing on my jeans, needing them off. I wanted to stuff my hog in her so bad! But then her breasts were right there too, also stealing my attention.

Undecided, I used one hand to yank the top of her dress down, letting her tits protrude and then bust out, while my other hand managed to tug my jeans off far enough to suffice. The seams were still digging into my shaft but not hard enough it was cutting off the circulation.

I buried my face in her tits, her soft skin engulfing my face, kissing every inch of them. Wanting to leave no place untouched, I traced her body with my lips, her breasts, ribs, neck, and then kissed her lips once again, entwining our tongues and savoring her sweet piney taste. She started kissing and sucking on my neck and ear lobes, an area I didn't even know I enjoyed being sucked on.

The sensation made me groan and consequently I gripped her ass cheeks tight. Clawing them like an animal.

I jerked my hips up, unintentionally, my body's automatic response to the want, the desire building in my loins. Wanting to penetrate her, bury my dick in her! A feat I'd only dreamed would happen for the last seventeen years or so. But I couldn't take it any further without her consent.

Luckily, she shared my enthusiasm. Kissing me and then biting her big pouty bottom lip seductively, causing shivers to work up my spine, she almost whispered,

"I want you."

Her eyes pleading for my cock. That was all the encouragement I needed. Within seconds I finished unbuttoning my fly and whipped my pants off, tossing them to the side.

My erection bouncing up dripping with eagerness, I slid her panties to the side, feeling their dampness. My dick twitched, knowing her need was as strong as mine.

It was dark, but I could make out her well-manicured cunt and marked my target. Easing in, it was all I could do, her pussy so tight, it took several small thrusts for me to let her juices pour down my shaft lubricating it along with my pre-cum and stretching her out enough that I could bury my hog in her as deep as I wanted. She gasped and moaned as I finally got it in, her arousal stimulating me more! I felt her nails dig into my back, and like a shotgun start she was riding me, bouncing on my dick. Her clam squeezing with each plunge, and more juice flowed from her.

Clearly, she was enjoying me as much as I was her. Gripping her waist and hip bones, I guided her bounces, showing her the angles that she could get more and more of me in her, hitting right where I liked it. I found a "ledge" of some sort inside her and feeling my shroom catching on it added a whole new sensation that made us both quake in pleasure.

I let her go to work and busied my left hand with her airborne breasts, as with all the bucking they were more in the air than at rest. My right I brought downwards, wanting to pay the proper attention to all her bits. Watching my dick sliding in and out of her, seeing her drapes part around my shaft allowing access. Seeing how glossy my shaft was after each heave into her, the knot in the base of my cock was building. I wasn't normally so quick to cum, but I knew it wouldn't be long.

This was far too much of a turn on. I thumbed her pearl like I was Dimebag Darrel strumming out one of his killer chords, hoping to catch her up to me. Her pace accelerated, and her pussy tightened, choke holding my meat. I pushed her thighs out wider so I could barrel into her even deeper. Digging my heels into the floor, I lifted up letting her weight sink herself down on me so she was suspended on my dick like a tripod, and I thrust wildly into her. The knot rising up my shaft, she started moaning and screaming in ecstasy and my cock was squeezed even tighter, causing me to lose control. I gave one last heave into her and shot my load. Fuck that felt good.

Reveling in the moment, I finally disclosed my long-awaited desire for her and why I hadn't made a move sooner, seventeen years sooner to be exact. I could tell it made her think, and that was enough for me. I wanted her to connect the dots on her own, for her to know she should've been with me all those years ago. I never would have hurt her the way that ass wipe Chad did. But feeling the desire between us, I was certain she already knew.

I decided it was likely time I retrieved the keys and uncuffed her, releasing her from my lap. She eased off of me. The moan she let out as her tight pussy pulled off my still hard cock made my shroom pulse. Out of her was not any place I wanted to be.

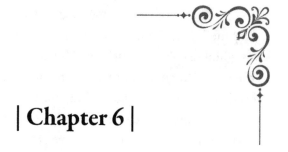

| Chapter 6 |

Slam! The hotel room door banged against the wall when it opened. Our bodies intertwined, I had Dustin pinned to it, kissing him deeply and lustfully. We had barely managed to make it to the room after our short walk to the hotel and check-in. It was all I could do to keep my hands off him until we were out of reach from curious eyes, and he seemed to be having a similar struggle. I tossed the code card onto the floor and we shuffled inside, neither of us making any attempt to unlock lips in order to get where we were going. We giggled through our stifled lips as we tripped on each other clumsily and made our way to the bed where we flopped down together in a tangled heap.

Once on the bed, we lifted our heads and took in our surroundings. The room was actually nice, two big queen sized beds, both with mountains of pillows. A huge bay window overlooked the city. All those twinkling city lights were pretty breathtaking, like a galaxy within our reach. All the colors and their glowing auras reflected off the evening fog settling in.

Alongside the window was a glass shower. It had two doors, one from the window and another entryway through the bathroom. I had seen a layout similar to this before. I had to think for a moment to recall, Sparkling Hills! Their set up was far more elegant and had a bath as well, but I'd say for the price of this room we'd gotten a good deal.

Dustin jumped up to check the mini fridge and found a not so mini bottle of champagne chilling inside it as well as two plastic bottles of water and a few tiny liqueurs.

He looked at the bottle and then at me for a sign of approval, to which I smiled and nodded. He grinned and grabbed the two glasses set aside the coffee machine.

Pop went the cork, and he filled those cups up a good three-fourths of the way.

"You must like me intoxicated!" I giggled.

His smile got goofier and he nodded,

"I do indeed, but then again, I also didn't hear you complaining either."

He winked as he handed me a bubbling glass, and we clinked them together before having a sip. He turned to put some music on using the TV.

While he was distracted I once again found my eyes landing on that shower...

I jumped up and went to the light dimmer and lowered the brightness until the whole room was basking in a dusky glow. I then skipped into the bathroom and started the taps, which was perfect timing as Dustin had just turned the music up, so the sound of the water was muted behind the bass vibrating off the walls. I went around to the front entrance of the shower by the window as he turned around to see what I was up to.

I saw him take another sip and at that second, I slid off my dress entirely, and leaned against the partially open door of the shower. The glass reflected the curves of my naked body back at him. I heard him choke a bit and try to clear his throat, and I instinctively ignored him and slunk into the shower.

With my back to him, I glanced back enticingly just before disappearing. I stepped under the hot stream of water, letting it soak me. I closed my eyes as the water ran over my face, shoulders and breasts before turning my back into the jet stream.

He stood on the other side of the glass, just watching me. Normally, I'd have shied away embarrassed of my body, but either I'd had enough liquid courage to cause me some misled bravery, or I was still high on the night's sequence of events and was suffering from an unsubstantiated boost of self-esteem.

Instead, I unleashed my inner sex goddess and lifted one leg onto a small shower seat off to the side, aiming my front in his direction. I then started touching myself.

At first I was pretending he wasn't there, but then as it started feeling good, I began to lose myself in my play, until he dissolved away completely.

It was just me, myself and I. I rubbed in slow sensual circles, with just the perfect amount of pressure; the water aided my sensitive slit, still raw from its vigorous activities not even twenty or so minutes ago.

My clit buzzed, ready for more action, my fingers working her, reviving and exciting her. I sighed and sunk against the tile wall.

My free hand squeezed my own breast, and the water continued to beat down on me. I was all hyper-sensitive and each droplet that hit my pussy caused me to shake.

I heard some rustling outside the door and allowed my eyes to open. There he stood in his boxer briefs and white tee, fully erect, watching me, staring. Seeing me see him broke his trance and he ripped off his shirt as hastily as he had his pants earlier. He tossed it aside and I had the opportunity to admire his gorgeous masculine physique. His muscles rippled under his golden tan, pecs bulging, each feature perfectly etched. His lean figure caught the dim glow of the lights. It played like candlelight flickering off his abs and belly button. A tidy finely trimmed treasure trail led downward.

Just then he reached down and removed his drawers, kicking them behind him on the floor. He opened the steamy shower door and walked forward. I could see the muscles of his thighs and buttocks rippling as he strode forward. I swear I felt my jaw drop taking in his whole figure. Then I let my eyes settle on the showstopper once more.

That monstrous dick of his swooped up towards the ceiling. A small, well-groomed patch of pubic hair nestled below his treasure trail. I licked my lips looking at it. Never had I seen a more delicious looking cock!

Sitting up and jumping to my feet, I grabbed him by his shoulder and swung him up against the damp wall, pressing my naked body against his. I could feel his sizable erection pressing against my abdomen. Both our heartbeats pounded, his through the robust veins in his dick, and mine through my engorged clit.

We remained against the wall kissing for a moment, feeling each other's bodies thoroughly, exploring them and getting familiar. My hands loved their new playground, tracing the ridges of his abs, up the middle of his chiseled chest and around each pec muscle. Then I slipped them around to the nape of his neck before gliding my fingers down the middle of his back, finding his back dimples then delicately sliding to his front again.

His shivers under my fingertips made me feel powerful and I was thrilled to feel that kind of power again. I took full advantage and grasped his hips, then slid down to my knees into a slow forming puddle in the shower drain.

I was almost eye level with his dick and he immediately knew where I was going with these actions as he leaned back into the wall a little further, reclining, getting comfortable. I sucked the base with only a partially open mouth, tasted his sweet salty skin, then licked from base up his shaft right to the tip, where I circled his shroom slowly and seductively. Then I began easing him little by little, centimeter by centimeter into my mouth, sucking ever so gently and barely hovering my tongue over his skin. Tantalizing and teasing him.

I went straight down to his balls breathing my hot breath on him, never quite allowing my mouth to close around him, until I got right down to the bottom and could feel him deep down my throat. I then sent shock waves up him by clamping my lips around him and sucking him hard, pulling all the way back up to the tip again before sliding back down thus the rhythm continued. His body jolted back.

Alternating between shallow gentle sucking and tongue bathing, to long hard spit swashing deep throats, fondling his balls in between every few rotations. Then I would break and give him some hand action in addition to my mouth, letting both my hand and mouth mimic the way my pussy would clamp and unclamp around his cock.

He moaned his appreciation and stroked my damp hair. Every once in a while, he'd grab my hair and guide my mouth down his cock and show me exactly how he wanted it.

I looked up at him, a motion I didn't usually divulge in, but had heard males enjoy. I wanted to watch him though, this handsome being, enjoying the services I was delivering him. Beads of pre-cum once again formed at his tip for me to lick off and savor his flavor. I was hungry for it. The more I squeezed and seduced out of him, I hungrily lapped it up, like a thirst quenched traveler in the desert with the first drink of water she's had in days. Licking, sucking, enjoying.

I'm not sure how long I was even down there, entranced in giving him satisfaction. However, he must have sensed that if he didn't put a stop to it, we would have missed out on more *activities*. He grabbed my shoulders and lifted me up to a standing position, then did something completely unexpected.

He squatted in front of me and scooped his biceps under my thighs and then lifted me. Sliding me up, back against the wall, burying his head between my thighs and started tongue lashing me in a craze. I nearly fell in alarm. Pinning myself against the wall for balance and grabbing his head. I finally got over my terror and succumbed to the ecstasy!

"Holy Hell!" I practically screamed, my head rolling back against the wall, my back arching.

His fast paced tongue circles, and this crazy flicky-click thing he did was driving me nuts. The soft bristles of his scruffy beard cushioning his face between my legs was a soft comfort that complimented his rapid tongue strokes. My breathing increased, coming out more like panting.

Every few seconds he'd slip his open mouth over my entire slit and suck, kissing it, before surfacing again and once again lapping at my clit. Sliding his tongue up and down my labia parting them and paying attention to every crevice. There were no complaints on my end!

Each time I thought I might cum, he calmed his tongue and let it lightly lap at me until the urge had numbed. Then he would continue flicking, licking and sucking. He was building my orgasm, he wanted me to explode. He was giving me my treatment right back to me.

"*Well played sir!*" I thought in my head.

When my clit was swollen as a ripe grape, he finally lowered me back down with ease, and turned me away from him, pushing my top half forward pressed against the glass, and jutting my ass out towards him. My breasts and face were squished against the pane of the shower door.

I could see him through the reflection of the big bay window outside the shower. He had positioned me this way on purpose, so he could see me pressed against the glass and see my body and expressions in the reflection! Just then I felt his dick pummel into me, my eyes bulged and I gasped!

His beefy meat pushed in and out. I could feel my labia part around him, his bulge leaving no room for my vagina at all. It consumed any vacant space I may have had. Stretched tight right around him, I could feel my pussy tear a bit at the back, but the pain was a turn on. Knowing his massive girth was enough to split me, was super arousing! I knew I was wet enough. There was plenty of lubrication to help him glide, but his thickness still caused there to be so much friction, I could once again feel his cock skin roll and pull inside me. That's saying a lot as there wasn't much skin there on his circumcised shaft.

I arced my back for him more, so his dick would scoop up and hit that g-spot again, he let out a deep throaty growl and I stuck my ass up higher and pressed myself on the glass even more. He spanked me. Once... twice... three times! The sting made me cry out unexpectedly, but then made my clitoris buzz! I started heaving myself back into him matching his rhythm, his speed kept building, and I sensed he must be close.

I took my hand down between my legs and began to rub, feeling the pressure build. I started panting and could hear his breathing also quicken.

Then all at once, my toes went numb and my eyes dark. I felt his cock swell up inside me again and we came simultaneously. Our cries echoed across the shower walls, reverberating off the many tiles before finally bouncing into the room and fading into the drywall.

He hugged me from behind as I up righted myself, squeezing my breasts, and he brushed my hair to the side so he could kiss my neck.

"That was fantastic!" He breathed, still panting in my ear.

I smiled slyly, then had to ease him out of me so that I could walk again. I rinsed and turned off the water. Once the shower door opened, steam poured throughout the room. I grabbed a nearby towel and draped it around myself and walked out to boldly take in the view.

I let my towel hang off my body slightly, opening the front and once again pressed my body on this new pane. It was chill and cooled my body down, making my nipples erect, and the flushness started to recede from my cheeks.

He stood, watching me from the shower door. He had wrapped a towel around his waist and began walking out.

Stepping towards me, he turned me around to face him, goosebumps now surfaced on my skin. My hard nipples pressed into his chest as he then hugged me and whispered,

"You're beautiful."

| Chapter 7 |

Beautiful? Well, that wasn't a word I'd ever use to describe myself. He had me curious though, I mean he himself was a stunning specimen, I had no idea why he'd be interested in me, surely, he had no troubles getting *some* if he tried. I scoffed out-loud at his comment, an action I regretted the second it escaped my throat.

"Why do you do that? Why do you act like you can't see what I see when I look at you?" He queried in a more aggressive and almost pleading manner.

"You are beautiful, you always have been. That's also just one of the many reasons I was interested in you in high school, and still am now." He spun me around to face him looking at me imploringly.

"I...I don't know, I guess I just don't see it, and I definitely don't feel like it." I shrugged and tried to break his stern gaze.

"I'll never understand how you can't see it. You're stunning! Look at you, your long auburn hair, your skin always looks tan year-round. You have the most gorgeous hazel green eyes and the longest lashes I've ever seen. Your perfect big pouty lips drive me crazy. I want to kiss you constantly, and don't even get me started on your body. Even after three kids you look amazing!"

"Oh don't even!" I growled.

I was no idiot, no one could look at my body and think that *THIS* was amazing!

"Don't do that," he growled back.

"Well, I'm not exactly in the best shape Dustin, especially next to your body! I have stretch marks, extra skin, and extra weight. I'm not perfect by any means!"

"Nobody is." His tone raised.

"I work very hard for my body because quite often my life and my job depend on it. Women are supposed to have a bit more cushion to them, especially after kids! It makes you soft, feminine and supple. It accentuates your curves and gives me more to grab. I've felt my fair share of both younger tits and fake tits, and your tits are by far my preference. They're real. And having kids has made them even softer and more voluminous than any other breasts. Men love having tits swinging and bouncing in their faces by the way. And as for your stretch marks, you can't even notice them, but they're more like badges of honor. They just make me appreciate you and your body more. It's attractive that you're a mother, that you put lives ahead of yours every day, that you live for people other than yourself and they always come first. It's very selfless, and I find it super sexy! It makes me want to spoil you, knowing you don't spoil yourself."

I blinked, letting his perceptions soak into my brain. So many years of thinking I wasn't good enough anymore, that youth was my only attribute, and that was gone so I was just useless now. It was a hard thing to unlearn, after telling myself for so long. I hugged him, breathing into his chest and feeling his warm embrace back. It felt so good to be held.

"Thanks for the pep talk, I needed it." I mumbled into his armpit, finding solace in his grasp.

He began toweling me off until I was relatively dry. I then returned the favor and we both slipped into bed. He set an alarm for work the next day and we both snuggled up close to one another, his arm behind my head and me resting on his chest.

I laid there listening to his breaths get heavy and steady, until eventually the odd quiet snore escaped him. I used those as my white noise machine. It wasn't long before I drifted off, eyes falling heavily down until sealed shut.

When I woke, rays of sunshine were bursting through the curtains, warming the room. Dustin was gone. Looks like he had made some attempt to make the side of the bed he had been laying on. I felt bad that he had to get up so early for work after our late night exertions.

I had been so tired I hadn't even heard his alarm or him get ready and clear out. I sat up and checked my phone. Ten o'clock, the digits flashed at me. Wow! I had really slept in.

I checked to see if I had any messages. Erika had texted to let me know they'd finally been able to take off and to expect her by 4pm as it was a connecting flight.

I climbed out of bed and made my way to the shower, the fond memories returning as I viewed the bodily streaks on the glass. I started the water and got in, actually washing this time. I made it a quick shower. I figured I had wasted enough water the night before already. My mouth tasted terrible. I longed for my toothbrush and some toothpaste. I settled for a table mint resting overtop the hotel pamphlet on the bedside table.

The taste of peppermint rushed to my taste buds and faded the awful morning mouth aftertaste. I brushed my hair as best I could by running my fingers through it repeatedly, gave it a quick blow-dry and threw on the previous night's outfit. I didn't feel overly fresh, but I at least felt fresh-er.

I walked down to the lobby and checked out. I'd have to walk back down the street to get back to the O'Flannigan's parking lot where I had left my vehicle for the night.

The day had already begun to warm up and the last of the cool morning air had almost completely evaporated into steady heat. I walked briskly, eager to get behind the wheel and go find the nearest strip mall so I could get some essentials. I still really wanted to brush my teeth. Also, I felt like a change of clothes would be worthwhile.

The sun glistened and warmed my chilled bare legs. I steered my head into its rays and let the heat envelope me. I could see my van in the distance, getting closer with each purposeful stride, the clicking of my shoes on the pavement keeping in tune. Within minutes I had arrived and unlocked my door.

Climbing in, I searched my phone for the nearest shopping location. I found one not far away and headed there promptly.

The lady at the till looked at me, likely guessing my story, last night's evening wear, and tousled locks; purchasing a toothbrush, paste and a change of clothes. Her expression indicated she probably saw it often, but her lips still pursed in disapproval. I did feel the heat of shame rise into my cheeks and tried to ignore it. I was a grown woman! But oddly enough now that I was back to reality, my actions last night did come off as a bit immature, and of a college mentality.

I used an old plastic half empty bottle of water I had in my van from the day before for my rinse water and gave my teeth a thorough scrubbing. Ahh, much better! Then I shimmied into the back seat again and changed outfits.

I pulled on some jean capris, a black tank and a loose pullover shirt that hung loosely from my frame. I had also found a cheap pair of leather ankle boots and bought those as a selfish impulse purchase. I loosely braided my hair, strands too short to secure fell around framing my face.

I stepped out the side van door feeling much more appropriately clothed and ready for the day.

Dustin and I had made plans to go for an early dinner with Erika after his shift. I knew she'd want to approve of any man I might be involved with, and they could catch up as well, since we were all friends in high school. I hoped she wouldn't grill him too hard, but I didn't have high hopes.

| Chapter 7.5 |

I rolled over and slammed my hand down on the bedside clock, turning the alarm off. Five o'clock came too damn fast. I stretched and felt Naomi's warm body next to mine. A smile crept across my face. This was really happening. I'd been worried I'd wake up and find it to all be just another one of my many Naomi centered dreams. Not this time. She was clearly exhausted after our night spent together. She hadn't even stirred with the sound of the alarm clock howling. I sat up, taking a moment to admire her once more. I leaned in to kiss her shoulder before going about my usual morning ritual.

Stretch, knead toes, 5...6...7. Then climbing out of bed. I collected my clothes quickly and with one final glimpse at her sleeping body, I reluctantly walked out the door enroute to the station.

I figured I had washed enough only hours before and opted to skip my usual morning shower. The station house was fairly empty still, so I took advantage of the empty locker room. Taking my time dressing in my uniform and getting all my gear. Grace happened to observe my subtle grin and commented on it.

"Well don't you look happy this morning? She must be pretty special, I never see you without your usual stony gaze this early in the morning." She winked at me.

"Is it that obvious?" I smirked, unable to hide my emotions as I normally would have.

"It's about damn time."

She nodded in approval.

"A young lad like yourself should have a lady friend about ya. Last time I saw yer' half this happy was months ago with that older lady. Didn't approve of that nonsense myself, but you're a grown man, ye' can make yer' own decisions. Keep this one though, I can tell she make ye' happy."

"Thanks Grace, I'll see what I can do about that."

I fully intended on doing whatever I could to keep this ongoing. Following our conversation though, I couldn't help but reminisce, back to when I first moved to Kelowna and was really making groundwork on being promoted. There was definitely a story there, more than Grace had even ever picked up on. With plenty I wasn't proud of either. But it all led me to where I was now, so I couldn't regret any of it, it was just the path I had to take. However, I drifted off in my mind, reliving it all, as if I was there all over again.

Tanya Bonafete, the name echoed around the station house that morning. She was our regional executive, or Deputy, and it had been announced at debriefing that she would be doing rounds. Making sure everything was up to snuff. I was a Constable. Fresh on the force but making good headway on my career.

Always eager and energetic, taking whatever tasks were thrown at me and rising to the occasion. I'd been told many times that it wouldn't be long before I would rise up in the ranks. I looked forward to adding a few more gold stripes to my sleeves.

I couldn't help but feel my nerves like many of my fellow officers rise up though. You never knew what was going to be dug up when the Deputy came to visit. Whose name would be besmirched, who would be found at fault for something. It could be a minor grammatical error in your daily paperwork. Or an ink smudge on a ticket. Something completely minor, but the Deputy would always find it and make it into any reason to demote someone or taint their good name. I hadn't yet met Deputy Bonafete, but after all the stories I'd heard I can't say I was eager to.

It was roughly ten o'clock when the distinct clicking of heels rebounded off the cement walls, reaching every officer's ears and causing necks to crane in their oncoming direction. In strolled Constable Martens accompanied by Deputy Tanya Bonafete.

Her tall lean figure towered over Greg Martens. Her grey pencil skirted suit hugged her body tight. Long sandy brown highlighted hair with ironed curls draped down her shoulders. She appeared to be in her late forties I guessed, forty-five or forty six? Her thin features prominent. Pursed painted lips. Chiseled nose and cheek bones. She really was quite striking. Her legs went on for days. Her suit jacket didn't hide her bosoms, they bounced with each long-legged stride she took. Constable Martens had to take two steps to keep up with her every one. She strode confidently to the front of the bullpen to address everyone.

"Good morning everyone. I'm sure you're all aware by now of my presence today. I am Deputy Tanya Bonafete and I will be overlooking all your files today. I would also like a rundown of operations here. If you have any questions, please feel free to approach me. I will be sure to come around and speak to you all in turn as I will likely have my own questions as well. Please go about your business as per usual. Thank you."

Direct and to the point. I didn't really expect anything more from her. She didn't seem like one to beat around the bush or add more "fluff" into her commentary.

Throughout the day, my fellow officers were called into the office space she was occupying. They would all reappear a short time later looking paler than they had previously and all with somewhat grim expressions on their faces. I was sweating bullets awaiting my name to be called. This was a new experience for me, and I didn't handle change well. I dug in my desk drawer, rummaging until I found what I was looking for amidst the cluster of loose papers. I turned my back to my co-workers and popped the top off the little orange pill bottle. Tossed two back and swallowed hard as I heard my name bellowed.

"Trail!"

My chair legs scraped across the floor, squealing unpleasantly as I stood up. I quickly re-buried my bottle in my drawer and slammed it shut before heading towards the office. I wiped my forehead and tried to shake off my nerves before walking through the doorway. Time to put on my mask, I thought.

"Mr. Trail, thank you for coming. I've been looking through your file. I have to say, I'm surprisingly impressed thus far. I'm not used to a fresh face having such crisp and concise paperwork, nor the outstanding performance reviews by your superiors."

Her eyes were examining me hard. I felt a weight off my shoulder hearing her words, however I still felt there had to be more.

"Thank you ma'am."

I remained standing in front of her, my hands pinned behind my back. Feeling like I did back in my cadet days as the drill sergeants circled you, ready to pounce on any imperfection in a seconds notice.

"Furthermore, your records are impeccable. I was really thorough reviewing them. I found only one error. Luckily it was an oversight on the judge's end as well and it went through unnoticed. I'd like you to come have a look so I can show you for future reference."

She indicated she wanted me to come around the desk and view her computer. I obliged.

She scrolled down her screen and tapped the point of error.

"Right here. See that?"

I had to bend down and lean in close to see where she was indicating. I was right over her shoulder at this point.

"You indicated that this was on a rural route. However, it couldn't possibly be as your map log has it marked as Highway one. It's an easy mishap to make, but for future, make sure you reference your zoning on your map. If a lawyer or judge caught this in a higher stake case, it could cost you the verdict. Thank goodness this was just a minor traffic violation however."

I could feel her looking at my face as I read over her screen. She was of course correct but,

"May I?"

I asked reaching for her mouse. She nodded.

I scrolled to the screen shot of the map she had gotten her information from. I fingered the small dot and GPS coordinates I had typed in small font on the roadway I had pulled the suspect over on.

"This side road here, see, I marked the coordinates. It is actually labeled as a rural zone according to Kelowna's jurisdiction as it's just off Highway one, enough for it to be missed. I added it to the map so if it was ever deemed an error I had my proof."

She squinted her eyes and looked over my small font and the roadway she had missed. Sitting back, she peered up at me, with admiration?

"Well done. That's a first for me. Having a newbie put me in my place."

I gulped. Perhaps I was going to be thought of as a threat now. Her eyes kept casting up and down over me.

"Excuse me for being so forward, but I'd like to take you out for a drink later. I feel like you have a lot of potential."

I felt my chest puff up. Flattery from this woman was not a common thing so I had heard. Drinks though? I worried perhaps this would be overstepping some boundaries professionally. I didn't dare say this though.

"I'd be honored to have a drink with you, Deputy."

She promptly grabbed a card and scrawled an address on it and handed it over to me.

"Meet me here at nine and don't be late." She said curtly ending our conversation there.

As I walked out of the office I looked down at the address. It could have been an oversight on my part, but I couldn't think of an establishment in that area.

I pulled up to a gated community in a ritzy part of the city. The guard asked my name and jotted down my license before letting me enter. I drove to the end before locating the address. My gut served me right, no establishment, this appeared to be Deputy Bonafete's house. My gut knotted pulling in.

I approached the door and rang the bell. Within a few moments the door swung open into a grand, well-lit foyer. A finely dressed footman held the door for me.

"Welcome Mr. Trail, come in."

Tanya's voice rang down from the stairway as she leaned over the railing.

"That will be all Fletcher, thank you."

Her footman nodded in her direction and grabbed a jacket from a nearby wall hook before walking out the door.

I wasn't sure if I was impressed by the facade of her building and presence of a footman, or just plain intimidated. I removed my footwear and began to climb the spiral staircase.

She greeted me warmly with a smile and handed me a whiskey glass abundantly filled with the potent smelling amber liquid. She raised her glass to me, took a sip and I followed suit.

I grimaced. It had been awhile since I'd drank whiskey, and I never usually drank it straight. This woman meant business.

She guided me into her home giving me a grand tour. It was a whole lot of house for one woman. As I noted there were no pictures of children or a spouse and no ring on her finger.

She talked plenty, mostly about politics and her plans for her region and "assholes" she had to deal with to get what she wanted. I didn't speak much, I wouldn't have known what to say regardless.

Luckily, she didn't seem to be unsettled by my lack of conversation. Each time my glass got close to the bottom, without asking she'd reach over and fill it up again. I was grateful for it being a Friday night.

"Would you mind if I had a smoke?" She interrupted my thoughts.

"No of course not, it's your place."

She smiled subtly and beckoned me to the patio doors leading me onto the veranda. A pack of smokes lay on a small table along with a lighter and she hastily lit one up and took a long drag.

"Ohh yeah!" She exclaimed as she blew a trail of smoke out. Her body relaxed. She looked over at me and extended the box out to me.

"You want one?"

"No sorry I don't smoke." I politely declined the offer.

I was still wondering about the purpose of the evening. I had thought she had wanted to discuss my potential. I didn't have to think much more about it.

"So back to our discussion this afternoon. You have a lot of potential like I said. But I do want to bring up one thing."

Her eyes locked on me now, her back leaning and elbows propped over the railing.

"How did you do it?"

"What's that ma'am?"

I queried, unsure what she was referring to.

"Falsify your medical records." The glint in her eyes scathing me, her smile now gone.

My heart stopped.

"Your file was too perfect. I looked harder. Your physical, pristine. I'm not doubting that at all."

She once again looked me up and down approvingly, like a rack of ribs at a meat market.

"But I've seen my fair share of forms; your clinic's header was off by a fraction of an inch and was notably scanned versus faxed. The signature too, you wavered on your "Rs". Dr. Murdoch has very concise and scratchy "Rs". I could report you, have you stripped of your badge."

My eyes fell downcast. I couldn't help but think, so this is how it ends.

"I guess I just want to know why? A fine specimen like yourself, smart, organized, obviously devoted to the job. Why go to those lengths? You know fraud is a hefty crime."

I gulped.

"I wouldn't have been allowed in."

My voice was a hoarse whisper at this point.

"I never would have had a chance."

"Why's that Mr. Trail?"

She wanted me to say it. I scanned my surroundings looking for some kind of voice recorder.

I couldn't locate one, just an outdoor surround sound system. My paranoia had served me well this far into my life, I preferred airing on the side of caution. I flung the last of my whiskey down my gullet and cleared my throat.

"I was diagnosed with a condition at an early age. I am medicated for it. They never would have let me into the academy if they'd known. I've known all my life I wanted to be a cop. I couldn't let them turn me away."

She didn't blink. But her expression appeared to soften. She took another long drag.

"You realize it would cost me my career as well if I didn't disclose what I know now?"

It wasn't really a question. More of a statement.

I nodded. We fell silent, and the moments felt like hours. She took another swig of whiskey, emptying her glass and promptly walked over to a small outdoor wet bar next to a hot tub. Retrieving another bottle from behind the counter, scotch this time, she poured herself another glass. This one considerably fuller than her previous glasses. She waved me over and filled my glass as well.

"I have somewhat of a solution for us both."

She took another long drink and doused her cigarette in a nearby ashtray.

My eyebrows raised, curious that she had any form of a solution, let alone one she would be willing to share with me.

"I have something on you, career ending. However, you also have information, if I were to not report you, that could end my career. I propose this... Fuck me."

I choked on my scotch and looked at her, eyes wide.

"Well! Then we're both bound to secrecy. I get something out of it that piques my interests, and you get to continue to be a cop."

She eyed my crotch, her eyes locked on their target.

Was I being blackmailed?

"Listen, Trail, I want what I want. You proved your intelligence to me today in the office. You intrigued me. I've spent my whole life concentrating my efforts on this career. I am divorced. No kids. And all the men I meet are all bottom feeders, beneath me. I do have standards, and you're the only man that has come close to meeting them in a long time. I have an itch. I'd be most appeased if you'd scratch it."

She said it more like a command, and as she did so, she began pulling her clothes off.

She stood stark naked in front of me. Her boob job had been done exquisitely, her thin muscular frame balanced them proportionately. Her long legs walked backwards towards the hot tub. Her confidence never faltered.

I wasn't sure what to do. She was an attractive older woman, there was no arguing that. But this was a fine line. I didn't see any other alternative though. I had made it this far, I couldn't just throw in the towel to protect my professionalism. If my cock could buy her silence, then sacrifices had to be made. I took another drink and walked forward to meet her.

The lid was off the hot tub already and the lights were changing color in the water, setting her skin aglow. Her eyes met mine.

"Undress." She commanded.

I did so. I didn't dare not follow orders. She once again looked me up and down, smiling slyly.

"I had a hunch." She said as her eyes landed on my dick.

I felt it begin to stiffen. I was unsure of how to start. There wasn't exactly chemistry between us. This was a business arrangement, a deal. I awkwardly approached, trying to kiss her. She backed up.

"No kissing, just fucking." That made it easy. Fucking I could do.

She grabbed me by the dick and led me up the stoop into the hot tub. Her aggressiveness I wasn't accustomed to, but I didn't not enjoy it. It excited me.

She sat herself on the ledge of the tub and pulled me down onto my knees in one of the seats within the tub.

The jets massaged my muscles with their powerful stream. Tanya lifted each leg up out of the water, spread eagling herself. Her manicured snatch eye level with my face. I didn't need her cues to figure out what she wanted, but she pointed to it anyway,

"Eat." she directed.

I buried my face in her twat. Enveloping it. I could hear her purring at me like a mountain lion after a satisfying meal. My tongue lashing at her vulva and clit. If this was what it took to be survival of the fittest, I was going the distance.

I spit up her cunt and sucked it back out, introducing my fingers forcefully. She was a tough bitch, she could take it. She wouldn't settle for any light one finger prodding shit. She wanted the real deal.

I three fingered her pussy easily. Her walls closed in on me with each thrust, juices flowing out of her. She hissed cuss words at me and yanked my hair, shoving my face deeper between her legs.

I was scuba diving, coming out for gasps of air only when able. I spit on my pinky and on my next heave in, I slid it up her ass. She swore extensively but didn't demand its removal.

In and out I finger fucked her and swathed her clit in my spit. Sucking it and humming my A B C's over top of it. She growled a deep hoarse growl as a gush of lady cum shot in my mouth and she screamed.

"FUCK ME!"

I was more than willing to oblige at this point. My dick rock hard. I stood up and slammed it into her dripping hole.

I lifted her up by her ass and fucked her mid air, her titties bouncing in my face and against my chest. Her long legs wrapped around me and she clutched my neck to stay aboard. Each forceful buck dared to send her flying.

She bit my neck aggressively. I swear she drew blood, but I kept my focus, slamming my meat in her again and again. Water sloshed up and around us.

"Put me down." She ordered.

I was reluctant to stop, but I still wasn't about to not follow orders. I set her down, she unwrapped her legs from around my waist and slid once again onto the hot tub's ledge. She then took those long legs of hers and stretched them up and around her head, both of them!

Clearly, she was flexible. Now she was just a head, tits and two holes. I dipped my dick back into her slit, parting her now engorged drapes. I grabbed her knees for support and followed her lead as she commanded,

"Harder!"

I jack hammered her pussy, plunging in and out of her depths, my cock warm and sticky with her fluids. I didn't want to be too bold, but I had an aching desire. I weighed the risks and decided she liked gutsy, so I went for it. Pulling out I spit on her ass and pushed my dick in. Then stuffed my three fingers back in her box. She hissed in pleasure. Her ass hole was so much tighter, it was just the friction I needed! She started talking dirty to me or more, screaming dirty to me.

"You like my ass, you dirty little fuck stain? Get it! Fuck it hard! Rip me open!"

I'd never been with a woman who was so forward and so aggressive. I found it to be more of a turn on than I'd likely ever admit to anyone. Her tits continued to bounce, slapping up and down on her pubic bones as I continuously barreled into her. Watching all the action right there, pussy parting, ass stretching, tits flopping! I was going to cum.

I quickened my pace, plunging into her deeper, harder and faster. I felt my balls shrink up, the knot in the base of my cock swelling. She reached forward and spit on her fingers and began vigorously rubbing her clit while I still three finger death punched her box and fucked her ass.

Her clit swelled up quickly, it didn't take much more stimulation. Her pussy and ass simultaneously started tightening around my hand and dick. That was all I needed.

Her howls could likely be heard a mile away. I blew my load half up her ass and managed to pull out and blew the rest on her face and tits. There was a lot of buildup. She licked her lips and sputtered the jizz as she uncurled her legs and sat herself up.

We both sunk into the tub, where she then splashed water on her face to clear it off. Her tits were afloat, the semen melting off them into the jet stream and seeping out her ass, forming a milky froth of bubbles atop the water. It reminded me of a Starbucks coffee with their fancy creamers. As a result, I'd likely never consume fancy coffee the same way again.

She grabbed her drink and took another shot of scotch and lit another cigarette before standing abruptly.

"I'll call you a cab Mr. Trail."

Her professionalism back, she handed me her cigarette then wrapped a towel around herself and stalked off to use the phone. I was being dismissed. I took a long drag of her cigarette. What the hell. I might as well.

This went on for months. A workplace affair. Deputy Tanya Bonafete would make me her sex slave in exchange for her silence. Did I mind? Not really. She was an attractive woman after all, and she was kinky as hell. We kept it a secret as much as possible, although I'm sure Grace had figured it out at some point. She would look disapprovingly when she'd see Tanya talking to me at all. Then, I was promoted to Sergeant.

She congratulated me in her own way, a stairway fuck at work. Not my finest hour on the clock, but she was happy about it. However, I was realizing that my promotion may not have been exactly an honorable one based on my work performance. I had made it so far on my own, now I was getting a helping hand. Perhaps it was Tanya's need for status. She didn't want to fuck "beneath" her. She enjoyed being on top, but according to her standards, I was a bottom feeder as well, just a well-endowed one.

It ended though, just as abruptly as it began. She made me her slave for those few months, and then she moved on to finer things.

It definitely had never been a relationship. Not like I'd had with Angel only months prior.

I missed my ex, Angel. But we had wanted different things, different locations. And deep down I knew she hadn't been the right one for me either.

I'd met the right one years ago, in high school. And now that I was off the radar at work, I could finally continue my search for her.

I shook my head, trying to erase my memory like an etch-a-sketch. That was enough of thinking about my past. I just wanted to live in the moment now.

The workday was long. The hours seemed endless. It could have been because I was tired, or maybe because I couldn't wait to be with Naomi again that evening. We had planned a reunion dinner with

Erika that night. I was nervous. I wasn't sure yet what to make of this woman who had reached out to me. It had been so random.

Many thoughts raced through my mind, but without talking with her I'd never get a concrete answer. Either way, I was grateful as it led me to Naomi quicker than I could have done on my own.

Dinner time couldn't come fast enough. I watched the last seconds tick by, handed in my stack of forms and clocked out. Time to shower and shine.

| Chapter 8 |

I pulled up to the airport at quarter after four, I wanted to give myself enough time to find parking in case she was early. I wasn't planning on meeting her at the terminal. She could come out and I'd flag her down there.

I wasn't a huge fan of crowds and Erika was well aware. Plus, it was easier than paying for parking.

I did two laps of the lot before I managed to locate a spot near the doors. I wiggled in just as a cab pulled out, sent her a quick text relaying where I was and then waited.

I left my iPod pumping through my van speakers, keeping me entertained while waiting.

At four forty–five, a rush of patrons proceeded out the exit doors. I watched studiously and hopped out, eager to greet her.

As the crowd minimalized, I saw her near the back, a flash of bright red hair lugging a large cart full of bags and another large duffel slung over her shoulder.

I ran over to her, screeching her name, and she returned the gesture once she looked up and saw that it was me fast approaching. She dropped her duffel and we embraced, both of us talking fast, not pausing to hear what each other was actually saying, just bursting with the excitement of seeing each other after so many months.

It took a few moments of feverish jibber jabber before I grabbed her cart and pushed it towards the van and began loading it up. She then was able to talk at a pace I could decipher, and we could both carry on a sensical conversation.

"Tell me about this hurricane! What happened?"

Erika then divulged a story about the storm that had delayed her flight and dealing with the emergency services and the border patrol.

"I wasn't scared, I knew we'd be fine, but it was a mess! But it always is after a large storm like that! My biggest issue was just trying to deal with the airport. They tried to be accommodating, but it sure is a headache! Wait a second. Where are we going? You're headed back to Kelowna. Shouldn't we be headed back that direction?"

I smiled smugly and felt my cheeks once again get hot.

"I thought we'd go to dinner." I said a little too blankly. Erika didn't buy it.

"Oookay, what's going on? You're blushing! Is there something you want to tell me?"

And so I began my own tale of a day and night of sexual bliss with an old comrade. Erika's eyes bulged when I mentioned his name, and again when I went into detail about what a great lay he was.

"You dirty slut!" she squealed at the end, laughing and punching me in the arm.

Although I noted that similar angry glint deep in her eyes that she always had anytime Chad was ever mentioned as well. But I shrugged it off as the response of a protective best friend.

I bowed my head, laughing and faking a shameful smile.

"You would have done the same thing!" I defended myself.

"Ha ha! You're probably right! But I would've done it ten times better!" The glint had left her eyes. She stuck her tongue out at me and smiled a big shit eating grin. Erika was always super competitive, so of course sexual conquests wouldn't be any different. I just laughed.

"So, then where are we going?" She probed again.

"Well, I thought maybe we could all go for dinner together? I'm sticking to girl code here. IF, I decide to pursue something, I'd need your approval first!"

Her head turned; I could feel her eyes boring into me.

"Something? You're thinking of considering a relationship with Dustin after a one-night stand?"

I was taken aback by her tone of disbelief and disapproval. Her body language now rigid. My chest tightened and my own body became tense.

"Well, not a relationship per say, but why not? I mean we really got along, and it's not like he's some random stranger. We did attend high school together after all. Plus, he's a cop, seems like he has his shit together, and he's a good-looking guy. I'm not saying I'm going to marry the guy. I'd maybe just like to see where it would go! I mean if anything, I'd like to at least maybe sleep with him a few more times."

Erika kind of half rolled her eyes and looked back out her window.

"I think you're moving too fast again, and you already have your hopes up for something more than what this clearly was, a *fuck*."

She emphasized the word *fuck* to make her point.

"That's *not* what I'm doing." I defended myself.

"I'm just curious if there's more to the chemistry I felt. I'm not going to throw myself at him or create a relationship where there's not one. And that's why I have you. You can come feel him out at dinner and give me your verdict."

I could tell I made my point with the last comment.

She sighed, and her body relaxed.

"Alright, that's fair. I actually am pretty eager to meet him and see why you're so taken with him already. So where are we going to eat?"

We pulled up at the place Dustin had suggested. Blue Gator Bar, the neon sign flashed against the afternoon sunlight. The staff must've turned it on early in anticipation for the crowd to come. Either that, or forgot it was on all night and all day.

A black 4x4 GMC truck pulled up just down from us in the parking lot. I could make out Dustin's form through the window. He must've exchanged his squad truck for his own personal one at shift's end. We both clambered out of the cabs of our vehicles and he spotted us almost immediately and walked over.

"Hey! You remember Erika?"

I gave a not so formal introduction as if Dustin and I hadn't already just discussed this very topic. Dustin jetted his hand out to meet Erika's and gave it a firm shake.

"Of course! How have you been?"

She smiled smugly. I could tell she was eyeing him up and was approving of his physique.

"Great! Good to see you again!"

Erika flashed him a flirty grin and squeezed his hand in return.

"You ladies did not age, I tell ya!"

Dustin complimented, a gesture that made us both giggle like schoolgirls. He held out an arm to guide us to the front door.

"Thank you both for joining me! I know you're probably tired after your long flight, Erika."

"Ohhh, probably not as tired as you two."

She said half under her breath but still loud enough to make us both flush.

"Ahem," Dustin cleared his throat, clearly a bit uncomfortable.

Erika quickly changed the subject as we walked towards a booth.

"Yeah, I'm not bad, I slept on the plane. Just glad to be home. It was a great trip. But it's always so nice to finally return."

"Well, I'm super glad you're home. I've missed you like crazy!" I gushed.

"We have a lot of catching up to do. And a lot of drinking! Speaking of which..."

Erika snapped her fingers obnoxiously at a nearby waitress. I covered my face embarrassed.

"Can we get a round of shots please? Tequila!"

The waitress nodded and walked away, clearly a little annoyed.

"I wasn't really planning on drinking, Erika." I said.

"I have to drive us home later."

"Oh lighten up!" She brushed me off.

"We can afford to have a little fun, I just got here!"

Dustin looked at me sympathetically and shrugged. He then let a small smile emerge on his face as he and Erika burst into conversation.

When the waitress returned, we all took our shots, me a little begrudgingly, before chasing with my slice of lime. We all slammed our shot glasses down, and Erika hooted and ordered another round as well as a round of beers for us all.

The waitress smartly started up a tab before walking away to retrieve yet another round of drinks.

Surprisingly, Erika was friendlier than I expected her to be towards a potential beau of mine. The way she dug her heels in, on the car ride over, I thought maybe she'd be gruff with him. But they were getting along famously, and we all chatted up a storm.

We drifted between the past and the present, laughing and teasing one another, and re-living funny stories as if they'd only just happened. I'm sure the liquor was definitely helping the conversation flow.

I could see Erika getting looser and more flirtatious. She'd reach out and touch him often, either his shoulder, or his hand. She would lean in close to his face and laugh.

I was trying not to feel jealous, but I couldn't help but feel like my territory was being moved in on. I knew this could just be drunken Erika, or competitive Erika coming out to play. But I couldn't be sure, and I found myself feeling insecure once again.

We ate, and she continued to order us drinks and shots. My BLT club disappeared quickly, as I was needing something to help absorb the alcohol. I kept ordering water to wash down all the tequila and beers as well, sipping on them steadily, but it was a losing battle, and

I eventually felt the warm fuzzy sensation of drunkenness wash over me.

It was then that I was fully able to let go and really had fun, which was a welcome relief, as then I wasn't feeling those rising insecurities any longer.

I excused myself to the bathroom and Erika tagged along. Sitting in the stall beside me she exclaimed.

"He is a hunk, Naomi! Does he have any friends, because I could totally go for a slice similar to that."

"We actually haven't even discussed his friends or co-workers much; you could always ask."

Hoping maybe if there was a friend brought up that Erika would ease off Dustin a bit. Erika was already washing her hands and checking her makeup when I stepped out of my stall.

Her usually pale skin tanned a deep bronze from her vacation sun, and a million freckles added to the appearance of her tan as they were in even more of an abundance around her shoulders, chest and nose.

Her bright red hair tousled down her back, her slender figure leaning forward into the mirror reapplying her lip-gloss.

She wore a loose-fitting tank with braided knit T-straps on the back, and a pair of khaki shorts that were barely visible under the hem of her tank.

Her strappy sandals clicked as she leaned back onto the ground. "Hmm, maybe..."

She hummed almost to herself. She spun and exited, leaving me with my hands still soaped, rinsing under the running water.

I looked steadfast at myself in the mirror, locking eyes with my reflection.

What the hell is going on? I thought to myself.

Was I already so incapacitated that I couldn't decipher if my best friend was hitting on the guy I like? Or was I being jealous and paranoid? I shook my head and splashed some cold water on my face; tequila and I were not friends. I let the water drip dry off my face before I headed back to our table.

Upon arriving, I found Erika was sitting beside Dustin, cuddled right up. My heart caught in my throat and I gulped it down. I felt myself getting hot, and I briskly plopped down across from them, fuming.

Dustin glanced at me uncertainly, but just then Erika brushed his sideburns with her fingertips and made some joke about not being able to keep her hands off him. He laughed, almost nervously.

"Excuse me a minute."

Irritated, I again stood up and stormed up to the long L-shaped bar. I waited politely, trying to choke down my feelings until our waitress, Emily, saw me waiting and walked over.

"What can I get you?"

"Can I get a gin and tonic please? Actually, can you make it a double? And what's the strongest thing you have?"

Emily looked at me, clearly could read the pain in my eyes and nodded.

"We have some absinthe in the cabinet?"

I nodded in return. It doesn't get much stronger than that! I turned my back to the bar and leaned against its top and stood glaring at the top of their heads.

Why is she doing this to me? We're supposed to be best friends. I get that she's competitive and has been traveling the globe this past year, but you don't just forget how to be a friend.

Erika took a sip of her drink and waved at me from across the way. Dustin looked up too and quickly took a swig of his beer, then stood up, heading for the washroom.

"Here you go." Emily said as she plunked my drinks down on the bar table.

"Go slow with this one, okay?" She looked at me with a pitying look, indicating the small shot of absinthe.

I could already smell its strong odor and choked back a gag.

"Thank you." I muttered softly.

Wasting no time at all, I held it up to my lips, trying not to breathe it in. I blatantly ignored Emily's warning. With a toss I slammed it back, choking on its potency. I quickly grabbed a nearby empty glass and water jug and poured myself a chase, sloppily sloshing that back as well.

"Ugh!" I groaned, already regretting my decision.

I will not be driving home tonight, that's for sure. Grabbing my gin and tonic, I saw Dustin ambling towards me, sliding up effortlessly alongside me.

"What are you doing over here by your lonesome?"

I didn't want to let on that I was perturbed by his and Erika's closeness so I replied simply,

"Just grabbing another drink."

"Ok well, don't be too long," he smiled reassuringly and cupped my shoulder with his palm softly before heading back.

I planned on waiting a few moments before I returned. I wasn't in any rush to witness more of Erika's displays of affection. I sipped my gin, and sucked in a long deep breath, blowing out through my nose to calm my nerves.

A guy in a ball cap and black t-shirt slid up next to me from a seat over. He was decent looking, a little more boyish than my usual type, if I even really had a "type," but he was pleasant and introduced himself as Kyle.

"What's your name?"

"Naomi. Nice to meet you, Kyle."

We smiled politely at one another and he began to make small talk. He was super nice and came off very wise and gentlemanly for such a young buck. And in all honesty, I appreciated the distraction.

I did notice my companion's eyes looking over the top of their booth to see what was taking me so long at one point though, and if I wasn't mistaken, it appeared to be glares I was receiving. I humbly ignored their presence and continued conversing with Kyle about his travels.

Turned out he was a trucker, only been driving for a few years so far, and he was on his way to Calgary. He was very sweet and seemed so lonely and eager to talk to somebody.

It must have been twenty minutes or so when Emily slid him his bill.

"Thanks Em!"

He slipped some cash under the receipt and stretched out his hand for mine. I extended and he kissed my knuckles softly, his five o'clock shadow just starting to tint his skin. I smiled at him.

"It was such a pleasure talking to you, Naomi. Thank you for the company."

"You as well, Kyle! Safe travels."

I waved as he turned and strode for the exit; I then proceeded back to our booth to join as the third wheel.

"Who was that?" Erika and Dustin both asked in unison once I sat back down.

"That was Kyle." I answered coolly, I didn't bother to elaborate, just took another sip of my drink and returned their gaze.

"You two seemed..cozy." Dustin dug for more.

"Yeah, that was a pretty long interaction for just small talk." Erika threw in, digging for more information.

I just shrugged; they didn't need to know it was just an innocent conversation between two strangers.

Plus, it felt good to see that perhaps Dustin had a bit of a jealous streak himself. I grinned smugly and took another sip, then pretended to busy myself wiping some condensation rings from our glasses off the table with a napkin.

They seemed to take the hint and moved off the subject, although Dustin kept surveying me, his blue eyes steely and hard.

It was already starting to get late, and we still hadn't made plans for accommodations for the night; but Erika brushed it off when I brought up the subject and pulled Dustin onto the small dance floor when a bass dropping song began thudding through the speakers. She beckoned me over as well. A few other people were already dancing and bopping around.

My earlier absinthe was now taking effect and I could feel the dance floor swirling beneath my feet, and I swear I was seeing things flying above us through the laser lights.

Erika grabbed my hand and yanked me over to her and immediately started puppeteering me, making me dance and move along with her.

Dustin laughed, took another swig of his beer and joined us. It was obvious he likely didn't usually dance much. Not that he was bad at it, but you could tell he felt awkward at first. It was exactly how I felt, until I found my rhythm and got lost in the song. My body swayed and moved to the beat.

The speakers cranked up as more people got brave and joined us on the dance floor. Before I knew it there was a crowd forming and more people were lining up out the door to get in.

There were bodies pressing in on us from every direction. I could feel the muggy heat from everyone's liquored bodies. The floor shook every time the bass boomed, trebling up my legs. I loved to dance, but I was usually too shy.

I was glad to be equipped with my liquid courage once again to push me to cut loose and enjoy. My hips rolled and curved to the music.

I looked up and saw once again the swirling shapes flitting through the laser lights, dancing on everyone's sweaty faces.

My head was spinning and I thought maybe I'd have to go sit down, but as I moved to find a resting spot, I felt two big hands slide around me, cupping my hips from behind, stabilizing me but also guiding my rear end out and down, deep into a jeaned crotch.

I looked over my shoulder. Dustin was there peering down at me, grinding into me. He moved his hands down further on the front of my hips and landed them on my pubic bones, and my heart started palpitating!

That familiar bass boom was now making me more aware of that treble up my legs, making my clit hum with desire. I couldn't help it.

I had been so upset thinking Erika was hitting on him all night, but I had never stopped to notice if he had truly been reciprocating or if he was just being polite. I took his hands wrapped around my lower waist as a win, and fully unleashed my libido on the dance floor.

I was swaying and grinding my ass into his crotch, letting him watch and savor the view. His hands started massaging me gently, his fingers still pressing into my pubis.

Not wanting to risk his fingers wandering any further than they already were, I spun around to tease him face to face instead. I stroked his chest, running my palms up and down his breast bones and trailing them down to the hem of his jeans. Letting my fingers trace the tip of the hem line, just inside his pants, all the while still matching his gaze and swaying to the music.

I hooked his belt loops and pulled his body in close to me until I could feel his breath and smell his sweat.

He grabbed my arms and gently guided them up around his neck, and then settled his own on my lower back and ass. Our bodies rubbed and pulsed against one another, the fabric of his jeans and my shorts bunched and caused friction. I felt like a teenager dry humping again.

He leaned down and kissed me, his lips soft and supple. I leaned up and kissed his neck, nibbling on it and his ear lobe slightly, his skin moist from the muggy heat. He tasted like salt and I licked my lips.

Suddenly Erika's head appeared right over the shoulder and it startled me. In my drunken state, her hair appeared to be glowing green, and those damn floating lights were hovering around her face, drawing my focus away from inquiring eyes. I hadn't noticed that she must have asked a question.

"Huh?" I looked at her blankly.

"Do you guys want to get out of here?" She shrugged her head towards the exit. Dustin and I exchanged looks, and without hesitation, we nodded in unison, neither of us blinking.

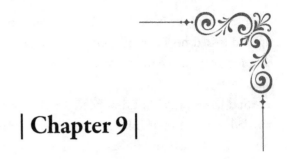

| Chapter 9 |

The cab pulled up, not five minutes after Dustin called to summon it. The two of them had me supported on either side. I was starting to get tipsy and wasn't walking quite as straight as I should. I guess while dancing, at the end there, I had been relying on Dustin's strength to keep me from teetering a bit.

Erika bought a water bottle and was thrusting it into my fist. Making me hydrate and hopefully flush some of the effects of the absinthe out of my system before I got too badly intoxicated, although I think I had already surpassed that point. Erika opened the door and climbed in. Dustin assisted me to ease into the middle seat and then he slid in after me. He gave directions to the driver, and I heard the engine rev and the clicking of the turn signal as we pulled out.

I felt like I was in a spaceship, and all the lights whizzing past were stars shooting past us as we warped into lightspeed. Of course, this was likely just my delusions talking, but it felt cool! Erika continued to shove the water in my face, forcing me to drink.

Dustin stroked my back and played with my hair in an attempt to be soothing, but really the sensation of his touch was just making me "itch" again.

We approached a tall white building, with large floor to ceiling windows overlooking the city. Small patios were the only obstruction of the clear glass view, and it wasn't much of an obstruction. The modern details of this condominium were artistically done.

Structurally, it was breath-taking for a building. I peered up through the cab window and had to lean over Dustin's lap and gaze way, way up to see it all. As the cab completely halted and Dustin tapped his Visa on the driver's square terminal, we all began to pile out of the cab.

"Umm, where are we?" I asked, for I really had no idea.

I thought maybe we were on our way to a hotel. Neither of them responded. They just both strode forward towards the doors.

Dustin punched in a code on the keypad and held the door for us as we followed him in. A meticulously designed lobby greeted us. White marble floors and bright LED pot lights lit the way to a stainless-steel elevator door. The door opened as we arrived in front of the elevator, and following suit, I clambered in after my companions, using the railing for a safety net.

Dustin punched the number 4 button, and seconds later the door closed and the elevator did its usual jerk into motion, sending me off balance.

I steadied myself and took another sip of water, determined to shake off this blurry off-balanced beast I had transformed into.

I still had no response to my question outside, and I couldn't understand why. Unless I was even more out of it than I originally thought and had only imagined myself asking it? The chime dinged, announcing our arrival on the fourth floor. The doors slid open and we proceeded into the bright hallway, which was just as impressive as the lobby.

Wide open corridors, one whole wall was glass. I didn't dare get too near it for fear I'd fall. Yes, I was hallucinating, but I'd say only minor hallucinations. That glass was pretty damn clean!

We had only walked a short distance when we stopped at a big white double door with the number 469 in a silver oval above it. Dustin punched in a code on a pin pad off to the side then replaced the cover on it so it once again blended in with the door frame. He then clicked the knocker seven times, or did I imagine that? Seven seemed like a lot of times. I must have just still been drunk. He swung open the door and guided us in with an open arm.

"Welcome to my home ladies!" he announced gallantly.

My jaw dropped; we were at his place? And what a place! The entranceway was large and spacious. The whole condo was open concept, with tall ceilings, white crisp walls, oak colored vinyl plank floors, and in the middle of the living room, a huge white shag rug.

He must've really liked white, or the clean look of it, because most of his belongings were white.

He had a large white leather sectional with some storm gray and black throw cushions. A large TV was mounted on one wall, and I could see surround sound speakers strategically placed to blend into the walls and ceiling.

The pot lights were dimmed and set off a serene amber glow, warming the space. The city lights blinked and shone through those huge, floor to ceiling windows lining one whole side of the condo.

A fish tank was against one of the walls near the back of the living area. It bubbled and glowed with the changing light shades of the lasered filtration system. Bright colored fish swam around rapidly. They almost seemed happy to see him arrive home.

I removed my shoes and placed them in the entranceway hall tree in one of the cubbies, then slowly made my way further into the room, taking it all in.

The kitchen was attached to the living area, and only a big butcher block top island separated the two areas.

A large gas range stove was behind that and a huge double door stainless steel fridge. The sink was a traditional deep farm style one but with the modern squaring of the corners.

A large linear glass chandelier hung above the island lighting the area, as well as under cabinet lighting.

The clean lines of this place were immaculate! I was in sheer awe, and my face must've shown it.

"My humble abode m'lady," he joked.

"Humble, my ass!" Erika chortled. "This place is lit as fuck!" I shook my head up and down in agreeance.

"Well, I figured I'd waited this long to buy a place, I might as well get something I really liked."

Erika found a built-in bar and began mixing some more drinks. Using the ice machine she filled three small scotch glasses and then began to pour.

"Make yourself at home." Dustin half rolled his eyes at her.

She smiled.

"Don't mind me."

Dustin led us down a short hallway, indicating the washroom on the right and then a huge doorless entrance leading into a game room of some sort.

Another white shag rug was on the floor and a pool table was just off to the left of the center of the room.

An electric fireplace was inlaid into the wall and he flicked the switch on; the flames burst on and began flickering against the glass instantly.

A few autographed jerseys hung in shadow boxes along another wall, and some leather bar stools beneath a small wet bar.

In the far corner a small gym was set up on some rubber mats, weights placed very orderly in their pyramid casings and a treadmill and pull up bar sat beside them.

Dustin put on some music and Erika placed our drinks on the ledge of the bar, grabbed some pool cues and threw them at us. Dustin caught his, but I barely saw it coming and fumbled the catch horribly. At least I managed to not allow it to fall completely to the floor.

Erika laughed and started putting the balls in the triangle. Apparently, we were going to attempt to play.

This wasn't exactly how I imagined the end of the night going after that spicy dancing at the club, but I guess the distraction of having to focus in order to play pool might help me sober up a bit so I seemed like less of a goon.

I was grateful Chad had the kids for the weekend, as this was turning into a whole weekend affair instead of a one day return trip as was originally planned.

I was thinking of the hangover I was likely going to face tomorrow and hung my head, ugh! Why did I have to react so perniciously?

Erika yelled.

"Break!" and the pool balls shot every which way across the table, three finding their ways into pockets.

"You're on my team Naomi, girls against guy." she declared.

That was a relief. I was terrible at pool. Perhaps Erika's skills would save me some further embarrassment.

Dustin took a sip of the scotch Erika had prepared for him, and then approached the table in order to make his first shot after Erika failed to pocket any more balls after her third shot. He leaned forward over the felt surface, lining up his shot precisely.

Crack!

His cue made contact and four balls ricocheted off the rails and one another before landing in their appointed pockets.

"Ooo, he plays hard ball!" Erika taunted.

I gulped. There was no way I could hold my own at all, especially if they were both this talented. As the number of balls dwindled after Dustin took each shot, it got harder and harder for him to pocket, until eventually he missed altogether and it was my turn.

"Shit." I sighed under my breath.

I attempted to line my cue up with my ball. I'm sure my positioning was all wrong because I heard them both stifle their giggles. I felt completely awkward and stupid. I pushed my cue forward as I had witnessed them both do effortlessly; but instead, my cue veered along the green felt and right around the ball I'd been aiming for. Nothing moved.

Dustin and Erika could stifle no longer, and they both burst out laughing. I paused for a second, mortified, until I couldn't help myself and I burst out laughing as well.

Finally, I was able to really cut loose and started having fun again. We clinked glasses and drank our scotch, cracking jokes and teasing one another. They both gave me pool tips and we eventually got a half decent game going. Dustin still ended up winning, but he did let it be known that he spent a lot of free time in that game room, so that eased our shame.

The bottle of scotch had made its way to our wet bar at some point in the game, and now only a quarter of its contents remained. Well, that was until Dustin grabbed the bottle and he and Erika fought over the last few sips.

I helped by putting the cues and balls away. Dustin seemed like a fairly clean and orderly guy, and I already felt bad for us consuming all his scotch and for the liquor splashes all over his wet bar.

The music was turned up. My back was to whomever had the controller, but I was digging the tune. I couldn't help but dance a bit whilst I tidied. I could see Erika dancing as well out of my peripherals. I danced around to the front of the pool table, when I felt his hands cup me around the waist again and spin me around.

Caught off guard, but pleasantly surprised, I shrieked and giggled a bit, and that's when his lips collided with mine.

We started kissing, his tongue massaging mine, and then suddenly his hands grabbed my ass cheeks and hoisted me up onto the edge of the pool table. My heart raced. I looked around for Erika. I didn't want to be too affectionate right in front of her, but instead of seeing her, I heard her knees scuffling behind me on the felt of the pool table.

Her hands swept my hair to the side, and she kissed the side of my neck from behind. I was floored. What was happening?

Dustin wasn't taken aback at all. Instead, he leaned forward again and kissed me deep. Erika's arm reached over my shoulder and scooped his neck and head over in her direction where she began kissing him as well. I felt my mouth gape open. I was so taken aback I didn't have time to react! *Should I be mad? Appalled? Turned on?* I had no idea! Maybe I was just imagining all this! That's it! This was all a hallucination, and really, I passed out on the couch an hour ago or something. That sounded more like me anyways. Tame, predictable, boring.

Dustin's lips once again locked with mine and as soon as they parted, Erika spun my head and latched her lips onto mine as well. What should I do? I was stunned. The only time I'd ever kissed a girl before was way back in my early twenties or late teens. I couldn't even remember, so it likely hadn't piqued my interest much.

I was quite obviously inebriated at the time, and I think it may have been a dare or a game of some sort. But since then, nothing. It had never been an avenue I'd explored or had much interest in. I was typically a one guy kind of girl.

I stared at her, as she pulled away slightly trying to read me; but again, she gave me no chance to react and dove in again, kissing me deeper this time.

Her lips were soft and thin, plumper than Dustin's but not by much. Her tongue tasted sweet, the remnants of scotch and her strawberry vape lingered.

The scent of her perfume wafted into my nostrils, flowery like honeysuckle. She broke her latch on me and I started to say something, but before I uttered more than a pitiful,

"Ah!"

Dustin had once again started kissing me.

Erika leaned in so we were now cheek to cheek, and he drifted back and forth between the two of us kissing us both. I could taste her on his lips, on his tongue; he grabbed both our heads gently and turned our faces together so we could kiss again.

Of course, him being a male and seeing two girls kiss, would be the ultimate turn on. I decided then, rather than be insulting or a mood crusher, I wanted to arouse him, wanted to make his wildest dreams come true. Seeing how Erika was willing, I might as well rise to the occasion and blow his mind. So, I gave in...

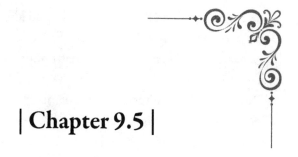

| Chapter 9.5 |

I hadn't let on that Erika Crane and I had already spoken prior to me actually seeing her today, and Erika hadn't let on either. We had a nearly unspoken agreement that I hoped would benefit in the end.

Now here I was after just reacquainting with not one but two ladies I went to high school with, letting them into my condominium late at night. I had high hopes for how the evening would play out. I wanted Naomi, that's for sure! But Erika was pretty decent looking herself and seemed up for anything. I was intrigued by the thought of possibly seducing the both of them.

Naomi was a little tipsier than I would've liked, but I had a feeling she felt she needed it. Hey, if it helped her draw out her inner deviant, I was all for it!

Out of habit, I made the mistake of clicking my knocker my lucky number seven times. In doing so, Naomi dawned a kind of weirded out expression, while Erika didn't seem perturbed.

In order to distract from my slip up, I announced their arrival as I swung open the door. It seemed to work. Naomi's face especially looked awestruck.

I quite forgot what an impression my place could make on people.

Trying to lighten the atmosphere that followed, and the silence that fell, I made an attempt at cracking a joke.

"My humble abode m'lady" I jeered.

Erika's comment that followed and Naomi's drunken nodding told me my joke had fallen short of my goal.

Erika walked around to my built-in bar and began mixing some more drinks. I rolled my eyes. I didn't like when people touched my things. In some cases, I made exceptions, but it was another thing I needed to work on.

I led them down the hall to my multipurpose room. I walked over and put some music on for background noise, as it would seem

Erika began making herself comfortable once more, helping herself to the pool cues and setting the drinks she prepared on my bar's ledge *un*-coastered, yet another *faux pas* of mine.

I caught the stick she threw at my head, possibly a little too forcefully. Looks like we're going to play...

The extra scotch Erika had poured for us, a really good year I might add, was going down fast. My bottle was nearly empty, and all of us were feeling the effects, Naomi more than obviously so.

The game over, she began fumbling trying to put things away and wipe up the spilt liquor off my bar. I appreciated her efforts and loved watching her do it.

She was dancing away as she wiped up the spots where booze had been sloshed. Erika, catching on to her vibe, also began swaying. I sat back admiring, watching as Naomi maneuvered her way in front of my pool table once more.

Being an opportunist, I made my move. I snuck up behind her and wrapped my hands around her waist, turning her around to face me.

I silenced her shrieks by locking her lips on mine, kissing her passionately. She didn't hesitate to kiss me back, our tongues intertwining, so I decided to take it one step further. Grabbing her by her ass cheeks, I lifted her up, placing her on the wooden rail of my pool table.

Erika must have been waiting for me to make my move, as she wasn't far behind. She caught my eye and gave me a subtle nod. The plan was in motion.

Crawling across the green felt, she brushed Naomi's auburn hair to the side and began kissing her neck. Naomi looked stunned, like she might stop everything if I didn't act fast. I pushed forth, kissing her again, calming her momentarily.

Erika was a lady of action, and as soon as she saw an opening she grabbed me and kissed me as well. Her lips were thin, just like her frame. Her kiss felt how most one night stands feel, cold and strange. She didn't emit the kind of warmth Naomi did. Perhaps that was because Naomi kissed with feeling, and intent. Erika was likely just kissing me for a sporadic threesome; sheer lust.

Naomi's face still looked aghast, her reaction held at bay as she likely didn't know how to react, given that the liquor was likely fogging her brain.

I was hopeful, if I kept the momentum going, things would turn out in my favor. Erika was even faster though. She pulled off of me and went straight for Naomi's big lips. She showed more passion kissing Naomi than I had felt when she kissed me, that's for sure. I sure did enjoy watching them kiss, the crotch area of my pants once again grew tighter.

Each time Erika pulled off her I pushed myself in again. It felt like a kissing competition at first, battling it out for Naomi's affections. I had to remember, this was a collaboration, we were a team.

Erika placed her face right next to Naomi's, cheek to cheek, and I kissed one then the other, picking up on Erika's cues. Then I turned their heads so I could feast my eyes on them kissing each other once more.

Watching them tongue bathe one another, my erection near prodded a hole in my pants. Naomi looked at me, a new expression in her eyes. I tried to read her. A sudden confidence, an allure.

Whatever it was, I liked it!

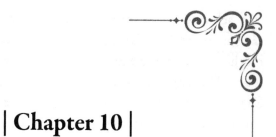

| Chapter 10 |

Back and forth, our tongues all took turns caressing one another's. I felt Erika pull off her shirt behind me, and heard it hit the floor after she whipped it across the room. She then reached forward, assisting Dustin to pull off his black t-shirt as well. He eagerly removed it and it dropped on the shag rug below. I felt both Erika's and Dustin's hands grasping my shirt and pulling up.

I hesitated, and they must've sensed my resistance because they both started kissing my shoulders and neck, motivating me. All the while sliding my shirt up and kissing my abdomen and back, tracing their fingers seductively. I hate to admit it, but I completely melted.

As soon as my arms relaxed Dustin guided them up, and Erika lifted the material up and over my head. They kept me occupied by taking turns kissing me and then making their way back to my neck and body.

Erika's fingers swiftly unclasped my bra, and my defenses came up again. I grabbed my breasts in an attempt to cover them.

She kissed my neck and collar bone, softly, and slowly, it seemed she was savoring each suckle of my skin. Dustin's hands glided up my naked sides and settled under my arms before sliding forward forcing me to uncover myself. I shivered, not because I was cold, although I was a little, but because this was so new, and quite honestly frightening for me.

I compared myself to a lab rat with two scientists manipulating my body, testing for different boundaries and responses until they got the one they wanted. Erika's breasts pressed into my back, warm and soft on my chilled skin.

Goosebumps rose up all over my body and they both made efforts to warm me with their bodies by waffling me between them even tighter. Dustin fondled my breasts, my nipples firm with the cold and uncertainty. He began tonguing them and kissing their curves.

I didn't know what to do with myself. That one extra body in the mix had thrown me for a loop, and I didn't know where my hands should go or who I should focus on.

I felt useless, but neither of them seemed to mind. Instead, I was more of a prop in the center of this *menage a' trois*.

I decided to take some action and caressed Dustin's chest, started kissing his body as well. Erika would turn my head to kiss her every now and again after pausing from kissing and licking my body.

I wasn't sure how far this was going to go. I knew where I wanted it to go with Dustin, but the Erika aspect had me lost.

I lost my patience and pulled his belt loops towards me. He stumbled into me and I immediately went for his fly, unbuttoning it with ease then pulling down his zipper.

The huge swollen dick imprint bulging through his jeans told me my plan to *blow his mind* was working.

I wrapped my hand over top of the bulge and rubbed, outlined the shape and felt his cock swell even more with the contact of my touch. It felt like Christmas, as I peeled down his pants and boxer briefs, having his girthy dick spring up at me once again.

He slid me back onto the table further and Erika moved to allow it. His pants and briefs hit the floor and he kneeled up onto the pool table as well.

The temptation was so strong, I licked my lips hungrily and got on my hands and knees like a cat on the prowl. Licking up his lengthy shaft from balls to tip, then sucking on his head.

Mmm!

That was better. Erika followed suit and joined me on all fours. Getting into the atmosphere of this sharing, I allowed her the privilege of also lapping at his glistening and swollen head, which she did graciously. We both licked and alternated sucking down the length of his cock, lapping our tongues at the beads of pre-cum protruding from his tip in thanks. Erika took to fondling his balls and sucking on them while I worked his dick; plunging it deep down my throat and coating it in saliva before sucking it right up and stirring it around in my mouth.

Dustin was moaning and grasped our hair like a bridle, this time more in an attempt to withhold us from stimulating him too much more for fear he might blow prematurely.

Erika and I kissed, ignoring his hints. I was enjoying kissing her more and more. There was no whisker rub. She kissed like me, and since I consider myself to excel in this area, it made it quite pleasant.

Our eyes met and we configured a plan with no speech necessary. Simultaneously, we both licked up his shaft, then taking turns, I'd suck his head, then her, back and forth, working him like a lollipop. Our eyes watched him, seeing his immense pleasure and quivering with ecstasy. His six-pack glowed in the flickering of the flames from the fireplace; he was quite the sight!

I'd never felt so powerful as I did at this moment. Abruptly, Erika caught my gaze, grinned and jumped off the table and disappeared behind Dustin's kneeling frame. Confused, but not wanting to lose momentum, I continued to work on him. Sucking and jerking him off, pulsing his pole up and down into my mouth and down my throat.

I heard whispering and looked up and in that split-second Erika's head disappeared from Dustin's shoulder. Before I had time to register, he was flipping me onto my back and Erika was dragging my bottom half to the table's edge.

My shorts were ripped off my body with such force, I thought for sure I'd be drug from the table all together. Caught by surprise, I was definitely not anticipating what happened next.

Erika thrust apart my legs and plunged her head between my thighs. She licked up and down my slit, encircling my clit, blowing cool air between my legs that sent goosebumps all up my thighs and caused my nipples to once again harden.

I gasped and moaned, then choked on my moan when Dustin's dick drove itself down my throat. I reached my arms around, grabbing his ass cheeks and using them as my handles to jack hammer his dick into my mouth again and again.

Erika also picked up the pace, lapping my pussy thirstily. She paused for one second, and I felt why! She must have sucked her finger, making it wet and lubed, and then she slowly eased it up inside me. She began fingering me, still lapping and sucking at my clit.

My legs began shaking with the titillation being bestowed upon me. I glanced up while continuously working Dustin's shaft and caught him watching Erika eating me out.

I got excited knowing how aroused he was watching me being pleasured, and I allowed myself to really unleash and release. Erika's tongue lashed wildly against my pearl, slowly swiping her tongue down my slit again, parting me then engulfing my entire snatch with her mouth, sucking me dry and repeating; causing me to weep my juices like an ever-flowing fountain.

Dustin seemed to notice my toes beginning to curl while he was looking back watching Erika work me, and he grabbed her hair to get her attention. She stopped and he helped lift her onto the table.

We both got up on all fours again and turned, our rear ends facing him and sticking up. He started fingering Erika and slid his dick into me, pumping both shallow and then deep, a rotation of seven pumps before pulling out and switching.

He buried his dick until it was fully immersed in her crater and pumped in and out of her in the same motion, he had delivered to me, fingering me all the while.

Then he'd pull out once again and switch, submerging himself inside me again.

I felt his cock skin roll up and back and then glide forward, catching inside me. Every time he pulled out and switched my pussy ached for his meat.

My clit vibrated with anticipation to be slapped by his nuts swinging forward as he pounded me. The pause in between, as torturous as it was, also added to the intensity when he'd slip it back in.

There wasn't a dry second, Erika and I both slathering wet, his dick dripping with it, and swapping back and forth.

Never in my mind would I have ever in any normal circumstance considered this arousing, and yet here I was, afire with passion. I could hear our pussies slopping as he slammed in, his hips thrusting against our butt cheeks. I rocked back and forth allowing him to get even deeper, rotating again so he hit all the spots. Erika saw and followed suit. We were a team, both arousing him and ourselves.

His manhood was so engorged, I could feel every vein, his pulse throbbing through his shaft, beating against the walls of my cavern.

Smack!

Like lightning, he spanked us both across our asses. I could feel the sting and heat from the blow. Instinctively I raised my ass even higher, arcing my back until I was nose down in the felt.

Thwack!

He struck us again! I bit my lip, absorbing the pain and loving it! Someone's empty scotch glass was off to the one side of the table's ledge and he grabbed it.

I heard the clinking of the ice against the rim of the glass. I was unsure why he would need an empty glass, but I was too immersed in being fucked to give it much thought. Ice cold water dripped onto my asshole from above before that ice cube was placed right where that droplet had landed. I sucked in my breath and held back a yelp. So cold!

It was in such a private area, and the shocking sensation from the sudden temperature change caused me to whimper. He held that ice there with his thumb, applying pressure, and letting the ice melt beneath his thumb. It was only a few seconds before the cold made the area feel numb, the cold droplets tracing down his thumb and rolling down to my labia. I shivered as his pole pushed the cold beads up into me with a few thrusts before again swapping to Erika.

The pressure of his thumb as the ice melted, slowly disappearing, allowed his thumb to push inside me. The numbing of the ice caused me not to feel any of the discomfort that would normally occur when a foreign object was placed in such an area. His thumb swirled and made contact with what I can only explain as another sweet spot.

I shuddered with pleasure as he hooked his thumb there and then rewarded me with a few extra deep thrusts.

He thumb fucked my ass, while still going back and forth between mine and Erika's pussies until I could sense he was close, and I chose to change it up.

I slid up from my position and pushed him to lay down. Erika stretched her leg over his head, straddling his face and his tongue got down to business, lashing in and out, lapping at her. Her tuft of soft ginger pubes resting on his chin, she ground her muff down on him until he was full on frenching her pussy with such veracity, I'm surprised she didn't erupt just then. I sucked our juices off his meat, tasting our flavors combined, the taste of sex ingrained in my taste buds. I slurped him, savoring the tartness.

Erika reached for me and pulled me atop Dustin's lower half and I instantly got her drift. I mounted his still saliva-soaked knob and eased myself onto it. He slipped inside me with little resistance, but I still gasped at the depth his dick reached in this new position. I leaned in and Erika and I kissed.

I always enjoyed kissing my mate while getting it on, but in this case, I was kissing my best friend, a female, while grinding a man's rock-hard prick.

She groped my breasts as they bounced, and we continued to kiss. I was so aroused!

My hands surveyed her thin body, so perfect and unscathed by the effects of child birth yet. I bent her head forcefully and kissed her neck and collarbone, biting her softly.

She exhaled heavily and lunged at my mouth kissing me intensely. That was enough. I lost it and began riding Dustin's dick like a rodeo clown, bucking and thrusting. This of course in turn caused him to tongue lash her pussy in a frenzy.

Erika and I both reached forwards and began rubbing each other. Her clit swelled, as did mine. We both started screaming and cussing in satisfaction in between feverishly kissing one another. I tongued her nipples and she bit her lip howling. Watching her ride his face and enjoying and feeling his fat cock pounding my g-spot again and again, that familiar numbness crept up my toes.

My back began to arch and legs tingled all the way up. My pussy clenched and I could feel his shaft bulge and then explode with force inside me. I released one final squeal,

"Fuuuuuccckk!"

Erika heaved and groaned with pleasure. Then we both collapsed.

Laying on our sides, Dustin still on his back, his face damp with Erika's sweet juices and he was panting. Cum was oozing down my inner thighs, but I could not yet find the energy to walk to the washroom.

Instead, I burst out laughing, then all three of us were laughing. Hard gut-wrenching laughter, it was like another release. Eventually we collected ourselves, and I managed to heave myself up from the table and hop down, racing for the washroom before I dripped on Dustin's immaculate floors.

I cleaned up promptly but stared a moment in the bathroom mirror. Who was this woman? I wasn't sure anymore, but I wasn't hating her.

She was exciting and powerful. I peered at myself, naked in the mirror, and had new appreciation for my body. The same body I turned my nose up at only two days ago, the body I hated for not looking like all the bodies in magazines and in movies. This body carried three children, and still entranced two of the most unlikely and good-looking people to both make love to me tonight. I promised from now on to give her the appreciation she deserved.

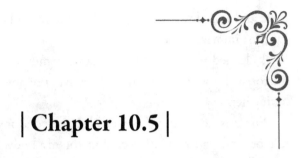

| Chapter 10.5 |

No more hesitation, no more stunned demeanor, Naomi was now kissing with the same matched intent that Erika possessed. Kissing us both intensely, back and forth. Erika stripped off her shirt and then assisted me with mine.

We locked eyes, as if making a game plan and we both reached for Naomi's top pulling it up and over her head, kissing her seductively, coaxing her to allow us to strip her down. Her arms relaxed with our gentle reassuring touches and I lifted her arms up while Erika pulled the top off completely. Erika's swift fingers unclasped Naomi's bra, and she immediately tried to cover her breasts, her insecurities and uncertainties ringing clear. But I wasn't about to let her. I'd come too close, and she was too gorgeous a specimen to have these fears and reluctances.

Erika sensed her resistance as well and had already laid the groundwork, kissing her collarbone and neck ever so softly and soothingly. I went for the bigger prize, sliding my hands up her sides, lifting her arms up and off her ample breasts. Her areolas hardened and goosebumps rose over her flesh. I loved how her tits looked.

I grabbed them, tongued her nipples, tasting her skin.

Looking a little lost, she caressed my chest, stroking my pecs and kissing me wherever she could reach.

Erika, not wanting to be left out, turned Naomi's head towards her intermittently between sucking and licking her body as well, and kissed her.

Naomi reached for my belt loops and yanked me into her, and taken aback by her sudden enthusiasm I stumbled, driving myself between her legs. Her fingers quickly worked my fly loose and my jeans fell to the floor. My boxer briefs still on, her fingers traced the shape of my cock, then pulled them down as well. I could feel my dick spring forward as soon as she removed the elastic of my boxers, the freedom of the night air felt good against my bare skin.

I pushed Naomi back further onto the table, and Erika moved to allow it as I then mounted the table as well on my knees. I had one plan, she had another.

She changed her position, tucking her knees under her and her hands on the table, very cat-like. Erika followed suit onto all fours, and they both began licking my length, lapping at my head and taking turns sucking me. I didn't mind their changes to my plans!

Feeling their lips wrap around my cock, one after another, the different feels of their lips and mouths suctioning my meat, it was glorious! When they were finished "sharing", Erika's red hair hovered above my sack, massaging and suckling my balls, while Naomi took over deep throating my hog, she did it so well.

She churned her spit around him, swathing it in saliva, like sticking my dick in a jet pool without the potential negative repercussions.

Over and over they worked me up and down, overloading my nerves, stimulating me with every pleasurable sensation possible.

I dug my fingers into their hair, needing to grasp something, anything just to ground myself to the fact this was reality, this was happening! Pausing, they turned over to satisfy me visually again, kissing one another then once again sharing my veiny knob. Sucking and lapping at my tip all the while watching me, with those sexy alluring eyes.

Without notice, Erika hopped up circling behind me. Whispering her very provocative intentions to me, to which I was very agreeable.

At her signal I flipped Naomi over onto her back and I crawled further up onto the table closer to her head, feeding my meat to her which despite her shocked expression, she devoured fervently.

Erika could be heard rustling behind me, reefing off Naomi's shorts and positioning her in a way that suited her objective. I felt the jerk of her legs being thrust open and then heard the sounds of her feasting ravenously, further adding to my arousal.

As a result I energetically throttled my cock down Naomi's throat, and she, obviously feeling the vibe, grabbed my ass and helped drill my rod in further and more rapidly.

I couldn't resist the temptation to watch. Craning my neck backwards as far as I could in order to watch Erika's red head go down so vigorously on Naomi's snatch. I could hear the slop, as saliva and pussy juice mixed, knew how aroused Naomi must be and my tip throbbed with anticipation.

Not wanting to leave Erika out of the mix, I let her go at Naomi for a few minutes longer before I had to help hoist her up on the table as well, her face dribbling wet with Naomi's sweet pussy juices.

I wanted to kiss her, suck off all that delectable flavor, but the need for more than a kiss, stung my brain. They must have read my mind and positioned themselves on all fours, asses up facing me. Hungry for penetration.

Accepting the challenge of extreme multitasking I drilled my dick into Naomi's eager cunt and sucked my two fingers, lubing them with saliva before pushing them into Erika's slit.

Bouncing back to old habits, I pushed in my lucky number seven times before pulling out and swapping. Now stuffing my hog into Erika's glossy muff and fingering Naomi.

Three shallow pumps and four large thrusts, and repeat, my rhythm going strong. It felt so good! Fucking not just one but two pussies! Alternating between their two holes, each one feeling a little diverse from the other, each one pleasantly tight and succulent. My knob swelling with all the amorous energy and friction.

They began rocking back and forth, rotating, allowing my dick more depth and to hit a variety of more angles. I spanked them both, letting them know I was the boss. Such good girls, even with the reddened areas prominently rising on their cheeks, they followed their instincts and pushed their asses up higher into the air, begging for more. I obliged, smacking them even harder across their rear ends. Feeling the vibration of my smack reverberating down into their pussies, quivering the shaft of my rod.

Having their asses up so high in such promiscuous settings, ideas flooded my mind. I found an almost empty scotch glass laying within reach and grabbed it. The partially melted ice cubes were the perfect tool.

I grabbed the two largest ones and placed them strategically on their back doors. I pressed my thumbs in, using just my hips now to guide my cock in and out of them still swapping back and forth. Feeling the ice melt beneath my thumbs as they slid deeper and deeper into their assholes with the pressure I applied. Their tight holes enclosing around them, as I pushed in, in search of that magical spot.

I knew as soon as I hit it. They squeezed tighter in both holes and tremors shot up their legs. I hooked my thumbs there and then proceeded to fuck them with my thumbs. Rubbing those same spots with each push in. Still thrusting my raging hard dick into them, my orgasm growing.

Naomi got up pushing me down, Erika mounting my face and pulling Naomi aboard my cock. I tongue lashed the shit out of Erika's pussy, her ginger pubes holding all the scents of our hormone driven affair, and I breathed it in sensually.

Naomi began riding me, slamming her cunt down around me as she and Erika kissed and fondled each other above me. I felt Naomi's walls close around me, clamping me inside her clearly wanting to claim my cum as her own orgasm was peaking. She was bucking, like a mad person. She must be close.

In turn I started whipping my tongue around, working Erika's clit like a seizuring snake. She started twitching like mad, and I could see Naomi's fingertips rubbing her as well.

I moved my attention to working between her fingers and tonguing her slit, eating every inch of her out. They both started shrieking in euphoria, pushing me over the top. The bulge in my shaft rising up before exploding like a volcano in Naomi's convulsing cunt.

My own moans muffled by Erika's pussy still smothering my face until she and Naomi both collapsed beside me. My face damp with pussy juice and Naomi soaked with my cum. We all began laughing, I wasn't even sure why, but it was a great end to a triumphant night.

| Chapter 11 |

I awoke in an entangled heap, legs and arms entwined; the sunshine pouring in casting rays into my eyes. My head throbbed. I needed a drink of water so bad.

I heaved Dustin's leg off mine, lifted Erika's arm off my chest and carefully tried to wedge myself out without causing the others to stir.

Untangling the sheets from my feet, I managed to break free and tiptoed to a door on the opposite side of the room that I assumed must be the ensuite. Funny, I didn't remember this room or even going to bed at all last night. My foot retracted slightly when it made contact with the cold marble tile, but I pushed forward.

Seeing the tap, I basically dove my head underneath it and turned on the cold-water full bore. Letting the water pour over my tongue, gulping large mouthfuls, I must've guzzled a whole liter or more by the time my thirst was quenched and I turned off the tap.

Looking up, I cringed seeing my reflection. Mascara shadows around my eyes, my hair was a tangled mess standing up off my head.

I found a comb in a nearby drawer and tried to tame my mane with little to no success, but at least it wasn't standing straight up anymore.

I turned the hot water on and cupped my hands under the faucet, splashing water on my face, erasing the circles under and around my eyes. A hand towel was in reach and I patted my damp face dry.

Figuring I'd done most of my morning routine already, I applied some toothpaste to my finger and did a rough scrub over my teeth and tongue. Morning stale liquor mouth was not my favorite, and I wanted to erase that before I spoke to anyone that morning for fear it likely smelt as bad as it tasted.

Clothes. I need clothes. My bare body still exposed to the world, and without a bunch of alcohol on board, my insecurities were back in full force. I remembered fuzzily wanting to give my body more appreciation and acceptance, but right now all I wanted was to cover myself.

I once again tip-toed out and around the room where Erika and Dustin's soft snores hummed, reassuring me I had time to find my stuff. Looking around at the scattered items, and the bedraggled sheets draped half on the floor, I couldn't help but think that this was probably the messiest this condo had ever been.

I didn't find any of my items in the bedroom, so I crept out into the hall. I should've gotten a tour of the place sober before losing all my things, I thought to myself.

Picking the direction that looked most likely to have a game room, I headed down the hall. There was another bathroom on the left, and a bit further down, the large opening to the game room greeted me.

Clothes were strewn all over the floor and the furniture. I found my panties in a clump on the shag carpet alongside Dustin's jeans. I slipped back into them and decided to be a good guest and began gathering everyone else's clothes as well. I found my bra and shirt thrown over the back of one of the stools.

Not ready for the confinement of a bra just yet, I passed on putting that back on. I saw Dustin's black t-shirt on the floor a few feet away and smiled, walked over and put that on instead.

I loved wearing men's roomy shirts. They were so loose and comfy and always smelt like them. I lifted the fabric and sniffed, *God he smelt good!*

I found all the articles of clothing that this room contained and brought them back to the bedroom, folding them and dividing them up into piles for each person. I then returned and collected all the dirty scotch glasses and brought them to the dishwasher and loaded them up.

Grabbing the dish cloth and getting it wet, I then commenced washing down all the sticky, wet spots our glasses and our bodies had left throughout the room. Erasing the physical memories of the night's activities.

I stood back and stared at the area...This is where it all happened. I still wanted to believe it had all been a crazy dream, but the soreness I felt between my legs from Dustin's engorged manhood told me differently.

Shaking my head, I began looking for Tylenol, anything to relieve my head of this constant throbbing. I went to the bathroom and checked the medicine cabinet first off.

It didn't take me long rummaging to locate what I was looking for. The red and white capsule bottle stood out amongst all the other orange and white topped lids as well as suaves for muscle pain. I twisted open the lid and popped two capsules into my mouth, then ran some tap water into my mouth again, swallowing them down.

I stood up again and wiped my mouth on Dustin's sleeve, when something caught my eye.

One of the pill bottle labels was pointed out towards me. I wasn't trying to invade his privacy at all, but when a nurse sees a medication name it just gets processed. *Clozapine*, a well-known antipsychotic med. I looked at the label harder.

It indeed had Dustin's name imprinted on it as well as his doctor's name, *Dr. R Murdoch*. Against my better judgment, as this put red flags in my brain, I turned a few of the other orange pill bottles so the labels faced me and read. *Haloperidol, Ativan, Risperdal, Zyprexa.* *"Oh shit."* I thought.

I didn't want to be judgmental. Some medications really helped and stabilized people, but this was still concerning for me. I did take the time to note the expiry date on several of the bottles. Most of them were outdated.

Wouldn't he just throw the expired ones out? How many of these was he currently taking? No doctor would put a patient on all of them at once, so obviously some must have been unsuccessful, but just what was the reason he needed them in the first place? I was attempting to rationalize my fears when a voice startled me.

"Good morning."

I jumped and almost toppled over.

"Dustin! You startled me!" I gasped, clutching my chest.

He rubbed his eyes sleepily and chuckled.

"Sorry, that wasn't my intention. You're up early though."

He snapped his cabinet shut, almost forcefully and then lifted the lid on the toilet seat and whipped himself out of a fresh pair of boxer briefs to urinate. I had backed against the wall to allow him room to fit in, but also a little shaken by his actions.

"Yeah, I had a really bad headache. Sorry, I thought I'd grab some Tylenol."

I explained, trying to let him know I wasn't intentionally snooping through his belongings.

"Did you find some? I'm sorry to hear your head hurts, but I'm also not too surprised."

He smiled, winking at me.

He seemed back to his usual self.

"Yes, thank you, I found some. And yes, I know, I overdid it."

I half laughed; half rolled my eyes in embarrassment. He finished voiding and tucked himself away and then washed his hands.

"Would it be alright if I made breakfast for you guys?" I asked.

"Are you sure?" He asked, turning towards me.

"I don't want you feeling obligated to slave over me."

"No, no, I want to, as a thank you for all the accommodations."

I said, before thinking how silly that actually sounded and I immediately regretted it.

"It was my pleasure."

He laughed. My face turned bright red. I followed him out of the bathroom and strode towards the kitchen.

"Would you guys like pancakes and eggs?" I asked.

"That sounds perfect."

"Coffee first!" Growled Erika as she groggily made her way into the living area and threw herself on the white leather sectional.

We all laughed at her, and Dustin prepared his coffee pot, readying it to percolate. I busied myself getting all the ingredients and utensils ready to cook with.

As I whisked the pancake batter, the aroma of coffee filtered throughout the air, awakening all our senses.

Dustin retrieved three mugs from a corner cupboard and poured some cups. Erika drug herself up to one of the island stools and almost laid down over the table until Dustin pushed her mug in front of her. She took a long sip and sighed.

"That's better!"

The sunshine bounced off the white walls of the living and kitchen areas, creating a bright and elated atmosphere. The griddle reached temp and I poured the batter onto its sizzling top, then spun to stir the eggs frying on the stovetop.

The smell of pancakes always comforted me, reminding me of my grandma. I breathed deep and sighed out. The tops of the pancakes began to bubble and I flipped them with the rubber spatula, their underside a golden brown.

Dustin was reading the paper and sipping his coffee, while Erika hugged her mug tightly sitting crisscrossed in her stool, still blinking trying to wake up fully.

I plated up the food and presented it to each of them, handing them all forks and placing syrup in front of them.

In truth I did not feel like eating, but I forced myself to because I knew if I ate, I'd eventually feel better. Everyone wolfed down their food.

"Hangover food tastes so good!" Erika barked with a mouthful of pancakes and I smiled.

I cleared and rinsed everyone's plates once done and loaded the dishwasher again. Dustin pinched my butt as I walked by him, wiping up the counters.

Dustin fed his fish, and I excused myself to the deck outside to call my kids. I missed them, and after these last few days, I could use a dose of reality. Dialing Chad's number, I listened to the steady rings. On the third ring, he finally answered.

"Hello?"

"Hey Chad, it's me. I was just missing the kids and was hoping I could talk to them?"

"You get them back tonight, Naomi, is this really necessary?"

"I know, I'm sorry I just really miss them, please?"

"Fine, but only for a few minutes, this is *MY* time, remember?"

His attitude always perturbed me. Why does it matter whose time it is? I would never disallow him a phone call with his kids when they're with me. I felt like they're still both our kids, and they should be able to talk to their parents whenever they wanted.

I paced the deck, running my fingers through my hair when Aeda's voice came up over the phone.

"Mom?"

"Hey Aeda! How are you guys? I miss you so much."

"We're good, just hanging at dads. We miss you too. We went to the pool yesterday, Everley swam the length of the whole pool in one breath. She's pretty proud. And we all competed on how far we could jump off the Tarzan swing. Austin and I tied!"

"Wow! That's great honey! Sounds like you're all having fun."

Everley's voice piped up.

"Mommy did she tell you? I did it in only one breath!"

I laughed.

"Yes, she told me. That's fantastic! I'm so proud of you! We'll have to go swimming and you can show me."

"Yeah!" she squealed.

"Love you Mommy, see you tonight!"

"Love you guys too. Tell Austin as well. See you guys tonight."

I heard them all yell,

"Bye!" into the phone before it clicked off.

Knowing Chad, he likely had them on a timer. Austin was so quiet, I'm sure he came over just to hear my voice on speaker, but would only really talk in person other than his "Bye," yelled out with the others.

Man, I missed them. I still wasn't used to being away from them for so many days at a time. It was so hard going from seeing them every night, to going days and whole nights without, I didn't think I'd ever get used to it.

Being proactive, I quickly called and ordered a taxi. After pinning the location and sending it to the driver, I took one last look at the cityscape before re-entering the sliding doors, feeling the A/C's cool air hit my skin.

Erika had hopped in the shower and Dustin was getting dressed and washed up. I decided to follow suit. It was probably time I got out of his dirty shirt and dressed in my own clothes.

Locating my clothing pile, I went about slipping each garment back on, pulling off Dustin's t-shirt and throwing it in his hamper. I still felt dirty, but I didn't really feel like showering at Dustin's place.

Despite all our "connecting" we'd done in the past few days, I was still on edge after seeing those pill bottles. Schizophrenia is a pretty serious mental disorder, and as a cop, that could have some serious adverse effects on his judgment or career if things ever went sideways.

I brushed it off, sure I was digging too far into it, as usual, always assessing and considering the worst. I used the ensuite to once again try to fix my hair, this time putting a bit more effort into it and managing to make it look half presentable.

Dustin and Erika were sharing the main bathroom and sounded like they were both done. The shower water had ceased, and I heard them talking above the roar of the fan. Just garbled speech, but I was curious what they were talking about, nervous if it was about last night.

My palms were instantly sweaty, I made my way through the condo, slinking past the bathroom door, but I couldn't make out anything that was being said.

Disappointed, I finished tidying up his place, even sweeping up the floor, more or less just to kill time until we could leave.

I just really wanted to see my kids. I'd had my fill of "fun" for a long time now. I missed them and wanted to get home.

Still wrestling with my shame and desire to be a typical mom again when Erika and Dustin exited the bathroom, I scurried and beckoned Erika to come. I didn't mean for it to come off so pushy or rushed, but I was.

"Whoa, dude what's your rush?" Erika protested.

"I want to get home to my kids, sorry, and I don't want to wear out our welcome." I nodded in Dustin's direction.

"No need to worry about that. You're both more than welcome here anytime." He smiled slyly.

I'm sure in reference to the unsolicited fun he got to participate in. I squirmed uncomfortably.

"Don't you get them in the evening?"

"Yes, but I still want to get home, get cleaned up and get the house ready, grab some groceries."

I danced on the spot to signal to Erika my desperation to leave. I get antsy, and she knows I do when I've been in a place too long or when it comes to being with my kids. Call it separation anxiety if you want, but I get to the point I just need to go.

"Ok ok, we'll hit the road. Let's thank our oh so gracious host."

She swung her way around Dustin's back and then pulled his hair back so as to kiss him. He returned the gesture and then watched her prance towards the door happily.

I stood there awkwardly again, not knowing my place in all this, but Dustin got up from his seat on the couch and walked over to me.

Peering down at me, my eyes downcast and shuffling my feet. He cupped his fingers under my chin and tipped it up towards him tilting his head so we could lock lips. I was thinking it would be uncomfortable, just because I was feeling awkward, but it wasn't.

His lips were so soft and welcoming. His tongue caressed mine and I felt my arm raise and wrap around his neck, holding his lips to mine. I'm not sure how many moments passed, but the solace I found in that kiss, the reassurance, melted away my discomfort and anxieties. A calmness washed over me, and I was suddenly reluctant to leave, but Erika piped up.

"Ok you two, time to hit the road!"

Her tone sounded annoyed. Maybe because I was in such a rush when she was saying goodbye, and then I was taking my sweet time. Perhaps the jealousy I had felt last night in the earlier portion of the evening was mutual.

"Bye," I muttered shyly.

"It was really nice bumping into you again ladies. Text me, ok?"

He looked at me earnestly and slipped me a piece of paper with his cell number scrawled on it. I gave a short nod, pursed my lips, then turned, pocketing his paper and walked out the door Erika was holding open for us.

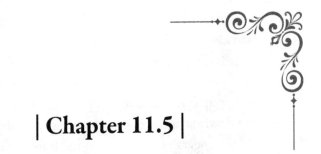

| Chapter 11.5 |

The sun was pouring through the windows, seeping into my eyes. Being that I was usually up before the sun, it was a tribulation attempting to ignore its brightness and not let it rouse me. But to no avail, my eyes couldn't squint it away. I stretched and yawned, rubbing my groggy eyes.

Feeling the warmth of a body pressed against my back, I smiled. Perhaps a little too cockily, reminiscing the night I'd had.

Two girls, one guy, I'd lived the dream.

Quite frankly, it hadn't been the first time I'd conquered this feat, but this was the only time it mattered to me, wasn't just another fuck. How could it be when one of the girls was the perfect girl for me?

Rolling over to kiss her good morning, I was surprised to find that the body laying next to mine was in fact not Naomi's, but Erika's. I instinctively put my other arm out searching the bed top for another body, none. *I wonder where she got off to?*

Leaning up and pulling myself into a seated position, I did my routine. Making knuckles with my toes for a count of seven before standing up and pulling out a fresh pair of boxer briefs from my nightstand, adorning them and then making my way down the hall.

I could hear the tap flowing in the hall bathroom and made that my destination. By the time I approached she had turned the water off and I creeped up behind her.

My medicine cabinet lay open and she was reading my bottle labels. Rage billowed up inside me, but I knew I had to conceal this. If I acted out of ordinary, I'd just raise her suspicions.

"Good Morning." I said coolly.

I obviously startled her as she jumped and barely caught herself on the sinks ledge. A sight that despite my anger, made me chuckle.

"Dustin, you startled me!"

I rubbed my eyes again. I apologized and made a curt comment on her being awake so early while I reached over, snapping my cabinet door shut over top of her head. Perhaps with a little too much force.

In an attempt to calm my nerves, I aimed to distract myself. I lifted the toilet lid and pulled out my dick to take a long-awaited morning piss.

"Yeah, I had a really bad headache. Sorry, I thought I'd grab some Tylenol."

She tried to explain her actions.

Clearly, she read that I was upset about her going through my shit, but I tried my best to keep my tone neutral.

"Did you find some? I'm sorry to hear your head hurts, but I'm also not too surprised."

I said, forcing a smile and her face relaxed.

"Yes, thank you, I found some. And yes, I know, I overdid it."

I could see she was feeling uncomfortable about our activities last night, I wished she wouldn't. It was fun, and natural. Polyamorous was getting closer to normal than monogamy.

Although if I had it my way, I'd have only Naomi. Others were just added bonuses. I finished and began washing my hands.

The silence in those mere moments must've further unsettled her and she quickly jumped to task, likely to keep herself busy.

She offered to make breakfast, and I was only too eager to accept. But didn't want her to feel like she *had* to.

"No, no, I want to, as a thank you for all the accommodations."

I smiled slyly.

"It was my pleasure." I couldn't help but laugh.

I was glad she felt that my *"accommodations"* were worth thanking me for. The red rising in her cheeks added to my amusement. Clearly, she was embarrassed about what she had just admitted.

Erika's disheveled hair floated into the kitchen and living area before she flung herself onto my sectional growling about coffee.

There she lay strewn over the lounge portion, lifeless, and Naomi and I shared a laugh at her expense.

I began prepping my coffee pot. A nice hot brew would taste amazing right now, while Naomi worked on breakfast. She sure looked good in my dirty tee and her panties, I mused.

Pouring three cups, I handed them out, having to push Erika's practically right under her nose now that she was draped over the breakfast bar.

That first sip tasted like heaven, hot and awakening my senses. I grabbed my newspaper and started perusing the articles while awaiting our food, casting the occasional side glance over at Naomi, watching her, admiring her.

After breakfast Naomi went out to the patio to place a call to her kids. I took the opportunity to go get washed up and Erika joined me.

Turning on the shower, she climbed in while I washed my face and brushed my teeth in the sink. She was bold and didn't appear shy in the slightest, quite the opposite of Naomi. She could've gone to any of the washrooms in the house, but she chose the one I was in.

Her ginger bush and perky breasts highlighted her thin athletic frame. I averted my eyes, not wanting to linger where my gaze may not be wanted.

"I know your secret," she disclosed, nonchalantly.

Ignoring my manners, I turned to look at her through the shower glass, staring.

What exactly did she think she knew?

| Chapter 12 |

B *ang!* Erika slammed the cab door. I was already in and looked at her reproachingly. She ignored my gaze and so I went ahead, giving the driver our destination. The blinker was clicking and a few seconds later we pulled out and merged into the HOV lane.

My cell was nearly dead, so I sat back and took in the view as we drove. The drive took longer than I thought, and Erika's silence was deafening as she was usually such a chatterbox. I wasn't sure what to say, and anything I would have said I didn't want to say in front of a stranger.

I shifted in my seat, trying to read her expression, but I was truly puzzled. I hoped she wasn't upset about our goodbye kiss; I mean she'd had one too.

There was too much uncertainty in all this. It was too much drama for me. I like knowing for sure that someone is mine and likes me, and that I'm their only one and vice versa. That way it isn't so damn complicated. But again, I was getting ahead of myself. That may not have even been her issue. There might not even be an issue!

The minutes drug by before we finally arrived back at the Blue Gator. The cab driver pulled up next to my van and I paid our fare.

Stepping out, I unlocked the doors and we literally went from one vehicle to another. Putting the key in and starting it while we buckled up, I couldn't take the silence.

"Do you want to talk about it?" I asked cautiously.

"Nothing to talk about," she responded flatly.

"Okay."

I couldn't help but feel there was, but I wasn't about to dig.

The radio and rumble of the engine were the only sounds as we made our way, weaving through the streets towards Highway 97. Car after car whipped by, and rather than concentrate on the uncomfortableness, I chose to zone out again like normal.

It was easy to lose myself in the scenery. The Okanagan was such a gorgeous place to live and was well known for it. Tourists from all over Canada came often to vacation here. Our area's many voluminous lakes, cascading waterfalls, hiking trails, fishing and camping locations as well as hunting. There were so many outdoor activities this place had to offer. I was proud to live here and felt privileged to be able to raise my children here as well.

It was twenty minutes into our drive before she finally broke the silence.

"What are you smiling about?"

"Oh, just thinking about home, looking at the scenery."

She snorted and snubbed her nose at me.

"That's all you're thinking about?"

"Yes."

I really couldn't figure out what she wanted from me, or what she wanted me to say?

"Figures." she mumbled.

"What's that supposed to mean?" I demanded.

Her attitude was coming off as really insulting. Was she insinuating I'm small minded? Or selfish?

"You're so incognizant all the time."

She rattled her fists in the air before plummeting herself back into her seat.

"Whoa! Ok, I guess you're right because I really have no idea what we're even talking about right now! Did I do something wrong? If it's about last night, I mean, we were all drunk and I'm sorry if it went too far. I didn't plan any of that."

I shook my head flabbergasted.

"You really think this is all about that?"

"Well, what else?"

"Nevermind." She put her head in her hand and leaned against her window.

A few more moments later she piped up again.

"Do you really like him?" Her gaze still cast out the window.

"I don't know." I shrugged.

"I don't *not* like him. I thought we had good chemistry, but I'm sure some things I'm leery of."

I thought back to the pill bottles, and the fact that a man as hot as he was and well established was single with no kids. Perhaps there was more to that story.

"Well, you certainly seemed all over him."

"So were you!" I defended myself.

"Are you really that freaking oblivious? Holy shit, you must be! I seriously can't believe someone as smart as you can be so daft!"

She was screaming at this point, spit spurting from her mouth as she inflected her words at me.

"What are we even talking about? How am I daft? If you really feel so poorly about me, why are we friends?"

I was vibrating with anger now. *Did she really think I was stupid? And for what reason? Liking a guy that she quite obviously liked as well?*

"We're friends because we've been friends since we met in school. We're friends because of how I feel about you. I don't think you're usually stupid. Like I said, you're a smart person, so I can't figure out why you're being so dumb! Or maybe you're just choosing to be on this particular subject in order to avoid it? Either way it pisses me off, because you just don't seem to care how it affects me!"

Her arms were flailing with anger, emphasizing her words.

"But I don't even know what the subject you're referring to is! Please explain this to me, because I seem to have missed it? And for the record, friends don't think their friends are stupid! I'd never think that about you! It's hurtful that you obviously think horrid things about me and are now lashing out! Had I known you'd react like this the following day, I never would've gone through with last night! I knew that was a mistake!"

I heaved my fist into my horn. My voice was breaking with the tension in the van's cab. .

"You knew it was a mistake, huh? Good to know. I'm done." Erika shut it down.

We both breathed deep breaths, calming our pounding hearts. The minutes ticked away.

Her voice reduced to an almost normal tone.

"Can we stop? I want a drink."

"Yeah, I need to get gas anyways. I'll stop in Vernon."

I tried to ease my tone as well, wanting to forget we'd even had this fight, still unsure what it was we were even fighting about. We had already passed Lake Country and I wasn't about to turn around.

I turned the music up and despite our heated conversation, we both started moshing our heads, singing. By the time we emerged into Vernon, things were normal once again. I summed it up to us both being sleep deprived and hung over.

I pulled into the Co-op station, gas was 152.9.

"Just keeps going up."

I muttered to myself, and hastily punched in my banking info before positioning the nozzle in my tank.

Erika had already stalked off into the store to grab her drink. I poured sixty bucks in and Erika was striding back across the parking lot, wind flailing her wild red hair.

She was slurping on her slushie and she had another in her hand for me as well as a water bottle.

"Hangover cure!" She announced as she handed it to me.

She knew my weakness for slushies all too well. I took it as a motion for a truce.

"Thanks!" We clinked our cups and started sucking away on our straws.

"Mmm, so good!"

I sparked the engine up again and we hit the road, ascending through the farm plains and neighboring towns. After numerous brain freezes and laughs, we were approaching Salmon Arm. I sucked the last remnants of ice from the bottom of my cup before plopping it in my trash bin.

I drove up to Erika's town house and helped her carry her numerous bags of luggage into her home.

"Ugh, it smells so stale in here," she complained.

"Well, you were gone for a year."

I said as I began opening a window for her to allow the air to circulate.

"Probably feels weird being home now after all that time away?"

"Yeah, it does. It's kind of nice but also makes me feel kind of empty as well, you know?"

I didn't really know. She forgot I've never been anywhere, but I knew I missed home when I was gone for a day or two, like now.

The emptiness, I thought, perhaps was like when I come home and my kids aren't there. That emptiness I understood and could empathize with.

"Thanks for picking me up. Sorry it took so many extra days. Good thing I caught you on days off!"

"Ah, you didn't catch me on days off. I booked extra days off because I knew I had to come get you."

I smiled knowingly, tapping my nose.

"Ok I've got to get going though. I still need to grab groceries and get my place sorted before the kids get there. Luv ya."

We hugged quickly before I walked out the door and left her to unpack.

The grocery store was a quick stop. I just grabbed fresh milk and cheese, some snacks for the kiddos, and a few more fresh veggies to replenish my stock before heading to my place.

Since the divorce I'd relocated to a small town house. Chad was in the process of selling our house and was shopping for his own new place as well. Rent was steep, and inflation was ever-rising, making it harder and harder even with my decent income to keep us fed and housed.

I was eager to split the income from the house, although I knew it wouldn't be as much as it should be. It never is. Sad to see our family home sold but eager for some extra financial security, as well as shutting the door on that chapter of my life officially.

Unlocking my door and walking in, I went to work putting the food away and cleaning up. Unpacking my bags, throwing laundry in, sweeping and vacuuming, and getting the kid's bedding fresh for them.

I finished with just enough time to start dinner and hop in the shower.

The hot water felt so good! I scrubbed my skin, cleansing off the memories of the previous night.

Lathering my hair and rinsing the bubbles down the drain, I stood letting the water pour down my face and body. It was going to be so hard to drag my butt out of the water.

Reluctantly, I turned the taps off and toweled off, the soft lush fabric drying on contact, then slipped on some fresh crisp clothes. I blow dried my hair quickly. It was still partially damp when the doorbell rang and I bolted to answer it.

I whipped open the door with a big smile on my face.

"Hello, my babies! I've missed you so much!"

Kissing all three of their heads, I hugged them close.

Chad had Everley's bag and he handed it off to me, once again without looking at me. This was his way of avoiding me, just avoiding contact as much as possible.

"Thanks." I said.

"What's for dinner mom?" Austin asked.

"Lasagna and salad."

"Yum!" He ran in, licking his lips.

I knew lasagna was one of his favorites.

"Parent teacher interviews are this week on Wednesday at three fifteen."

Chad relayed, finally turning his gaze in my direction.

"Ok, sounds good, thanks for letting me know. I haven't checked my emails yet."

His usual cool attitude towards me melted a bit and he looked at me funny.

"You seem different."

"Oh?" I responded, puzzled.

I hadn't had a haircut in months and looked no different than usual.

"Yeah, I don't know how; you're just giving off a different vibe."

I shrugged and he looked at me a second longer, trying to read me before he turned to leave.

"Anyways, see ya."

"Okay, bye."

I closed the door, baffled, and went to catch up with my kids. I was so eager to hear all the stories of their week.

The night went accordingly. We all talked and shared about our days away from one another. Obviously, I left out many details about my own.

Dinner followed, which was wolfed down before showers, a bit of TV and then bed.

"Everyone's got their alarms set for school tomorrow?"

"Yes!"

"Clothes are picked out?"

"Yes!"

"Brushed your teeth?"

"Yes, Mom!"

I laughed.

"Ok, ok I'll quit bugging. Give me a kiss, all of you."

I laid a series of smooches all over each of their faces and squeezed them all tight, then sent them to their beds. I sighed deeply, smiling and then proceeded to the kitchen to pack their lunches and do dishes.

The bubbles lathered and fizzed against my hands as I scrubbed the plates. I felt so tired. So much had happened these last few days, and so many late nights.

I started my set of four tomorrow morning early, so once I finished my tasks, I set aside my scrubs for the next day and my ID card before climbing into bed. As soon as I hit the pillow, my eyes closed, and in a blink, my alarm was blaring, announcing that it was 5:00 am.

Time to get up and get ready for work.

| Chapter 13 |

By the end of my set, I was spent. Understaffed every day, four out of six patients almost total care, and no float to help. My kids and I were excited to actually get to spend time together that evening. I had gotten home at twenty after seven in the morning and had a quick nap so that I wouldn't be a zombie when they got home from school.

My phone dinged and a text message popped up. It was Dustin. I had added him to my contacts reluctantly.

I hadn't heard from him since we parted on Sunday. I kind of thought maybe that was confirmation that it was just a little fling, but here he was messaging me.

I opened my phone to read what he had to say.

Dustin Trail: *"Hey Beautiful, been thinking about you all week. What are your plans for the weekend?"*

I blushed... beautiful? I wondered if that was just a line he uses? I hadn't thought forward enough for the weekend. I had only been trying to make it through the week.

Naomi Wilkinson: *"Hey, long week. How'd you make out? I hadn't even thought that far ahead honestly, how about you?"*

Laying down my phone, I went to try to figure out what to make for dinner, every mom's struggle! I weighed my options and what ingredients I had on hand, eventually deciding on a strawberry, goat cheese and cashew salad with balsamic dressing, and chicken. I needed to finish up my spring greens before they turned and this salad was always a hit, more or less for the fact that it had strawberries in it.

I got the salad ready and placed it in the fridge for later, then prepared the chicken. Washing my hands, I heard my cell chime again. I towel dried off and made my way over to it, picking it up.

Dustin Trail: *"I made out alright, but I really have been thinking about you a lot. Would you be opposed to a visit?"*

Oh my goodness! A visit? That seemed really soon. I mean I knew I was at his place and spent the night, but this was different. I had my kids and he'd have to drive here with the sole purpose of seeing me. No other reason like I had picking up a friend. It just seemed so committed, and that was not a step I was ready for. I sat stunned, hovering my thumbs over top of the cell screen, not sure what to put. I didn't think I could answer his question.

It was way too soon to have my kids get involved or meet him. I mean this was the first time we'd spoken since the "events" and I needed more than that. I literally knew nothing much about this guy other than, he's a very handsome, well-established cop, with an amazing dick, whom I knew previously in high school. We had good chemistry, but given all that, I had also only just found a bunch of antipsychotics in his medicine cabinet.

Aside from his possible condition, he was likely *the perfect man*, if ever a thing existed, but I was still hesitant. When things seem too good to be true, they likely often were.

I was about to text back declining, but once again my fingers froze before I started typing.

Was it possible that fate was throwing me a bone, and here I was throwing it away? A chance at happiness?

A knot swelled in my throat and I just couldn't bring myself to type. Instead, I opted to just put the phone down and walk away.

I kept myself busy the rest of the day. Did a workout, swept and mopped, did laundry, went for a walk and got mail.

Anything to have an excuse to not text back. I stayed occupied and eventually, once kids returned from school, forgot.

The kids and I went swimming at the beach in Canoe. I brought our salad with us and had a picnic dinner. It was a picture perfect night, swimming until the sun disappeared behind the mountains, before we packed up.

The drive home was quick and the kids got their pajamas on as soon as we walked through the door so that we could watch a movie and have popcorn. We all snuggled up on the couch with our fuzzy blankets, Everley in my lap and Austin and Aeda on either side of me, a big bowl of popcorn being passed between the four of us.

Everley had gotten to pick the flick and had chosen *Minions*, I always got a kick out of children's movies and thoroughly enjoyed watching them with my kids.

It was late by the time the film ended, and I briskly sent them all to brush their teeth before bed, then kissed them all before tucking them in. Austin and Aeda didn't often let me tuck them in anymore but on such occasions, they let me get my mom kicks in still and allowed me the privilege.

My heart was happy, it had been a wonderful Friday evening with my kids, I couldn't ask for more than that. I drifted to sleep that night in my bed, content and ready for another day of it tomorrow.

I awoke to the sound of Everley squealing and jumping on my bed, her dark brown curls flouncing around her face and demanding tickles and breakfast. I gave a thorough tickling, bringing her to fits of giggles before allowing her to surrender. Yawning and stretching, I rose and peered out my window. The sunlight was streaming in and I could feel the early morning sun already casting its heat over my floors. I put my face amidst one of the rays of warm sunshine, feeling the glow and enjoying, taking a deep breath and acknowledging the gratitude for the day I felt.

I cantered into the bathroom and began my morning routine, workout clothes on, hair up, then out to the living room where Aeda and I did our workout DVD together. Austin played on his tablet and Everley was impatiently awaiting her breakfast by playing with some toys a few feet away from us, piping up every few minutes to let me know she was still waiting.

Once done, I quickly washed up and dressed, so as to make breakfast for everyone, I made french toast with strawberries. Their smiles and full cheeks as they chewed ferociously, told me they appreciated and were enjoying themselves.

We planned our day as we ate. Everley never came up short on suggestions, but we had to reel her in as going to Disneyland wasn't a realistic option.

We decided upon a hike to Syphon Falls and a picnic lunch there, followed by a bike ride to the beach to spend the late afternoon there again. I started doing dishes and packing lunches, while the kids collected up the gear.

Erika called to see what we were up to, and I invited her along. She said she'd be busy working on some stuff for work until the evening and then she might meet up with us at the beach.

The kids busied themselves and were packed and ready to go in no time. We then proceeded to load up the van and hit the road.

Syphon Falls was a short drive, just up in Glen Eden. It was a very family friendly quick hike, but it was gorgeous. My kids always loved to go there. The falls itself was a sight to behold.

We pulled up into the small parking area, just a grassy patch on the side of the road encased in trees and wild grasses, the information board off to the left.

We grabbed the gear we needed, lunches, water bottles etc. We were about to set forth, when I heard a voice call out my name. I glanced back in the direction of the approaching footsteps on loose gravel and gasped.

"Dustin?"

He strode towards me, hand up in a wave gesture. His hiking boots scuffing the ground, and his tan cargo shorts and light blue tee showed off his muscular physique even with their somewhat baggy appearance.

He adorned a hiking backpack that buckled around his waist and chest, and a pair of aviators sat on top of his head. I didn't even know how to react other than to stare in shock.

He must have noted my dismay and excused my lack of welcome.

"Hey, yeah, when I didn't get a response from you, I decided either way I'd make a day trip and come check out some falls, do some hiking, maybe hit up the beach later. These falls came highly recommended. I didn't imagine I'd run into you here though. That's crazy!"

My mouth must have been gaping open, so Aeda asked.

"Mom, who is that?"

Her question snapped me out of my trance and I stammered.

"Uh this is ...Dustin, a friend from high school. I ran into him in Kelowna when I picked up Erika last week."

Then finally I responded to Dustin.

"Sorry, I got busy and forgot to reply. I've been packing in as much fun as I could with my kiddos. Dustin, this is Aeda, Austin and Everley."

I indicated with my hands whom each child was as their names were stated.

He held out his hand, shook each one of their hands, and made jokes about what firm strong grips they had, making them smile and breaking the ice.

They appeared responsive to him, especially when they were asking him what he did for a living and he said he was a cop. Austin exclaimed how *cool* it was that he had a gun. I watched the interactions and surveyed the situation. Was it just a coincidence?

"Are you guys just heading up now? Or have you already been? I just pulled in, so if you're just heading there, I would be honored to join you?" I looked at my kids, and they returned my gaze and nodded subtly.

"Yes, of course, we're just heading up as well, and we'd love to have you join us."

I didn't want to say no, and then have to explain to my children why I was being so rude. I was taken by surprise. This could all be a random coincidence, because the other options of him being a serial stalker seemed too far-fetched, especially since he was a police officer. There were just less complications this way.

He smiled at my acceptance and we all started walking. He immediately laid on his charm and began conversations with them all, entrancing them with stories and nature facts as we hiked up the trail. Aeda, who was usually more hesitant with people, took only a few minutes before her defenses melted away.

Dustin's good looks, despite her young age, still worked their magic on her as well, it seemed. She smiled and talked more than usual, gushing over what all he had to say.

Austin kept asking questions about his gun, tasers, cuffs, tackling people, and all other action-packed questions he could think of.

Everley was infatuated the second he gave her any attention. She loved being the center of attention, and a new audience was all that much more exciting. She clung to Dustin's hand as we clambered up the trail, smiling up at him and making funny faces to get his approval.

I walked at the end of the line, allowing them the freedom to talk, still a bit off-put that this was occurring, but I guess I had no one to blame but myself. Had I just taken the time to respond and tell him I didn't approve of a visit this weekend, I perhaps could have avoided this whole situation.

Oh well, at least they all seemed to be getting along, and no awkward topics had been brought up thus far.

We veered around the last corner at the rock wall canyon, and then it began to open up into where the roar of Syphon falls could be fully heard crashing down and thundering off the rocks below.

The trees, although hiding the waterfall somewhat, did not mask its beauty. The lush needled canopy offered a "*Secret Garden*" ambience that I always admired.

The children ran to the waterfall's base and Austin started balancing on the rocks crossing the creek it formed at its bottom.

We walked around appreciating all the area had to offer, sight-seeing and climbing. We captured two geckos and played with them for a bit before releasing them. Then the kids removed their socks and shoes and splashed around while I unpacked the lunches.

Dustin gallivanted with the kids in the water for a bit then came up to join me.

"Need a hand?"

"No, I think I've got it all covered now, thanks."

"I'm really sorry if I've made you uncomfortable today. I really didn't know you'd be here today, but I'm so glad I did bump into you. Your kids are great, and I'm really enjoying all your company. Anyways, I just hope I'm not spoiling your day."

He said it more like a question, imploring for me to open up.

I wanted to tell him that I did feel a bit uncomfortable, but was there really any point now? The kids were enjoying him as much as he was them. I loved seeing them having fun, and I didn't want to make the rest of our time spent together awful.

"No, it's fine. Sorry if I seem off. I just wasn't expecting this and wasn't really ready for it."

"That's understandable. Just know that I'd never intend to do anything that may upset you."

Just then the kids all sprinted up to feed their faces, each one grabbing a sandwich and stuffing it in their mouths. Huge grins adorned their faces and they chewed leaving little to the imagination. I couldn't help but laugh, and we all began feasting joyously.

Our sandwiches were consumed in no time at all, washing them down with water, and then finishing with slices of juicy watermelon and succulent cherries from our neighbor's tree.

It was a good thing I packed an abundance of extra food, as I always liked to be over prepared. I never knew when my kids would decide one sandwich wasn't enough. It paid off today and we had extra to share with Dustin who accepted it graciously.

The rest of our time we spent having a massive water fight in the pool below the falls. All the squeals of joy echoing off the cliffs was music to my ears.

The heat of the day was peaking and sweat furrowed on all our brows despite the cool misty breeze emitting from the waterfall and our water spattered clothes.

I announced it was time to pack up and make our way to the beach. We had spent so much time at Syphon we likely wouldn't be able to squeeze in a bike ride as we had planned, but at least we could go cool off at the beach.

It didn't take us long to descend the trail and reach the parking area once again.

Dustin was hesitantly looming around by our van waiting for an opening. I waited for him to inquire.

"So, I know you guys are heading to the beach, and you know that was my plan originally. Would you be opposed to me tagging along?"

He looked at me expectantly, and the kids, upon hearing this, jumped to his rescue.

"Yeah Mom! Can Dustin come?" Half pleading with me, half demanding.

"He can help me build my sandcastle." Everley pouted her lip out. If I said no, I'd be the bad guy.

"I guess so. You'll meet us there then?"

"For sure!" He smiled triumphantly.

"See ya in a bit!" He turned, trotting off towards his truck.

The beach parking lot was packed. I ended up parking up in the overflow, so we had a bit of a walk to the actual beach. I had my wagon to assist me with carrying all the beach accessories and towels, so it made the journey more manageable.

I still hadn't seen Dustin's truck, so I thought maybe he decided against the beach and went home? Walking through the shaded underpass tunnel to the waterway, the sun hit hard when we escaped the darkness on the other side. It was way hotter than it was in Glen Eden!

Scanning the beachfront for a spot to lay our things, I managed to locate one not far from the entrance and close to the park so Everley could play there as well if she wanted.

We made our way down to it and then unpacked, laid our blanket down and stripped down to our bathing suits. I had a pop tent umbrella and I put that up to offer a bit of protection from the heat.

Austin led the girls down to the water, and they walked in, leaving me to dig out their towels and set them up.

I wiped my brow when I heard Everley shriek in excitement.

"Dustin's here!" pointing up to the pavement.

I held my hand up to shield my eyes and squinted against the glaring light. I could vaguely make out his form walking towards us, his boots replaced with sandals, his aviators on his face this time.

In his hands he had a drink tray filled with slurpees, one for each one of us. The kids saw what he was carrying too and all ran up to him to retrieve their treat.

He handed theirs to them. With a flurry of

"Thank yous" they ran back, showing off to me.

"He got me rainbow, Mommy!" Everley rambled whilst trying to suck its contents and run at the same time.

I smiled as he approached.

"So that's what took you so long. I was beginning to wonder."

He returned my smile, passing me one which I took graciously.

"Well, I had to bribe your kids into liking me somehow," he joked.

"Yeah, like you needed any help getting them to like you!"

I rolled my eyes laughing at him.

"Thank you for this. It's so hot."

He took a long slurp and nodded in agreement, then set down his and my drinks in the shade.

"Time to cool down then, hot stuff."

Without any notice, he tore off his shirt and scooped me up over his shoulder and began barreling down into the water. I screamed and managed to hold my breath as I was thrown into the water.

The blast of cold hit me, shocking my system before I found my footing and shot out. It was refreshing and I got caught up in the fun and jumped on Dustin's back forcing him under the water as well.

The kids all jumped in and joined in everyone wrestling each other into the water. Dustin was throwing them all, plunging them in feet from where he launched them. They shrieked and laughed in enjoyment.

Austin and Dustin also recruited the group to swim out to the floating docks where we commenced a game of King of the dock, boys against girls, girls lost but we had put up a hell of a fight.

Forty-five minutes or so later, all panting and smiling wearily, we trudged our soaked bodies out of the water and back up the sandy shore to our towels.

Toweling off as best we could, we had only a half hour or so before we'd leave for dinner. I hadn't packed dinner in advance like I had the day before.

Dustin stepped aside to make a call and I rounded the kids up for a quick game of volleyball. Most of the other patrons at the beach were all packing up and leaving. We walked by them on our way towards the public net on the far side near the wharf. A group of teens had just finished up using it, so we took full advantage and moved in on the space.

I served, Aeda bumped and set Austin up, he tapped it over the net and Everley and I raced for it. She was still young, and wasn't super skilled at volleyball, but I always applauded her for trying and having fun with it. She bumped it and it deflected off her arms and to the far left.

I thought for sure it was headed out, but to all our surprise Dustin flew in and one fisted it up into the air. Austin met me at the net and we both jumped up to tip it onto the other team's side.

My height gave me a bit more of an advantage, although I was only 5'4". He was still growing and I had at least 4-5 inches on him still. I managed to tip it just over his fingers and we scored!

"Nice tip!" Dustin chimed.

Back and forth we rallied. We goofed many serves, many bumps and many passes, but we had a blast doing it!

The ending score was tight, but Aeda and Austin took the win 20-18, Everley was a bit disappointed for about ten seconds and then was skipping back to our towels again to pack up.

Our towels lay where we left them, and I gathered up all the empty slurpee cups and walked them to the trash can.

I smelt the air, that wasn't garbage I smelt. This smelt good! Like gooey melted cheese and fresh dough. I looked around, but there were only a few groups of people left and none had any food items that matched.

Weird, I didn't think I could be imagining something quite that vivid. Just then I saw the pizza delivery man handing over two large boxes and a bag with some cans of pop in it to, low and behold, Dustin.

Aeda, Austin and Everley were all hovering, breathing in the pizza's delectable aroma.

Dustin placed the boxes down and I heard him say,

"Dig in you guys."

"Thank you, Dustin!" they all responded, each grabbing a napkin as a plate and a pop flavor of their choosing.

"That was awfully nice of you! But you didn't have to!" I remarked as I returned.

"I wanted to." He shrugged his bronze defined shoulders.

"Is that what that phone call was about?"

"Yes, you caught me. I figured we'd been having so much fun, I didn't want it to end. What a better way to extend the day than a pizza party at the beach?"

I smiled. It was very attractive seeing his paternal side and seeing how much my kids were enjoying him. His efforts to spoil them were so sweet, and I couldn't help but admire him for it.

A flash of red hair caught my eyes. Oh my god. Erika! I had completely forgotten she said she'd try to join us at the beach. She was walking over with a picnic basket, a look of disapproval dawning her face when she saw our company.

"Looks like I'm late to the party." She slammed down her basket.

"What a pleasant surprise finding you here, Dustin." She smiled, a little too sweetly.

"Yeah, I came up when I didn't hear back from Naomi and decided to spend the day here. As luck would have it, I ran into them while hiking and they were kind enough to invite me along for the day."

Either he ignored her astuteness or he was oblivious to it. I, however, detected it and felt its wrath.

"Yes, this was not planned. But it ended up being a really good day. I should have let you know, but we just got caught up in all our activities and I completely forgot."

She waved her hand, brushing it off.

"Don't worry about it."

"What'd you bring us, Auntie Erika?"

Everley asked, jumping over and opening up the picnic basket lid. Erika made an effort to try to block her from opening it, but Everley was too quick.

"Ooo fancy!" She exclaimed as she pulled out a bottle of champagne, some strawberries and a charcuterie board filled with all my favorite goodies.

I exclaimed at her efforts.

"You did all that?" Her head turned away, once again brushing me off.

"Yeah, well, thought we had a lot to celebrate. You know, me being back and everything."

I could tell that the charcuterie board must have taken quite some time to assemble. It was her own board that I recognized, and all the salami roses she'd created, onion blooms, assortment of cheese slices, olives, pickles and an array of different crackers and breads with oils and vinegars to dip.

"I'm so sorry! We can still eat it, we haven't even started the pizza yet, aside from the kids."

"It's fine." She cut me off.

I felt so conflicted. Here Dustin had gone to the efforts of ordering and paying for these pizzas, and Erika had spent all this time planning and arranging this spectacular meal for us as well! I felt like no matter what I did, I'd be hurting someone's feelings.

"This was so kind of both of you, it's a good thing I'm hungry." I tried to make it so they could see I'd eat both their items. I selected a piece of meat and cheese off Erika's board, and she smiled smugly as I took a bite.

"So good! You know I love smoked gouda!"

She grabbed the champagne bottle and started spinning the cork in, Dustin also grabbed a piece of meat and I think measuring the sensitivity of the moment, complimented her execution of it.

The champagne bottle let off a *Pop!* and fizzed. She then positioned glasses she'd brought along and began pouring us some. I'm sure she only poured Dustin some to not appear spiteful in front of me, but I appreciated her gesture nonetheless.

We all dived in, feasting on charcuterie, pizza and strawberries. An interesting variety, but it was all so good, it went down easily.

We devoured a large portion of each. I think there was only three fourths of one pizza leftover and only a few pickled onions, slices of brie and crusty bread.

Erika had put aside her indifferences and been pleasant. We all had chatted and joked around as we had on the night we shared together.

The kids had eaten to their heart's content and played on the playground. By the meal's end, we were all satisfied and could feel the tiredness creeping over us.

"So, are you heading back to Kelowna now?" Erika implored.

"Well, I probably shouldn't drive after drinking that champagne, but I'll chug some water and then maybe rent a room at a nearby hotel for the night."

I hadn't even considered that we'd been drinking, let alone the fact that Dustin was a cop. I felt so dumb.

"Right! I hadn't even thought of that. Dustin, I'm sorry. I wish I could offer you a room." I apologized.

"No, don't be sorry. We hadn't planned for this. Heck, we didn't plan any of this, but I wouldn't have changed a second of it. It's been a wonderful day!"

I thought I saw Erika roll her eyes, as she started placing her items back into the basket she'd brought them in.

"I feel bad. I'm sure you weren't looking to cover the expense of a hotel tonight as well as pizza."

"Again, don't feel bad. I had a great day, well worth the price of a hotel for the night."

He said it in such a matter-of-fact way, I think he deemed the conversation as settled.

So rather than argue a moot topic, as I really couldn't offer him a spare room, nor could I cover his hotel, I just agreed and smiled.

"It was a great day!"

"Yes, Mommy, it was so fun! Can we do it all again tomorrow?" Everley asked as she wrapped her arms around my waist embracing me in a huge hug.

"Maybe not tomorrow, but perhaps another time?" I left it as a question, as I didn't want to push it if that wasn't something Dustin was interested in.

I was also hoping Erika was included in this proposition as we had had such a nice evening all together, and I didn't want her to feel left out.

"Oh, I'm guessing there will be more occasions such as this." Erika chirped cheekily.

"I hope so," said Dustin. His eyes met mine and we both smiled.

"Come on, let's get these kids home." Erika interrupted, shoving some gear into Dustin's arms.

We finished gathering up our supplies and made our way back to our vehicles. Ours was still up in the overflow, but I left my armload with them and ran ahead, driving the van back to load everything conveniently.

"This really did work out awesome having you both here with me and the kids. Erika, I wish you'd been able to join us for the whole day."

"Maybe next time," she said as she helped me load our last item into the trunk. I gave her a hug and didn't stop until she returned it.

I wanted to reassure her, no man would ever take her place. She was my best friend.

The kids all jumped in their seats and buckled up, hollering at me to hurry up.

Dustin had driven his truck over and hopped out to say goodbye. His engine rumbling, he walked over.

"I'm breaking all the rules for you." He swooped me into a bear hug.

"Thanks again for letting me tag along with you and the kids. I know I probably put you on the spot, but I sure did enjoy my time."

I felt him kiss the top of my head. His arms tightened their squeeze around me, and I felt my body turn to mush.

"It was nice having you along. The kids had so much fun."

I could feel Erika's eyes boring into our backs, and I pulled away. Maybe she was jealous, thinking I had more of Dustin's attention than her? I didn't want there to be any animosities between the three of us. I was worried about something like this happening after engaging in *such events,* but I always thought I would be the jealous one and the other woman would have stolen the man's attention.

I hated thinking like this. That may not be what she was thinking at all. I could be misinterpreting everything.

I backed away waving to them both and climbed in my van. I saw in my rear view, them exchanging words before walking to each of their separate vehicles. Pulling out, I took one last glance in my mirror to see Dustin's face over the steering wheel before driving away towards home.

| Chapter 14 |

Full and happy, my kids all jumped on me on the couch dressed in their pj's to say goodnight. They had called Chad when we got home, just because I felt they should update him, let him know how they were. I blushed a bit when they started telling him about a guy named Dustin joining them all day and how much fun they had. Everley also swooned over how good looking he was.

I had to break that up and knew I'd be getting some angry texts later about having a man around his children. It didn't matter how many times he'd cheated on me. If I were to pursue any relationships, it would always be an issue with him despite the fact that we were separated.

They scampered off to bed and I poured myself a glass of wine. I took a sniff and then sipped, relishing its grapey oak taste. I walked to my bedroom and pulled my hair out of its elastic. It was damp still, and I tousled it by rubbing my scalp.

I picked out one of my silk nightgowns from my drawer, a dark teal gown with black lace. I also grabbed my black silk bathrobe to cover it and laid them on the bed.

Reaching behind my neck, I pulled a string to untie my bathing suit top. It fell loose and I pulled off my shirt that I had thrown over top for the drive home and threw it across the room to my laundry hamper. I then reached back untying the bottom strings holding my bathing suit top on and it fell to the floor. I swore if I could get away with never wearing a confining garment over my boobs again, I would.

One of the best parts of my days was the moment I could remove whatever restraining device I wore that day. Unbuttoning my jean shorts and shimmying them off, I kicked those at the hamper as well.

I clicked on the sound system in my room and started grooving, taking another sip from my glass. I was full-monty-ing around the room, shaking and moving until my song ended. Slipping my gown over my head and robing up, I wasn't sure what to do with myself.

I plopped myself on the bed and picked up my phone to scroll. I had three unread messages. One heated one from Chad, which I decided to not even acknowledge tonight. The other two were from Dustin and Erika.

Erika Crane: *Can we have a re-do of tonight sometime?*
Naomi Wilkinson: *Yes! Definitely!*

I was glad she wasn't mad at me. I pressed send, then opened Dustin's.

Dustin Trail: *What are you wearing?* ☺.

I laughed. That old line? I seriously thought about pulling one over on him or telling him to nevermind, but I was enjoying my drink and thought, oh hell, might as well have some fun!

I described my negligée, making it sound slightly more exciting than it likely was on me, ending it with a winky-face sticking out tongue emoji. I went and grabbed the bottle of wine from the fridge and brought it to the bedside, pouring myself another glass.

I saw he had already responded. Opening my screen, a pile of very racy photos popped up.

The first was him taking off his shirt, his muscles glistening in the dim lighting of his hotel room.

The next was a close up of his shorts and him unbuttoning them. Then another of him reaching down his shorts, feeling himself. I hadn't ever received dirty pictures before via text. I felt so naughty and held the screen to my chest.

Holding my breath, instantly paranoid, I listened to make sure the kids weren't moving about.

Silence, other than my music. I didn't know how to respond. Looking back down at my screen, my fingers frozen above the keypad. Another picture popped up.

His big meaty cock gripped in his large hands took up my whole screen. My eyes bulged, and I couldn't help myself from swallowing hard.

Even when it was kilometers away, it looked intimidating, and...thrilling, like a mountain waiting to be climbed. The dots indicating he was writing a message appeared on my screen, and then...

Dustin Trail: *Touch yourself.*

I choked on my sip of wine, sputtering dribbles down my chin. I quickly ran to my ensuite and grabbed some toilet paper to wipe up my face. When I was clean and made my way back to the bed, I was unsure of how to move forward with this, or how to pass it up. I decided to be unrestrained, and just as I was about to change my mind, I hit send.

Naomi Wilkinson: *How?* hovered there, awaiting his response.

I saw the flashing dots, but then they stopped, and a window popped up over our messages:

Video Call from Dustin Trail

Accept Decline

My jaw dropped. *Oh dear god, what was he going to want me to do?* I winced my eyes, almost in a motion to brace myself, and pressed,

Accept.

It took a few seconds for the video to start. The screen pixelated at first before coming in clear. His hand working his cock up and down was what it opened to.

Startled, I nearly dropped my phone. I juggled it until I was able to steady my grasp. I could hear him chuckling on the line. Once he could see I had it secured he gave me firm directions.

"Put the phone where I can see you. I want to watch." He ordered.

I didn't even bother saying anything. I just did as he commanded.

"Good, now open your legs."

Again, I obeyed.

"Suck your fingers. Good. Now rub."

I could see his shaft rising and falling as he pumped up and down, and I compliantly slid my fingers down and caressed.

"Dip them inside you."

I pushed one finger in and then listened for my next command.

"Taste yourself."

I pulled my finger out and sucked it down to the knuckle, imagining it was his rod. The peachy tartness lingered on my lips.

"Now rub some more."

I rubbed, turned on by being told what to do. I was always the one telling people what to do. It was a rush being ordered about and having sexual favors being performed on either side of a screen. I lost myself in the motion, my body trembling.

"Spread your legs wider for me."

I opened my thighs, baring all, listening to his rattly breaths through the speaker as he pleasured himself watching me. I dipped my finger in me again. Getting it good and wet, then continued rubbing myself, playing with my clit, feeling her swell beneath my fingertips.

My arousal was heightening. I slid my finger down my slit, fingering myself then pulling out to rub my clit again. I continued that motion, and the wetter I got the better it felt.

"Good girl," he breathed in a deep husky voice.

I watched his dick gliding up and down, glistening with man gloss. I licked my lips. I wanted so badly to lap that up with my tongue, taste his salty zest. Suck him hard.

My fingers worked vigorously, rubbing and probing, juices now flowing out of me. The sensations amplifying under my fingertips, my clit engorged. I felt myself squirt a bit and it trickled down my fingers and thighs.

"Oh yeah, baby," he cheered me on.

I rubbed even faster, feeling my toes curl then go numb and fuzzy, my body shaking. I fingered myself again, imagining his rock-hard dick sliding into me, in and out. Instinct taking over my body, my back rounding my tits and abdomen rising towards the ceiling.

"Cum for me!" He ordered.

And as if on command, the fireworks filled my eyes, and the heat wave crept over my body, my clit vibrating with intense arousal as I rubbed and rubbed...and then I erupted.

My orgasm escaped my lips, making me moan tremendously. I hoped my kids wouldn't hear, but I couldn't stifle myself.

Dustin's moans echoed on the speaker as he let go too, cum flowing from his cock.

The gratification I felt was so immense. I grasped the bedding with my free hand, clutching the blankets until the pleasure had subsided enough that I could finally ease my grip.

As I lay there, I was then made aware of the puddle underneath me on the bed. I had squirted more than I thought. The longer I lay there, the colder and wetter it felt. I pushed myself up into a seated position.

"You are so sexy." His voice declared.

"Thank you, Master," I reciprocated softly.

"Have a good night." I blew him a kiss and hung up the phone so that I could get cleaned up.

Bundling my quilt into a pile I could manage, I walked down to the laundry area and put it on the large load cycle, packing it into the machine.

Then I made my way to the bathroom to wash myself up, snatching a spare blanket from the fabric cupboard along the way.

I left the washroom hurriedly, then wrapped the fresh new quilt around my body, engulfing me in its warmth. I slumped onto the mattress.

Exhausted, now in bed, I reveled in my lustful activities; my thirst had been quenched. I snuggled into my pillow with a candid smile on my face. Within seconds, I was out like a light.

The morning sun streamed through my window, and my eyes fluttered open. My glass was half full of wine, still sitting on my bedside table. I was awake before any of the children, which didn't happen often.

Everley was an early bird and always enjoyed racing into my room to jump on me. I still felt enlightened after my bedtime release, and got out of bed with minimal effort, scooping my dirty glass and prancing into the kitchen to pour the leftover wine down the drain. I rinsed the cup and deposited it into the dishwasher.

I then made my way back to the laundry area to switch my blanket over to the dryer.

My next stop was the shower. I took my time, paying close attention to the warmth of the water as I scrubbed my body and washed my hair. As I watched the soapy water circle my feet and trickle down the drain, I thought about the fun we had the day before and the provocative phone call with Dustin.

The memory still burned in my mind and made my loins feel electric. When the last of the soap washed away, I turned off the tap, climbed out of the shower and toweled off, ready to begin a new day, fresh and uninhibited.

As I dried off, Everley knocked on the door and shouted, "Mommy, I'm up!"

"Ok, you can watch some cartoons for a bit if you'd like, I'm just going to get dressed and then I'll come make you breakfast."

"Ooookay!" Her voice trailed off as she ran away to turn on the TV.

That was my cue to get moving. I had absent-mindedly forgotten to pick out clothes prior to my shower, so I was forced to wrap up in my towel and make my way to the closet and dresser.

Seeing as the weather was beautiful and sunny again, I opted for a pair of shorter jean shorts and a low backed tank with my cross-strapped sports bra. I donned the clothes as quickly as I could and dried my hair.

Hair still a bit damp, I brushed it and proceeded to the kitchen to make breakfast for everyone. I wanted something easy and decided on omelets. I sliced up some ham, peppers, mushrooms and onions and grated cheese. I had some spinach in the fridge and decided to throw some of that in too. In mere minutes the house filled with the delectable aroma of scrambled eggs and melted cheese.

Aeda and Austin filtered in, emerging from their bedrooms with winced eyes and wild hair, flopping into chairs eager for food but still too sleepy to fully open their eyes. Everley raced over and jumped right into a chair when hers was served, wolfing it as fast as she could manage in order to go watch cartoons again.

I sat down after serving everyone up, slowly savoring each bite. I hadn't yet thought of what we could do for the day. Sundays were pretty tame in Salmon Arm as many of the local shops closed so the employees could have days off with their families.

One of the perks of living in a city with a small-town feel is knowing all the shop owners and employees, their families and their stories.

Whatever I decided upon would have to be something outdoors more than likely, which was fine by me. More sunshine was always a good thing!

I came up with going on the bike ride that we missed out on yesterday, then we'd likely have to come up with something else because my brain power was severely lacking in that moment.

Ushering the kids to get dressed and ready for the day, I commenced clean-up duties in preparation for the kids to return to Chad's on the following evening. I remade my bed hastily so that the change in my bedding wouldn't be questioned before calling them all to the living room to discuss the plan. They all were game for the bike ride, but no one could offer up ideas for after. Oh well, cross that bridge when we came to it!

The kids and I went to the carport and dug out the bikes and helmets, dusting them off and checking the air in the tires. We didn't have a particular route in mind, but we did always enjoy the trail down at the bird sanctuary, on to the wharf, and then around McGuire lake before heading home. Aeda fetched our water bottles, and I helped Everley tie her laces, then we were off.

Tires spinning, legs churning, hair whipping in the wind, we sped down our street in order to cross the highway at the intersection.

It didn't take long for the light to change for us, and we crossed with ease, Aeda leading the pack and me following in order to keep an eye on Everley in case anything were to go wrong.

She headed towards McGuire Lake first which was likely a better route than ending there. Otherwise we'd have been climbing an incline, and I wasn't sure if we could all make it after our jaunt.

The little lake lay in the center of town, the hospital where I worked at one end of it, and a nice leisurely trail wound around the perimeter. Large willows draped over the water's edge, tall reeds growing in appointed areas, and a small creek overladen with a small rounded bridge were just some of the sights along our path. Birds of all shapes and sizes soared over-head, dipping and diving through the sky.

The notorious blue heron stood on one leg amongst the reeds in the water, a stunning spectacle to see. We stopped to watch him for a while, taking in all his glory. His dark navy feathers caught the sunlight and emitted a cobalt blue shimmer, and his feathered mohawk ruffled in the subtle breeze.

We pedaled on. Turtles sunbathed on drifting logs, and dragonflies danced past our heads as we made our way down the last stretch of the trail.

We exited back onto the road leading to the crosswalk a few streets down which would bring us across the train tracks to the wharf.

We weaved in and around other members of the public on the sidewalks and roadways, using our best etiquette.

Crossing the tracks, we sped down to the street where we could either fork right and head to the sanctuary trail or go straight ahead towards the wharf. I left the choice in Aeda's capable hands.

She approached and signaled her turn to the right; bird sanctuary!

Down this stretch, we got to view all the ritzy mansions along the lakeshore. It was fun to imagine we lived in them and what they looked like on the inside. The large stone one at the end was our favorite. We thought it resembled a castle. My girls had all taken turns throughout the years imagining they were princesses ruling the land in that castle.

Pedaling past its gate, my peripherals picked up the turning of all their heads, gazing in. I didn't doubt that was exactly what was going on in their brains.

My front wheel hit the bump that signaled we had exited the pavement and were now onto the dirt path that led through the bird sanctuary. The canopy of birch trees arched over the path creating an encompassing feeling of entering the wild.

It was a serene and picturesque background for many photographers in the area. I stared up at it, taking in its beauty. The leaves and branches all intertwining, beams of sunshine bursting through any small opening they could, birds flitting tree to tree singing. The treed area of the path came to an end and we were encased in sunshine once more as we entered the marshy landscape where many birds nested.

Pedaling slower so as not to surprise any unsuspecting mama birds, we wound our way along the trail, observing all the signs and hearing all the many sounds of wildlife: piles of scat, chirping and cooing, loose feathers, well-crafted nests both up high and down low, and beaver chewed logs. The water was a gorgeous choppy blue nestled against the horizon.

The further we went, the closer it got, and before long we were at the entrance to the island, where it was extremely rocky. Everley had always dismounted and walked this portion in the past. However, it appeared she was going to try biking the whole way. I watched as carefully as I could but also had to watch my own trek for any wrong move could cause me to biff it. She was doing great though.

I saw her stick her feet out after one larger bump in the trail to catch her balance, but she coasted along and never did put her feet down. Pride washed over me. It was watching all their little accomplishments that made me reflect on how much they'd grown from year to year. Some they recognized themselves, and some they didn't even notice.

The rocks protruded out all around the bike path, and the trail itself was bumpy and rocky. I had to swerve to miss one particularly sharp rock. Looking up quickly, I could see that we were nearing the end up the island trail, and then we'd be circled back onto the sanctuary path which would take us back to the wharf.

Hearing the gravel under my tires was my first indication that we had made it through. All the rocks had disappeared, so I turned my attention elsewhere and fully enjoyed the view once more.

A group of ducks had emerged near the trail opening and were playing in some puddles on the grass. Pulling up, we sat admiring them for a while. They were so funny to watch, the way they waddled and their different personalities interacting with one another. We all laughed when they'd wiggle their bottoms and shake. It was pretty comical! Everley especially got a kick out of it. A few minutes passed, and when the kids had finally had their fill of ducks, we headed off again. We still had to do the trail up the wharf before making our way home, and I wanted to save time for a little surprise.

The breeze was blowing, and we were fighting the occasional strong gust on our way back. The wind whistled past my ears, deafening the sounds of the nearby traffic down Lakeshore Drive and the passing train.

Pivoting around the last corner, we were now on the straightway to the wharf, the greenery bright and vibrant, against the looming endless sky ahead. Our tires thudded one by one as they made contact with the long wooden wharf boards, and we sped past all the railings, avoiding the foot traffic and keeping to our own made biking lane.

Approaching the end, we dismounted in order to view the scenery and give it the proper appreciation it deserved.

We parked our bikes, walked over to the railing and climbed up to look over. Eagles and gulls flew overhead, scoping out their next meal. The choppy water, lapping at the docks and harbored boats below. The algae covered pillars offering shade and protection to the fish whose shapes and shadows were barely visible from our location.

In the distance, boats could be spotted either fishing or pulling riders, their motors deafened by the massive area in between us and them.

I took my phone out and grouped the kids together for a photo. A passerby saw me taking the photo and offered to take one of me with them as well, and I graciously accepted.

I was rarely in the photos, especially the ones with my kids, as like a typical mom, I always found myself behind the camera. After a cheerful,

"Cheese!"

I thanked the older lady and smiled at my screen.

As much as I disliked pictures of myself, it was nice to see a picture of us all together.

Tucking my phone away, I opted to go ahead with my little surprise. I walked up to the counter of the ice cream shop at wharf's end and sing-songed the question,

"Who wants ice-cream?"

The series of screeches and

"Me, me, me's!" I received was enough to paint a huge grin on my face.

Of course I knew the answer before I even asked, but their response was half the fun. Everley requested cotton candy, Austin, moose-tracks, and Aeda, raspberry cheesecake, which I ordered as well because it sounded amazing.

As each child was handed their cone, they walked to a nearby picnic table and licked away, the younger two painting their faces with it as well. The frozen treat was such a wonderful end to our ride. I was so glad to have had such a great few days with them all!

Ice cream melted down my finger, and I licked faster, trying to beat the heat. It was a losing battle. The faster I licked it still seemed to melt twice as fast. I resorted to biting it and that made some difference. I was last to finish, mostly just due to the fact that I was last to receive my cone.

I attempted to wipe up Everley's face, but a faint pink and blue ring remained around her mouth despite my efforts. Austin wiped his on his sleeve. They all thanked me, and we picked our bikes back up again and headed home.

As I predicted, the way home was a bit more of a struggle, just with the gradual incline of the roadway. Everley ended up pushing her bike the last stretch, and I hopped off to accompany her. Ahead of us I could hear the excited voices of Aeda and Austin but couldn't make out the source of their excitement from where I was.

As we walked closer, I noted a black truck alongside the sidewalk in front of our place. When Dustin's lean form strode around the side where he must've been talking to the kids, he was smiling and looked up to wave at us.

Everley saw him and started running with her bike towards him, squealing.

I was in shock. I hadn't expected to see him today. I truly believed he was headed back to Kelowna this morning, and then another thought crossed my mind.

How on Earth did he know where we lived?

I raked my brain trying to recollect a time I may have mentioned my address but came up with nothing. I realized I hadn't been exactly coherent the entire time, but I wasn't even sure why I would mention my address while under the influence either.

I didn't have enough time to think before he was in front of me.

"Hello gorgeous!" He reserved a special smile just for me that made his laugh lines show around the corners of his mouth.

His blue steely eyes sparkled in the sun, and his bronzed skin off-set his gleaming white teeth.

I likely would have dwelled on the address thing more had he not been so freaking sexy. As soon as I looked him up and down, all my concerns disappeared.

"I didn't expect to see you today." I voiced.

"Well, what else was I going to do? Just go back home and be lonely? I had so much fun with the lot of you, I thought I'd do it all over again today. Unfortunately, I should've messaged you first or popped by sooner. You guys must have been up and at it early."

"That's sweet of you. Yeah, sorry, we were trying to squeeze in the bike ride we didn't have time for yesterday."

"Oh, no problem. I'm sorry I missed out on that, but I guess it worked out as I don't have a bike with me. I don't suppose I'd be able to take you all out for dinner tonight, would I?"

My kids stood nearby occupying themselves with something. All perked up and started cheering when they heard us get invited out for dinner, a luxury I hadn't been able to afford too often recently.

"Well, I guess you have your answer."

We laughed and I walked over to the car port to finally park my bike and put my helmet away.

I invited him in for a quick tour of the house, which would probably have taken about two minutes normally, since it wasn't a very large space. However, he was asking so many questions, and the kids were providing so many answers, leading him around and showing him each of their toys and beds, everything had a long-winded explanation or story behind it. I had to smile, especially when even Austin, my quiet one, was in on giving lengthy responses, and even struck up some of the conversations himself.

It was very moving for me to see. It made me wonder if Chad had been more attentive to the kids instead of his screens, or his affairs, if perhaps Austin wouldn't be so quiet. Maybe he just wanted that guy-to-guy relationship and didn't know how to establish it himself. Whereas Dustin was there asking questions, awaiting his responses and talking about things it was obvious Austin was passionate about. He was making a connection with him.

Once done with their rooms and the main rooms of the house, the kids ran off to get ready to leave, eager for their dinner out.

"Guess there's only one room left then?" Dustin walked towards the last room, my room.

I was on his heels. I had completely forgotten if I'd cleaned my room up. I knew Dustin was a little OCD on his cleanliness and wanted to avoid the embarrassment of not living up to those standards, or any standard of clean for that matter. He turned on me as I entered through the frame of my room's doorway, pushing me back and pinning me to the boards, kissing me intensely.

I pushed him back, panic stricken, looking down the hall to make sure the kids hadn't seen, but they hadn't. I looked back at Dustin, ready to scold him for being so bold in front of my kids, but before I could say anything he yanked me into the room and closed the door softly.

He locked his lips on mine before I had a chance to begin my scolding. His soft lips caressing mine, his tongue massaging, intertwining with my own, he pulled me into his arms, holding me. I couldn't help but melt in his embrace, feeling his warmth and big protective arms around me. I wrapped my arms up around him as well, returning his kiss passionately, losing myself.

Engulfed in his smell, his feel, it felt like our souls were connecting, even if just momentarily. We both knew exactly what the other person wanted right at that exact moment. I opened my eyes, and he looked deep into mine. Our gaze held, and then without a single word he guided me to my sliding patio doors, opening one side and closing the curtains. I followed him out and he slid the door closed once more.

My patio overlooked the small, shared yard. A big tree loomed over one side offering some privacy from the house over. I had set up a small privacy screen on the opposite side of the patio to try to somewhat block off the view from the adjoining townhouse renter's patio.

Dustin scooped me up, connecting my lips with his again, kissing me lustfully. He planted my ass on the railing and lifted up my shirt and pulled down the cups of my bra to expose my breasts. He squeezed them, then began kissing them, titillating my nipples with his tongue, causing them to harden. His breath blowing on them caused goosebumps to form all over my body. He sucked and blew on me all over my chest and sides, trailing his fingers lightly, almost tickling me, causing my skin to be hyper-sensitive.

I worried about being seen, or caught by my kids, but that fear also made it so much more exciting, the appeal of *public sex* revealing itself to me. Taking things one step further, Dustin sucked his finger and then slid his hand up the leg of my shorts, peeling my panties to the side and gliding his finger up and down my folds until he found my entry point. He then proceeded to do small circles, rubbing his moist finger around, arousing me, then ever so gently dipping it in and out, making me wetter and wetter with each motion, still kissing me all the while.

I ran my fingers through his hair, biting and sucking his bottom lip. I wanted him to know how much he was turning me on, to show him, as I knew he could already feel that he was. He plunged his finger up into me, and I let out a muffled squeal, his mouth silencing me.

Diving his finger in again, I could feel my juices on his knuckles each time he pulled out. It was so seductive. I thought he'd be more eager to bury his cock in me, and I leaned forward to paw at his fly, but he batted my hand away and kept fingering me excitedly. I was confused but didn't want to interrupt the momentum. Hell, he could keep fingering me if that's all he wanted to do.

I leaned back holding onto the railing with my hands, this new angle providing him with more depth and space to work, which he used to his full advantage. In and out, around and back, shallow then deep. My shorts began to feel damp, and he paused for just a moment, reaching with his other hand into his pocket. What on Earth?

He pulled out a small purple U-shaped thing and held down what must have been a button with his thumb, as the "thing" then began vibrating intensely.

He stuffed it up my shorts and hovered it on my clit. Like a jolt of electricity passing through me, I quivered under its tremors. He held it in place with one hand and started fingering me again with the other, never losing his rhythm.

The added sensation left me on the cusp of orgasm. The power jetting out of that little purple vibrator was unparalleled to any toy I had ever had the pleasure of using.

Each plunge of his finger, my pussy gripped harder, until he was barely able to pull it out. He began just thrusting while still being in me.

My eyes rolled in the back of my head as my climax built up. I heard a "*click*" and the power suddenly cranked up another notch on the vibrator. I lost it.

My body began convulsing in pleasure. He thrusted harder instead of stopping and I gripped the railing harder for fear of falling overboard. The ecstasy I felt, my clit was engorged, and I could feel jet streams of lady juice squirting from between my legs.

Dustin's arm was dripping, but he kept going, driven by my howls. I couldn't muffle myself. I was so sure at any second the kids would be opening the curtains and find their mother in this extremely provocative position.

Much to my surprise that didn't happen, and my howls went unnoticed, fading away until I was left panting and crumpled forward into a trembling heap on Dustin's shoulders.

He kissed me again.

"Let me grab you a towel." I said blatantly, looking at his soaked arm and hand. We both giggled.

I tip-toed back into my room and made my way to the ensuite. Grabbing a hand towel for him. He followed me in and washed in the sink while I disposed of my now cold, damp shorts and panties into the hamper.

I located a new similar pair so as not to attract too much attention to my change in attire. Wiping myself up as well before tucking my tits back into my bra and pulling my shirt back down. I gradually made my way out of my room with Dustin alongside me.

"And that's my room!" I proclaimed as if I had just ended a long spiel about my bedroom as part of the tour.

My kids, however, didn't even look up. They had busied themselves with their gaming console in our absence and didn't seem to have even noticed our lengthy vacancy.

Wanting to push the limits even further, I extended my hand backwards and landed my palm on Dustin's robust dick. I had seen the swollen outline of his erection through his jeans and had longed to touch it.

I took advantage of my chance. Tracing his girthy shape and gripping it. I wished for more time. I wanted to return the favor bestowed upon me. I heard him gulp, gave him a few tugs through his pants and then released him.

"Time to go!" I announced. Dustin gawked at me, and I smiled devilishly, winking at him as we headed towards the door, leaving him wanting more.

| Chapter 15 |

Hanoi 36 was a family-oriented Vietnamese restaurant located on one of the main streets downtown on Hudson. It was always very welcoming and served local fresh foods cooked up in their authentic style. Dustin brought us there for our meal and we were all delighted.

The family run business had the most amazing and generous owners, so it was a thrill to support their establishment and eat their mouth-watering food. Pho was a favorite amongst my kids so they each picked a different one off the menu. I had a harder time deciding, there were so many unique and tasty options to choose from.

The quaint little restaurant had multiple place settings filled with patrons. Artwork reflecting their homeland and heritage lined the walls, further adding to the experience.

Our booth was located near the window, so we were able to soak up the last rays of sunshine cast through the glass.

The kids talked feverishly, each speaking over the other in order to be heard. I kept raising my hand to motion for them to settle down.

Dustin spoke with each one, not put off by their demanding behavior. He played it cool, making them take turns and making them say *excuse me* if they wanted to speak.

I was impressed by his paternal skills. For a guy who didn't have any kids of his own, it seemed to come naturally to him, a trait that I also found quite attractive.

I sat admiring him. His eyes danced around from child to child, glinting in the light, his smile radiating as he spoke and induced laughter amongst them all.

The waitress broke my thought process as she laid down our hot plates and bowls of food meticulously. The kid's eyes all bulged at the sight of their meals, the presentation much more impressive than meals I usually served them.

Digging in, the flavors burst forth on my tongue, consuming my mouth with their savory tanginess. Catching my eye from across the table, Dustin smiled and suckled his fingers, clearly referencing our prior activities. I blushed and took a long drink of water, attempting to hide behind my glass.

Meanwhile, still not dropping his gaze, he tore a big bite out of his entrée, licking his lips and chewing insatiably. Everley, thinking he was trying to be funny, mimicked him, and before long they were all shoving food in their mouths and making silly faces and laughing. It was a great meal, thoroughly enjoyed by all, followed by many *thank-yous*. Dustin paid with a handful of cash and then herded us all out the door. We loaded back into his truck and made our way home.

I had no idea how to say goodbye to him. He had traveled all this way, and although unexpected, it had been wonderful having him around. He was so good with my kids, and they seemed to really like him. I felt as if we had gotten even closer and strengthened our connection to more of an emotional level than just physical.

However, I still wasn't sure how I felt about letting the children see me kiss him or show any physical signs of affection. I worried that maybe they only liked him this much because they thought he was just a friend, and that if they thought it was anything more than that, they might be discouraged from liking him anymore. I wasn't even sure how they'd feel about another man in my life, other than their father. It had never even crossed my mind.

Perplexed, I strummed my fingers on the door handle, antsy as we pulled up into my driveway.

Aeda and Austin jumped out as soon as the doors unlocked, once again thanking Dustin and bidding him farewell before racing each other into the house. They knew that they were going to need to prep for school and their return to Chad's tomorrow.

They had to make lunches, shower, lay their clothes out, pack up what they needed for the next four days and organize their bags. Everley was a little slower to leave. She reached over the front seat and hugged Dustin.

"Good bye!"

"Goodbye, sweetie! It was nice meeting you! We'll have to hang out again soon, okay?"

Her face lit up at those words and she nodded, grinning and biting her lip. Then she bolted, yelling at her siblings that she was going to hang out with Dustin again soon. Then it was just the two of us.

At first I squirmed a bit, avoiding eye contact, but my peripherals showed me he had turned to face me and was waiting for me to acknowledge him. I looked at him.

"I wish I didn't have to go. This weekend's been amazing."

"Yes, it really has. Thank you again for spoiling us. We all enjoyed our time, you've made quite the impression on them."

I nodded in the direction my kids had made off.

"It was mutual. They're awesome kids. You've done a good job. They've made quite the impression on me as well. I'd definitely like to see you all again."

That made me smile. So he was thinking more long term, and it was more than just a hookup. He returned my smile and leaned in, knowing he was serious about us was just the confirmation I needed to feel more comfortable. I hadn't wanted a relationship per say, because I was still in the process of being single, having fun, and figuring out who I was again. It was still nice to know someone was interested in being with me once I did decide to enter a relationship again.

I curled my hand around his neck, holding his head, and our lips met. Soft and sensual, we let it linger, opening our eyes and gazing at one another.

He lifted his hand and brushed my hair off my cheek. I sucked my bottom lip in and broke our eye contact, looking down.

"I guess I'd better hit the road; I'll text you." He affirmed, leaning back into his seat.

"Okay, I'd like that."

We exchanged long looks once again, then I opened my door and slid off his leather seat onto the dirt.

The door closed with a *thud* and I took a few steps towards my front entrance before looking back. I waved, and he returned the gesture as he backed out. Then with a quick honk, he drove away.

Encircling my eyes with a night cream, I stared into the mirror. The kids were in bed and the house was quiet.

Scenes from the past week kept going in waves through my head, playing over and over again as I tried to figure it all out.

Today felt so real, the feelings, that last kiss. I touched my lips where he had last touched them. The warm ember of it still remained. I closed my eyes whimsically, daydreaming of all the possibilities, remembering that single moment where it all seemed possible.

Re-opening them suddenly, breaking my fantasizing, I realized I needed to throw in another load of laundry before bed. I gathered the baskets from around the house in all the common areas and dumped them into my one larger hamper then hauled it to the laundry room.

I clicked on the load size for regular, and water started streaming out. I measured and poured in the soap then started adding the laundry items one by one into the machine, layering them evenly and checking through the pockets. It didn't take long before I found my shorts from earlier that afternoon, partially dried by now. I checked the pockets, all clear.

I finished the remaining soiled laundry and was about to close the lid when I realized my panties hadn't been in there. I was sure

I put them in the hamper at the same time I deposited my shorts in there this afternoon. I had removed them at the same time, but when I checked the shorts, they weren't entangled within them like sometimes happens.

I'd hate for the kids to find them. I searched the floor, and when I couldn't locate them, I began searching the house, starting in my room.

I checked under the bed, beside my night table and in the ensuite. I even checked the patio. Bewildered, I looked in my intimate's drawer just to be sure I hadn't been so distracted, I'd dropped them in there while grabbing the clean pair, but I came up empty.

Maybe I had somehow missed them and they were in the machine. Otherwise, I had no idea.

I scratched my head. Well, I had done all I could and crossed my fingers. I would be mortified if one of the kids found my sopping underwear somewhere random. Not sure how I'd explain that one.

It was late, and time for me to retire to bed. I walked around the house and shut off all the lights before pulling back my duvet and climbing in bed. I set my alarm and checked to see if I had any messages.

None. I sighed, somewhat disappointed Dustin hadn't let me know he'd made it home safe or messaged before bed. He's not your boyfriend, I reminded myself. He is just a guy! And with that, I reached over and clicked off my bedside lamp.

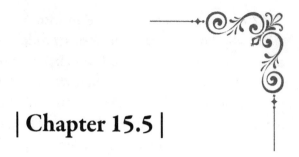

| Chapter 15.5 |

What a weekend! Meeting up with Naomi and her kids at Syphon falls was phenomenal. I hadn't heard back from her about coming up to visit, and I was certain it was more intentional than not. However, I couldn't not come, regardless of what she may or may not have said. I HAD to at least try! On the off chance she may have said yes...I wanted to be there already. Or at least be there to try to change her mind. So, I made the trip. I think it worked out in my favor.

Her kids were absolutely fantastic. I couldn't say enough good things about them. Spending the day all together like that, made me really rethink a family. Everything from our hike to time at the beach, dinner at Hanoi, to even just the conversation. I couldn't find a single fault.

Well, aside from the cold shoulder I felt in Erika's presence. I wasn't sure what grudge she had against me. We'd all had a threesome. *Why was I now being penalized by her for it?* Or at least that's what I assumed it was about. I had no indications otherwise. She didn't seem like she was all that interested in me, so I scrapped the idea that maybe she was jealous. After all she was the one that had basically set this whole thing up.

Oh well, I wasn't about to dwell on it. She and Naomi could hash out their own issues.

I loved how things were all coming together. Naomi was finally in my life. Her kids were fond of me and I, them. The sex was mind blowing! Now all I had to work on was convincing her to be my girlfriend, as that seemed to be a hesitation point for her. She always seemed to be weighing things out in that brain of hers. I admired her brains, and her beauty. If only she could know how gorgeous she was.

That would be my life's purpose, to make sure she was cared for, provided for, satisfied and most importantly make sure she knew how absolutely stunning she was. Every curve, every dimple, every scar, was just a part of her story, and I was quite sure I loved it all.

Everything she viewed as a fault, I found something to love about it. It made her unique, made her story all that more entrancing and made her all that more appealing. For every child she bore, for every man who scorned her, mainly Chad, I just admired her more.

Motherhood was a gift. I hated that women felt less attractive after bearing children, or while getting older. If they could see through my eyes, or any decent man's, they'd see that it all just made them that much more attractive. I knew Naomi would likely never see what I see or understand just how deeply I felt about her so soon in our *relationship*, but I could only hope.

I laid in bed thinking about everything following our erotic video chat and our patio rendezvous, trying to recall every detail, wanting to hang on to it, savor it, treasure it. I may just be a man, but there was more to me than that too.

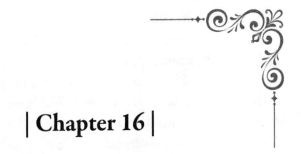

| Chapter 16 |

The sound of my alarm blaring jerked me awake. Ugh, Monday! I gave a good old Garfield stretch and adorned a face of contempt before rising, rubbing my eyes as I drug my feet to the washroom to void. I could hear the kids beginning to rise as well.

They had their routine down pat, and I could get ready at my own pace. I slipped into my workout gear, knotted my hair up on the top of my head and slapped on some deodorant before heading out to the living room. Everley was dressing with her door wide open.

"Morning, Mommy!"

"Morning, sweet pea!" I answered as I walked past.

Grabbing my yoga mat and weights, I laid it all out before putting on the TV and YouTube. With a few easy flicks, I had a home workout on the screen and ready to go.

I began my warm up as Aeda and Austin emerged looking as groggy as I felt and made their way to the kitchen for breakfast, waving their "good mornings" to me.

Aeda routinely made Everley's breakfast for her too, and she scampered up to the table to eat once she heard it served. I powered away, getting my sweat on.

As usual, I was dying by the end, panting and dripping. I drug myself to the shower to clean up quickly before taking the kids to school.

I started my set at work the next day, so they were headed to Chad's after school. This always bummed me out. I just missed them terribly, but I couldn't let them see that it bothered me.

I did a fast wash and rinse then jumped out, toweling off. Throwing on some clothes I had set aside the night before, I yelled,

"Are you guys almost ready to go?"

"Almost," was their response.

Brushing my teeth, I spat in the sink, rinsing it down with the tap water. I'd eat breakfast later but didn't want to leave the house with morning breath.

If this was a normal school day, they'd take the bus, but because they had extra bags to go to their dad's with, I always spared them hauling all that and drove them to school that first day. Plus, I wanted to savor every last moment with them before we said our goodbyes. There were only a few days left before school was done for the year and then we could look forward to enjoying our summer together.

Checking the time, I charged out of the bathroom.

"Ok guys time to go! You got all your stuff?"

All three shouted their answer in unison, sounding almost like one word.

"Yep-I do-Uh-huh!"

"Alright, out we go!"

I held the door and heaved Everley's bag onto my shoulder. She must have packed a few more items in it. The muffled sound of one of her toys singing inside told me I was correct.

Locking the door, we all hopped in the van and raced off, just making the bell when we pulled up.

"Ok, I love you so, so, so much! You have fun at Daddy's. Give me kisses!"

I jumped out to squeeze them all before allowing them to depart, they acted embarrassed. Well, Everley was overjoyed, but I could tell Aeda and Austin still enjoyed the attention, as much as they pretended not to.

Hugging them all, they turned and I blew one last kiss before they walked away into the school. I stood watching diligently, and once the doors to the school closed, I clambered back into my running vehicle and headed off.

I spent my day doing prep for the week, buying groceries, making meals, drying and folding laundry, mowing the tiny patch of lawn deemed a *yard* by our landlord.

Dustin finally messaged me, wishing me a good day and telling me once again how much fun he had with me and the kids.

We started chatting a bit, making dirty and witty jokes back and forth. Just enough banter to keep me smiling, before he took it to the next level and sent me a rather suggestive and steamy pic of him in the shower at the end of his shift! I grinned ear to ear for that one and clamped my legs together to restrain myself.

I'd return the favor later I thought and popped my phone in my shirt pocket above my breast.

It was five thirty when I thought I should probably eat something. I had gotten so busy puttering, doing all my prep all day, I hadn't eaten like I'd planned to, and my stomach was rumbling. I didn't want to use up any of my pre-made meals for work, so I began whipping something up quickly when I heard the doorbell ring.

I wiped my hands off and began walking towards the door to answer it. Before I made it halfway across the living room, the door thrust open, slamming into the wall, leaving a large gaping hole in my drywall. I screamed in surprise.

"What the hell, Chad!" I yelled at him as he barreled into my house.

"What the hell is right, Naomi!!" He screamed back at me.

"How dare you! With the kids here, *MY* kids!"

Spittle was flying from his mouth across the room at me, his face red with rage.

I had honestly never seen him this mad before. Usually he just didn't care. We'd argue, but this was different.

His pupils were dilated and he was breathing hard. I took a timid step back.

"What are you even talking abou..."

"Don't play dumb with me Naomi!" He cut me off mid-sentence.

"You know I'm talking about your slutty affair! What kind of mother are you going on like that in front of the kids!"

He was leering at me now, hissing his insults, knowing that trashing me about what kind of mother I am would hurt.

"That's what this is about? Dustin?" He was walking towards me, pacing and flailing his arms.

"It's sick! Displaying the things you have in front of them, seeing their mom act like a common whore! Who knows how many men you've had in here! This Dustin is probably just the tip of the iceberg! You'd better get your shit in order. I'm going to go for full custody!"

I was boiling inside. Livid! I stood my ground and lashed back.

"For your information, *WE ARE SEPERATED!* I can see whomever I'd like, whenever I'd like! You have no say! And this is my place! You have no right bursting in here spitting all over me! The number of affairs you've had over the years while we were married, or did you forget about those? How dare *I*? How dare you! Don't you ever insult my mothering ever again! You've barely participated in the parenting their entire lives, you hypocrite! If they were in your charge, they likely would have electrocuted themselves as toddlers chewing on your damn computer cord while you sat on your ass playing on it! Just try taking me to court! Fuck you! Get the fuck out of my house, you useless twat!"

I had my finger pointed at him, stepping forward, pushing him out of my house one step at a time. He definitely looked taken aback by verbal strength on the subject and shrank back aghast.

When we got to the door, he turned as if he was going to leave, when his arm reached back, suddenly ripping my phone from my shirt pocket. He ran and jumped over the back of my couch separating us. I lunged for him.

"Give me that back!" I screamed at him.

I saw him punching in my code. I knew I should have changed it when I left him. It opened right up to the picture Dustin had sent me, and like all text messages, his name was the header for the conversation just above it. *Dustin Trail.*

Chad looked up, that immense rage returning, his eyes narrowed.

"Dustin Trail is the guy you're fucking?"

I stammered. I couldn't even respond. I was terrified at this point, seeing the glint in his eyes and started taking slow, meticulous, shuffled steps backwards towards the doorway.

He was clenching his fists, balling them into large threatening balls and then cracking his fingers upon release before clenching them again, stepping towards me. He ignored the obstacles in his way, plowing over and through them. I had an abrupt urge to run.

Turning hastily, I bound for the door. Chad's long legs leapt over the couch. I heard the thud of his landing. With two lengthy steps, he clutched my hair, curling his fingers up in the locks and yanking back just as my shoulders were almost out the door.

I cried out in pain, and he used the force of the yank to throw me back, whipping me down to the floor. I stumbled trying to get up as fast I could, but he was on me in a second.

I had tunnel vision and could only see his big shovel sized fists barreling into my face, again and again.

The first blow stunned me and I swear I must've blacked out, but then the next one and the next one came. I felt all of them. He must've punched me about a dozen times, swearing at me, calling me,

"Bitch!" and "Whore!"

Then he rose up above my curled body, and an even harder impact knocked me in my ribs!

He was kicking me, again and again. He didn't stop at the ribs. He booted my back, legs, ass, stomach and arms.

The wind was knocked out of me, I hadn't even managed to scream. All I could do was whimper.

When the kicks stopped, I felt his hands grab my hair again, dragging my head up, his thumb forcing my swollen eyes open.

"Look at me, you cunt! Remember I own you!"

He lifted me up while still reefing on my hair. I could feel clumps of it ripping out of my scalp. Then he landed one last blow, slapping me hard across my face. He then released me and my body collapsed to the floor.

I had no energy or strength to catch myself. I slammed down. Then he spat on me and stormed out the door.

All I could hear was my rattled breath out of one ear. It hurt to breathe, I couldn't move, and I could barely see. My eyes were swollen up to the point all I could make out was a tiny blurry slit of light before they closed.

Ring! Riiinnng!*Riiinngggg!*

My eyes blinked, my sight all out of focus in one eye. I wasn't able to see out of the other at all. I couldn't tell the time by the lighting outside. It was like I was living in a shadow. Everything was dark and blurry. I was still on the floor, motionless. I couldn't move. I hurt so much.

I tried to think how I woke. My phone had been ringing! But I didn't know where my phone was at all. Even if I did, I wasn't sure I could reach for it anyways. The pain was so immense.

I wiggled myself in the direction I thought I had heard the ringing come from, but as I could only hear out the one ear, I might be motioning in the totally wrong direction.

Wrecked with effort, and writhing in pain, I gave up and laid there until exhaustion overcame me. I don't know how long I had been unconscious, but I heard a scream and crying, and someone was holding my hand.

The next thing I knew, I was being loaded onto a stretcher by two paramedics, or that's who I assumed was doing it anyhow. Even with their steady and experienced hands, being moved hurt.

Despite their extra efforts to keep me comfortable, there was no comfort.

The siren echoed in my one good ear, and every bump we hit sent a jolt of pain throughout my body. All I could do was lie there.

The bright fluorescent lights of the ER blasted my one partially functioning eye, and I cringed. I had no energy to shield my face from the brightness. The voices around me all sounded garbled and I wasn't able to focus on what they were saying. I could tell x-rays and a CT scan were being ordered. Someone drew up my eyelids and shone their penlight in my pupils to check for a concussion.

Being a nurse, I knew what their every move was going to be, but not being able to see, hear or move much limited me from knowing the extent of the damage done.

I felt a nurse insert an IV in my left forearm, taking multiple attempts, the tourniquet squeezing me tight until blood was drawn. They finally managed to get it in my dehydrated and flattened veins. I knew pain meds were coming now.

A few moments later, the cold, numbing sensation of the *hydromorphone* flowed into my vein and up my arm before covering me with a blanket of relief. Feeling my pain subside a bit was just what I needed, but then I could feel all the things my pain had masked before.

My mouth was so dry, like sand, and I could feel my lips like cracked and blistered scales. My clothes were damp and soiled. *How long had I been out?*

A team of nurses entered my curtained off zone and began washing me up, cutting my clothes off me, and eventually inserted a catheter. One assured me it was only temporary, until they could get my pain under control more and my skin back intact, as she smeared the oh so familiar thick zinc cream all over my outer labia, backside, and spots on my inner and back thighs.

I had applied this same cream to so many patients over the years, never imagining one day I would be the one getting cream applied to my personal bits, or at least not so soon.

They applied a brief to me as well, which only added to my embarrassment, and then finished my ensemble with a standard blue IV gown.

One provided me with a heated blanket and then covered that with another flannel blanket to seal the heat in.

I was so grateful for the care of my colleagues. I just hoped it wasn't anyone I knew too well, just for the sake of them not visualizing me in this state after I'd recovered. Assuming that that was a possibility at all.

A familiar tone snapped my attention back, and I slowly rolled my neck in that direction. A hand grasped mine and held it tight. Faint sobbing and a kiss was planted on the back of my hand.

A toothette wet with ice water was then sponged into my mouth, which I sucked at thirstily. The hand dipped again and again until I overdid it and choked a bit, sputtering water back and wincing in pain. My ribs were on fire from choking and coughing.

That's when the porter drew back the curtains, announcing he was taking me down for my imaging. My guest wasn't able to attend but was told to wait for me. I received a light kiss on the forehead before I felt the brakes on the bed un-latch and began the bumpy journey to the third floor's imaging department.

Overcome with fatigue again, I kept drifting in and out on the way there but got my wake-up call when they slid me over from the stretcher onto the cold hard surface of the CT scanner. I shivered as the images were taken. It was standard protocol to blanket the patient as they lay there. However, in this instance it was forgotten.

My catheter bag now with a bit of urine in it sloshed against my legs where they had propped it. The shivering was adding to the emerging pain as the relief of my pain medication was now beginning to subside. I ached silently through both the CT and the X-ray which they also had to take lying down.

By the time they were finished with me and returned me to my curtained area, I was once again in agony.

I dinged my call bell with the strength I could muster, and once my nurse made it over to check on me, she did not need words to see that I was due for more analgesic. With a push of her syringe, I once again felt the warm wave creep over me, and I fell asleep.

When I roused, it was to the flashing of a camera. I flinched at the brightness. I could hear a man's voice talking and questioning. A woman was answering. It was Erika. Thank-god it was her! She must've been the familiar voice who was with me earlier upon my arrival to hospital. She was telling the cop all she knew and how she had found me, while the other took all the photos, cataloging my ordeal one bruise at a time. I was grateful for the dose of hydromorph I was given when the other male cop began rolling me so he could take more photos. He handled me so roughly, like an object. I could hear Erika giving him shit, as she could tell by the look on my face that I wasn't handling it well. She ushered them out and they said something about returning at a later time, is what I gathered. I drifted away again.

The smell of food roused me this time. I was ravenous. My stomach rolled with hunger. Erika grabbed the tray and wheeled it over to me, and I made my first attempt at speaking.

"Th... tha... thank you." It was more of a raspy whisper, but she nodded and got me set up.

She handed me the utensils after cutting my food up for me. I couldn't imagine chewing at this point and concentrated on the soup instead.

"Come on, you can do it, you're stronger than this."

Her words of encouragement tugged at my heart strings and I pushed myself to lift my spoon. Pain shot up my arm and ribs, but I gritted my teeth and pushed through, almost spilling my soup when I dropped my spoon into it to scoop my first bite. I was shaky, and my muscles atrophied, but I managed to get a small slurp into my mouth.

Dribbles ran down my chin, but still, a small success. Erika blotted the soup away as I swallowed. I knew it was likely mediocre soup, but anything would have tasted amazing at this point. I slurped another bite; with every mouthful I felt a little more strength return and I kept on.

I was carefully slurping down my broth when the same male cop who was asking questions before entered again. This must be his return trip, I thought.

"I was hoping she'd be more alert and able to talk for herself this time round?" He asked, looking and analyzing me.

"She's still pretty weak." Erika began but trailed off.

"I-it's okay." I rasped, shoveling another bite into my mouth.

In all honesty, I just wanted it over and done with. I wanted that asshole charged. I hoped that my kids were someplace other than his place, but I knew that was probably not likely.

The cop, who introduced himself as Sergeant Webb, nodded his appreciation for my cooperation and strode farther into my room to speak to me. He pulled his notepad and pen out of his pocket, eager to write any information I may be able to provide.

I tried to find comfort in his face, but his expression was very flat and steely. No emotion escaped his eyes. His square jaw set, he began to question me.

"Can you give an approximate date and time this event occurred?"

I tried to think back and recall, and it occurred to me I didn't even know what date it was today.

"I believe it was the 17th around five-thirty in the evening. What is the date today?" My voice was barely an audible whisper.

"It's the 20th today, Miss. Can you explain the events that took place that evening?"

"I was doing all my preparation for work, making meals and what not, then I started making dinner when I heard a knock at the door. I went to answer it, but I didn't make it more than a few steps towards the door and it burst in. Chad, my ex, was there and he was screaming at me. Acting as if I was having an affair on him, but we've been separated and living in separate residences for months now. I told him off and thought he was going to leave, but he grabbed my phone instead and opened my messages. Then he started hitting me and kicking me. When he was almost done, he told me he owned me and spat on me."

My voice was so hoarse, and my throat dry and sore, I took a long drink of my water, attempting to rehydrate enough to make my words form with a little less effort.

"What did he do with your phone?" Sergeant Webb asked.

"He looked at my messages." I responded, not wanting to relinquish the exact message that had triggered the explosion, but I wasn't so lucky.

"What was in the messages that enraged him?"

I looked down, embarrassed.

"A picture, from the guy I'm kind of seeing." I think my expression told the Sergeant what the picture must have included. He asked no more questions pertaining to that subject but instead moved on.

"So, this Chad? Never had a key to your present residence?"

"No, not at all. We have a child custody agreement. We're able to pick up the kids at each other's places to exchange, but that's it."

He scribbled a few things down on his pad of paper, his face remaining flat.

"So, the argument was about your present lover?"

I hadn't considered that choice of words before and wasn't sure how to react.

"Yes, he was an old friend of ours in high school, and they had ended on bad terms. I started kind of seeing him and Chad found out somehow. Probably the kids, because we had all hung out together. I hadn't planned it at all, but it just happened. The next thing I know, he's bursting my door open screaming at me."

At this point, I was pushing my voice to my limits, and it was coming out more as a high-pitched screechy rasp.

"Where are the children now?"

"I'm assuming with him. It was his turn to have the kids as I was supposed to start work the next day."

Sergeant Webb hummed at this, clicking his tongue.

"Should we have any reason to be concerned on the children's behalf?"

"I don't think so? I don't know, this is completely out of character for him. I never would have thought him capable. But that part concerns me, if I never thought him capable of this..." I trailed off.

Sergeant Webb's pen scratched like crazy.

"Can someone please check on them?" I begged.

"Yes, we will be going to collect his statement as well and will make sure they are safe. Considering the violence in this case, we will most likely detain your ex until we can figure out how to proceed. The children, we will have to figure out a place they can go. Do you have any family local?"

"I can take them." Erika piped up suddenly.

"Are you sure?" I queried.

I didn't think Erika would want that much time with kids. I knew she loved my kids, but I also knew she enjoyed her own time as well.

"I wouldn't have offered it if I wasn't sure. I want to help." She sounded steadfast, so I agreed.

I'd rather them with Erika anyhow, close by and without the parental judgment that usually came with visits from my parents.

I smiled my thanks at her or attempted to anyhow. The large split in my fat lip pulled tight, and I don't think my mouth curled into a very convincing smile.

"Alright, Mrs. Wilkinson, I think those are all the details I need for now. I will follow up with you once we've taken care of a few matters. You work on healing up."

He looked at me somberly for a moment before turning to walk out the curtain, then paused a second.

"Just for investigatory sake, what is your present partner's name?"

I stopped a second, boy I hope this doesn't affect him at work.

"Dustin...Dustin Trail."

"Thank you, ma'am."

He jotted the name down on his pad with a mere few scratches of his pen, then turned his heel and departed.

"Fuck, Chad did this to you?"

Erika jumped at the chance to voice her opinion, having held back in the presence of the police.

"I knew that asshole was no good!" She looked at me sorrowfully.

"He screwed you up something awful, girl."

I gulped, I didn't know if I wanted to see or not. Erika was digging in her bag and procured a mini compact mirror, stretching out her hand towards me, offering me the chance to observe the damage. I sucked my sore lip, looking at the compact tentatively.

Temptation won and I grabbed it. Snapping it open, I had my eyes closed. Taking a deep breath, I held it and then released, opening my eyes and casting my gaze into the reflection. If I was expecting to see any sign of the old me, I was greatly disappointed.

My lips were fat and split. I had stitches on the inside of my lips where my teeth had gone through them. My cheeks were a crimson purple, matching my eyes, or the spots where my eyes once were.

Now there were two swollen baseball sized mounds, one completely closed and the other that I was able to see out of was no more than a slit, the cornea bloodied with all the burst blood vessels.

There were some staples in my hairline, dried blood encased them into my scalp. My hair was a tangled, greasy mess. I felt tears welling up in my eyes. I removed my covers and lifted my gown, I didn't care if Erika was there at this point. I just had to see.

My entire body was a massive pile of hematomas. There was more bruise than there was body. My ribs were clearly fractured as well as one collarbone. There was so much trauma to my tissue, my body was all puffed up. I felt like the Michelin man. I let out a choked sob. I was trying hard not to bawl.

Erika began to explain her side.

"The hospital and staffing office were looking for you when you didn't show up for work the next day. I was your emergency contact, so they called me. I started texting you and got no response. Then I called, and nothing. I was worried and drove by after I finished work. I just figured maybe you'd slept in, I don't know, but then I saw your front door ajar. I ran inside and you were in a clump on the ground, lifeless. I could tell you had been there awhile. I could barely recognize you."

She started to cry. Erika crying was super rare, so I knew she had to be very emotional over finding me like that. She hugged me and sobbed into my hair. It hurt, but her hug also allowed me to finally let go of my emotions too, and I sobbed.

"You've been basically in a coma. You'd hit your head so hard and all the punches you took, he fractured your skull too and cracked it open. Luckily it didn't require surgery though. You'd barely wake. I was so worried! I don't know what I would have done if you were…"

198

She couldn't complete her sentence, but I understood. Her body shook with sobs against mine. I squeezed her tight. I didn't know what I'd do without her either.

We held each other until we had both sobbed it out. Wiping our eyes and blowing our noses with the tissues on my bedside table, we collected ourselves.

"I'm so glad you're here with me." I squeaked.

"Me too. Also, I called your parents and let them know you're ok. I'll keep updating them."

"Thank you, and again thank you for taking my kids as well."

Her phone started ringing just then, and she answered promptly. My nurse entered with my now scheduled dose of analgesic.

I let the warm rush of relief wash over me again and thanked her as she hurried out to answer the next call bell. Erika hung up.

"That was Sergeant Webb, letting me know they've detained Chad and that I can come collect the children. I'll grab some stuff for them from his place. I'll try to bring them to see you tomorrow. I know they're going to be scared and want to see you for their own eyes."

I nodded, tearing again. I didn't want them to see me like this, but I knew Erika was right. They were probably terrified. I wished I could talk to them right now. She pecked my head and gave my hand a squeeze.

"It'll be ok. I'll see you tomorrow."

She'd only just walked away, when a male nurse I didn't recognize walked in holding the unit's portable phone out to me.

"A, Dustin Trail would like to speak to you?" He waited for my look of approval before handing the phone over to me.

"Hello?"

"Naomi? Oh my god! I just got off the phone with Clyde Webb. He told me you were in the hospital and was questioning me, asking if I could come give a statement. Are you ok? What happened? I was wondering why you weren't returning any of my calls or texts." The sound of panic and concern etched in his voice.

"I'm ok, a bit shaken, and sore, ok a lot sore, but I'm alive. My kids are taken care of now, and I'm not sure how long they'll keep me here, but for the time being, I need the pain meds."

I was hoping to not have to relay the story again, especially not to Dustin. I knew if anyone was going to be furious, it would be him.

"What happened Naomi?" His voice remained concerned but also stern. I knew there was no getting around it.

"Chad found out we've been kind of seeing each other, and well, he wasn't happy about it." I opted for the shorter, less graphic form.

"And he laid his hands on you? That friggen cowardly prick!"

The rage in his voice rang clear.

"I would have been there if I'd known, Naomi. I'm so sorry!"

"It's alright, I didn't expect you to be, and how would you ever know?"

"I wish I was there with you right now."

"Oh, no, I don't think I'd want you here. I don't look very good."

Thinking about it, I probably wouldn't want him to see me for quite some time. I didn't want my kids to see me like this either, but I did want to see them and hold them.

"I don't care about what you look like. I just want to be there with you."

"That's really sweet, Dustin. I'm hoping my recovery won't take too long."

"Me too. Let me know when they release you, and I'll come be your ride and take care of you."

"Ok, I will, thank you for calling."

"Bye, babe."

"Bye."

I heard the phone hang up and I clicked mine off as well. I sat for a moment. All I wanted was my kids.

That's when the nausea hit. I'd been without food and water for a few days and must have eaten too fast and my stomach couldn't handle it. I rang my call bell hurriedly and looked around for anything.

Across the room which was only a few steps, a garbage can lay. I leapt to my feet, not realizing just how weak and atrophied my legs were.

They gave out underneath me and I crumpled to the floor again but was able to grab hold of the counter to ease my fall. The garbage was right near my head and I grabbed it just in time as I began hurling into it full force.

My nurse arrived, shocked to find me on the floor and retching as vomit poured out of me. She called and assembled the same male nurse that brought me the phone in order to give me a hand getting up, and had a third go fetch me some IV gravol from the Pyxis machine.

Once I recovered enough, one of them perched on either side of me, lifting with their legs. It hurt something horrible, but there was no overhead lift here for them to get me up any other way.

I accepted my fate and attempted to walk with them, wincing in pain as they assisted me back onto my stretcher.

"I guess you'll definitely be needing some rehab and physiotherapy before you head home." My nurse concluded.

No shit, I thought to myself. I knew she was just making conversation, but I was exhausted and in pain, and I guess kind of bitter over the whole thing.

The third nurse pushed the gravol into my line slowly, and my nurse asked if she would grab me some more analgesic as well.

"You'd better get some rest today, because tomorrow PT/OT will likely come and assess you and hopefully get you working those legs of yours; and I'm going to have to start dialing back your IV meds."

I nodded; I knew she was right.

"Has there been any word on when I'll be released?" I asked.

"Well, your scans came back clear, thank goodness, so I think once we get your pain managed better with oral medications and get the approval from physio, I'd say the doctor will likely be okay to send you home in a few weeks, but I couldn't really give you a guess as to when, that's all up to you."

She shrugged and handed me a few kidney basins in case I got sick again and a cold cloth for my head, which I accepted graciously. She then scurried out at the sound of a nearby call bell once again leaving me alone in my cubicle.

I slumped back against my pillow, raising my head on the stretcher to a half-seated position, and let myself ease off into a deep sleep with the help of the meds I had on board, hugging my kidney basins.

I awoke to the usual bustle of the ER. With no daylight, I had no idea what time of day it was. Sitting up further, I had a small wave of nausea, but with nothing else remaining in my stomach, just stomach acid and dry heaving was the extent of it.

I wiped my face up with the kleenex on my bedside table and reached for my water. I took slow and steady sips instead of chugging it down like I wanted to.

My thirst felt insatiable, and the water felt so good on my chapped lips and throat, but I restrained in order to avoid another wave of uncontrolled nausea and hurling.

"Oh perfect, you're awake." A lady whom I recognized to be Michelle and a tall slender male named Greg followed behind her.

"We're here to assess your mobility and assist you with any difficulties you may be having."

They didn't seem to recognize me from working the floor with them, and I wasn't about to remind them. I'd rather people didn't know who I was right about then.

They began getting me ready to try to walk. Greg had a two-wheeled walker to steady myself with, and Michelle had a blue transfer belt. I was given a pair of hospital standard grippy socks, and with their help, I eased myself onto the floor and up into a standing position. They worked with me past their usual ten to twenty minute threshold.

Greg noted that I should have a sling for my broken collarbone just to support the arm better and help it to heal more aligned. I was very weak and unsteady, but they showed me exercises to stretch my muscles back into a place where they could support my weight. When we were finished for the day I was able to walk with the walker. Greg had adjusted it with an arm hold so I could rest my immobile arm and use the other for support. I could manage a full circle of the ward and almost down to the elevators with minimal assistance.

"Keep up with those exercises even when you're lying in bed bored, and within a week or two, you'll likely be strong enough to go home." Michelle said encouragingly.

"We'll try for two laps of the ward tomorrow. And I'll request they remove your catheter now too." Greg added with a little wink.

"Thank you both."

I waved as they left to see another patient. I couldn't wait to get this catheter out and get back to using the bathroom like a normal person.

Greg must have gone straight to the ER doctor with his request because it seemed like only minutes later a new nurse returned with the supplies to remove it.

I probably could have removed it myself, but again I didn't want to reveal my identity to anyone who hadn't already guessed, and I knew they'd want to chart on all the procedures done.

A few quick minutes and a stinging pull later, the catheter was out.

I shakily made my way with my walker to the bathroom just down the hall, wanting to clean the remaining betadine stains off my groin area from when the catheter was first inserted.

Hobbling in, I regretted my decision to come to the bathroom immediately. The big mirror over the sink, and the bright fluorescent lights showed every detail.

My reflection caused me to cringe and self-pity washed over me. From what I could visualize out of my one bleary eye, my hair was a greasy ragged mess, I was pale, and all the bruises covering my body stood out terribly. My face looked like a praying mantis got into a boxing match and lost, with my large swollen and blackened eyes.

"Ugh!" I let out a sound of disgust.

If I wasn't hard up enough before this, I most definitely was now.

I attempted to void, why waste a trip, and then washed up as well as I could with a few cloths and towels I found on the laundry cart along the way.

I tossed the dirty cloths into the soiled linens bin on my way back to my stretcher. Only mere steps away, I looked up hearing a familiar group of voices.

Erika led the way with Aeda, Austin and Everley in tow. The unit clerk following them attempted to tell her they were exceeding the number of guests allowed at one time in the ER, but of course Erika was ignoring her. I was so overjoyed to see them!

I hobbled faster with my walker in an attempt to greet them sooner, not wanting to take a single second for granted.

"My babies! You all came to see me! That's so nice of you. You must have known how badly I missed you."

I could tell by the looks on their faces they were taken aback by my appearance. Everley looked scared and hid behind Erika, peering around her at me.

"Mommy?..Is that you?" She half whispered, stunned.

"Yes hunny, it's me. I know, I don't look very nice. I'm sorry if it startles you."

I teared at the thought that my appearance was enough to scare my children. Aeda was the first to lunge forward after hearing my voice, embracing me in a big hug. The others, although more hesitant, followed suit.

Ignoring the pain in my body, I hugged them hard, breathing in their scents and kissing the tops of their heads. Erika looked sympathetically at us, knowing what their next question would be.

"Who did this to you Mommy?" It was Everley that spoke up.

I didn't know how to respond, I didn't want to be the person to taint their views of their father. That was never my intention throughout our entire separation. The silence following her question was long, but Austin saved me answering, his observation skills not having missed a thing.

"Dad did it. That's why the cops took him away." His tone was angry and choked, and I hugged him harder.

The girls registered my silence as truth and I heard them choke on their sobs.

"Oh Mommy!"

So much devastation all at once.

Erika ushered them into my room and closed the curtain as I ambled in behind them, then helped me onto the edge of my bed.

Everley climbed up next to me and cuddled in. Austin sat on the end and Aeda stood looking at me sorrowfully.

"Don't look so down, you guys. I'll get better soon." I tried to reassure them in an effort to lift their spirits.

Their faces remained dismal.

"Dad's in prison." Austin mumbled.

"Well he deserves to be there!" Aeda spoke up.

Everley whimpered beneath my arm.

"Okay okay, let's not get into this here. Erika is going to take care of you until I'm well enough to come home, and then from there we'll see what happens, ok? I'm going to need a lot of help in the first little while when I'm able to come home."

"I'll help you, Mommy!" Everley piped up, eager to help.

"We all will." Aeda agreed, nudging Austin with her foot.

"Yeah," he acknowledged moodily.

"I'd really appreciate that." I said with a smile.

"I'm so sorry you all had to see me like this, but I am so glad I got to see you."

They all reached for me, embracing me in a big bear hug. I winced but squeezed them back hard. This was my motivation right here. I just wanted to get strong enough to be home with my kids.

"Ok kiddos, short and sweet. You've seen her, but we're breaking the rules as is. Let's head out and give your mom some rest."

They all sighed in protest but didn't argue. They looked downcast and started to walk away, but Austin stopped, turned and walked back to me.

"I'm sorry Dad did this to you. That's not what a man does."

I instantly felt the tears well in my eyes, and I smiled at him and blew him a kiss as he turned to catch up with the others. Erika, who had hung back, came and gave me a swift hug and kiss on the cheek.

"Thank you for bringing them." I sputtered, wiping tears from the corners of my eyes.

"You needed it, and you're welcome."

With a swift pivot, she turned to follow them and guide them the rest of the way out.

Laying down on my stretcher and pulling the blankets over my chilled body, exhausted from all my efforts that day, I sobbed silently, and sniffed myself to sleep.

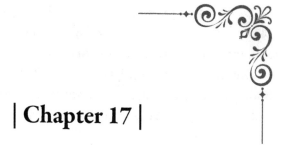

| Chapter 17 |

It was Friday morning, two weeks following the assault. I had been working with physio every day, and they'd been stretching their appointed time with me kindly to prepare me for discharge.

My pain was managed, and I had switched to oral meds and was finding I was tolerating it well. I had mostly just adjusted to the pain and was able to tolerate it now, but the pills did take the edge off when taken regularly.

Dustin had called me every day to check in, and Erika was doing well with the kids and also called or stopped by to allow me to see them and visit. The police still had my cell as evidence, so all communication was either in person or via the hospital's phone line.

I had been admitted to the fourth floor and was finally getting to shower today before I got the go ahead to go home.

My stitches were dissolvable ones, so no removal appointments would be necessary, just a follow up for my family doctor to find out how I was doing.

I was beyond ready to go home! Call bells, and dementia patients wandering around the wards jolting me awake, I couldn't wait to have a solid sleep in my own bed. I had finished my sessions with PT already that morning, had eaten and was gathering my clothes that Erika had kindly dropped off for me the day before in preparation.

Since I knew the floor, and the location of the showers, I just motioned to my nurse that day that I was headed to wash, and she nodded her approval from afar. Word had eventually gotten around that one of their own had been admitted as a patient, but after relaying my story multiple times, most gave me the privacy I desired and didn't make a big deal out of my presence. They did, however, allow me a bit more freedom of movement than the average patient, since I obviously knew my way around the hospital.

I grabbed a cloth and towel from the clean laundry cart and walked down the hall. I no longer required the walker and was walking on my own, so my pace was much quicker than it had been just those few weeks ago.

Arriving at the shower stall, I flicked the switch for the lights and stepped in, closing the door behind me. I was so eager to wash, I turned the water to hot and let it pour while I undressed, wanting to take my time and enjoy.

My bruising had faded to a black and yellow color on the majority of my body, and my swelling had gone down. I looked much more like myself than I had.

Stripping down, I carefully, eased my sling and gown off my fractured collarbone and threw them on the floor.

I put my foot in first, letting the water pour onto my toes, then stepped in fully. I gasped with how amazing that water felt! Hot and soothing, massaging my muscles, washing away the grease and pain.

I hoped it would also wash away the memories of the whole event, but that was just a heedless notion. I knew if charges were to stick I had to remember as many details as possible. I turned my face into the stream pouring from the shower head, losing myself, hearing nothing but the rush of the water barreling past my ears.

I cherished this small amount of privacy. It was the most privacy I'd had in over two weeks since I was alone, stranded, and immobile on my living room floor. Water dripped off my breasts and I ran my fingers and palms over them lathering suds, and then rinsing them away.

I hadn't seen my reflection since that first day in the hospital when I awoke. I had been avoiding mirrors at all costs. I fingered my eye that remained swollen. I had begun to see out of it in the last two days and had passed an eye exam performed by the ER physician.

I was so afraid to see my face, worried I'd see the same atrocious face, swollen and bruised.

Perhaps that sounded like the least of most people's concerns, but I didn't want to see my children withdraw or recoil from the sight of me anymore. That was truly heartbreaking. They cared for me and loved me the same as I did them, but I could still see the fear they'd displayed seeing my face, knowing it was me, but not being able to distinguish my face as mine.

I shook my head, pushing the negative thoughts down, instead focusing on my hands, washing and caressing my body.

I longed for warm muscular arms to wrap around me, wash me, comfort me. The daily phone conversations with Dustin were nice, but just not cutting it anymore.

As much as I didn't want him to see me like this, I longed for his touch. With a heavy hand I turned the knob, shut the water off, and grabbed my towel to begin drying off.

The cheap material of the hospital towel left my skin feeling raw and damp.

I had a new level of empathy for my patients, after my days on the other side of hospital care. From the subpar food, right down to these shitty ass towels.

Nothing was comforting. Nothing offered the nutrients to build strength in our injured or elderly. I always knew it was a problem, but to experience it really drove it home.

I promised myself that when I was able to return to work, I'd be a better nurse for it, and advocate more for better food and materials.

Pulling my pant legs on my damp skin, feeling the material clinging. It wasn't comfortable, but I took satisfaction in the fact that they were my own clothes and not another revealing hospital gown. Pulling on my shirt, I began re-slinging my arm to set that collarbone.

My damp hair entangled with the strap and I kept having to wrench it out. If I could lift that one arm properly, I could at least put my hair up and out of the way, but alas, this was not a possibility.

I gathered all my belongings and soiled laundry, opened the door and saw the fog emerge from the doorway.

I walked back to my four-bed ward, ditching my gown and towel in the bin along the way.

Mrs. Collingwell, one of my roommates I shared our four bed ward with, greeted me from her wheelchair, with her sweet smile and twinkling eyes under her wrinkled brow. Although her dementia caused her to forget where she was constantly, she kept me entertained with her stories of the past. She thought I was her daughter and would talk about "Papi"and her other children, my "siblings" often.

Speaking with her had filled all the empty moments of my days, and she had grown on me. I would miss her. She saw me folding my clothes and packing my bag and shuffled over using her toes to drag over her wheelchair.

Like any true mom, she began folding my laundry alongside of me. I didn't have many articles of clothing, but her gesture tugged at my heart strings. When we finished, I held her hand and we talked. She told me more stories all the while patting my hand, reminiscing on her youth and giving me advice, like mother to daughter.

I wished I could take her with me when I left but knew that was unrealistic. I gave her a squeeze and whispered.

"I'll miss you," in her ear.

She kissed my cheek and then let me go, once again shuffling away to color on a sheet of paper with some crayons a staff member had left in order to entertain her.

Heaving my bag on my good arm, I took one last look at my room before walking out towards the desk to get my final go ahead to leave.

The sliding doors parted as the motion sensor read my presence, lugging my bag past the many faces looming in the waiting room awaiting their turn to be assessed by the triage nurse.

I was in such a hurry to breathe the fresh air, I hadn't even bothered to wait for my ride. I figured I could wait outside and enjoy the outdoors. I didn't want to waste another minute breathing in the stale hospital air.

The outer sliding doors burst open and a rush of cool air hit my face. I breathed deep. A crisp breeze rifled through my still partially damp hair, helping to dry it. The rays of sun cast their warm glow upon my body. I closed my eyes and attempted to absorb every ounce of its goodness.

Reaching the bench alongside the building's outer wall, I set my bag on top of it in order to give my arm a break. It was close to noon at this point. Erika was at work and now that school was out for the summer, the kids would be with their babysitter.

I didn't want to be any more of a burden, so had opted to not call Erika for a ride home. I had reception call me a taxi, and also fax over my prescription for oral analgesics to my pharmacy so I could quickly pick them up on my way home. I sat down beside my bag, the heat of the sun-warmed bench enveloping my backside. If only it was more comfortable, I could have melted into it and remained for hours.

I didn't have hours though, only a ten minute wait and the yellow taxi pulled up ready to attend to my driving needs.

The driver, seeing my one arm in a sling, courteously got out and opened my door for me and assisted with putting my bag in the car. I thanked her kindly. She climbed in herself and asked my destination. I told her I needed to first stop at the pharmacy which she knew well, then gave her my house address. Her blinker clicked on and we pulled out, merging onto the street.

The taxi pulled up into my driveway, the crackle of gravel grinding underneath the tires. Thanking the driver and gathering my belongings, I handed her my voucher and climbed out. Tape was still over the door from the police investigation.

I had been given the go ahead to enter the premises again but hadn't anticipated the mess I'd be returning to. Yellow crime scene tape still draping the entranceway.

I hesitated at the doorway, a cold chill settling in my gut. I raised my hand to the doorknob, and sucked in my breath...pausing there momentarily, trying to build up the courage to turn the knob.

I swallowed hard, the sounds of cars zooming past my street ringing in my ears. Trembling, I pushed hard and stumbled in the door.

There were still items on the floor, and the stench of my excrement while comatose lingered. I gagged and tucked my fear away to tackle the smell and mess.

I buzzed about, opening all the windows, turning on my oil diffusers, and getting a bucket and scrub brush. I took one huge breath of air before kneeling down to scrub the area, urine had absorbed into the vinyl and I scoured it abrasively, the suds growing into a massive pile of bubbles.

The smell slowly dissipated under the lemony aroma of the multipurpose cleanser I had chosen.

Dumping my bucket and running a clean rinse water mop over it to get rid of the soapy residue, I sighed a great relief, thankful to be rid of that smell and the shame. I then began picking up and replacing any fallen objects and disposing of the broken ones.

Sweeping up the shards and emptying the dust pan into the garbage, I was sore after such minimal tasks. Doing them with one arm was not easy!

Wiping sweat from my brow I slumped into a seat, ready to pass out after my exertions. I didn't get that chance though. My doorbell rang.

Ding-dong!

Who on earth could that be?

I felt myself falter at the thought of answering it, my unwavering faith in people now altered. As I tread silently towards the entryway door, my mind raced.

Where was Austin's bat? Maybe I should get a gun? A taser? I peeked through the peephole, barely daring to breathe just as another,

Ding-dong, rang throughout the house. The shadows of dusk blackened my entranceway, but I could make out a flash of red hair, it was Erika.

Relief washed over me. I turned the deadbolt and opened the door.

She greeted me with a warm smile and hugged me.

"Glad you're home."

"Me too. Although I'm really feeling kind of sketched in here, reliving it all I guess. I just finished cleaning it up a bit." I allowed her in to examine my work.

"You shouldn't have done that. I was just on my way over here to do that for you."

"Well, I couldn't not. The smell was horrendous."

I let the look of disgust adorn my face and fake barfed, she laughed.

"Yeah well, it was bound to. Smells alright in here now."

"Thanks, I finished scrubbing and had my diffusers going trying to absorb the stench."

"You must be sore now?" She said as she looked me up and down, focusing on my slung up arm.

"Yes, I'm due for one of my pills. I haven't even unpacked yet."

I made my way over to where I had flopped my bag on the floor. I snatched my one pill bottle out of the baggy the pharmacist had made up for me and double-checked the label. Force of habit.

Satisfied, I twisted off the cap and popped two in my mouth before sticking my head under the kitchen faucet and gulping down some cold water.

"While you're doing that, I'm going to pour you a nice hot bath."

Not waiting for my response, as she likely knew I'd politely protest, she bustled off and cranked on the taps.

Alright, guess I'm having a bath. I shrugged. It wasn't a terrible idea.

I went and dug some pajamas out of my dresser and a fresh towel out of the linen closet, then headed for the bathroom.

Pushing open the door, the water was still pouring out of the faucet, and a massive pile of bubbles filled the tub. I could feel the warm humidity of the air saturate my skin, the smell of jasmine adrift in the air. Candlelight was the only lighting, and she was setting up her phone with some relaxing spa music.

"Wow!" I gasped.

"This is amazing! How'd you set this up so fast?"

She smiled and shrugged. I noticed she had blown up my old bath pillow as well and suctioned it to the back of the tub for me, so thoughtful.

"And don't worry about your kids either. I had Terry come over to supervise them."

Terry was my usual back up babysitter when I was truly desperate and couldn't find free babysitters. She was a nice girl, about eighteen, long dark brown hair, very sporty, and she lived only a few blocks from us.

Her mom and I were old workout buddies before I got too caught up in life to attend the gym regularly.

"You really have thought of everything."

"Well you get undressed and climb in." She ushered me towards the tub and stepped out to allow me some privacy.

I took a moment longer to take in everything she had done. She was truly the best friend ever. I felt so grateful, and blessed. I unhooked my sling and slipped that off first before starting on my clothes. It felt good to be bare, and in my own home.

This bath truly changed the atmosphere and gave me a feeling of contentment and solace. Dipping my toes in, feeling the heat of the water, I eagerly swung my other leg over into the tub and eased down inside it, letting the bubbles float around me, enveloping me. I sank into my inflatable pillow and let the anti-gravity lightness of the tub float me up, just enough to relieve all my body tensions.

I closed my eyes and felt the water lapping at my skin, relaxing and letting go of my inner afflictions, melting into that warm flowery scented water.

Hearing a creak, my eyelids flew open. I cast my gaze over to the door that was clearly the source of the noise, and watched it glide open with a tentative hand. Erika's face peeked around its edge.

"Are you enjoying it?"

"Yes, this is so perfect, thank you."

I expected her to turn and walk back out, but she didn't. She faltered, looking at me, then at her toes then back at me. She was always so bold and forward, this was a new side of her I hadn't witnessed before. Almost embarrassed? Or scared?

"Is everything ok?" I questioned.

She had me feeling nervous. Perhaps she had some bad news to spill on me and this had been her ploy to get me into a good state of mind before dropping it on me.

Quiet, she locked eyes with me, took a deep breath in and stepped the rest of the way through the door. She wore only a silk white robe, and as she stood there with her hair in a messy bun, I could finally read her expression. She was nervous.

She held my gaze and let her robe fall to the floor, settling around her feet, her body naked in the amber glow of the candlelight. She stood there, motionless, and I could see she was shaking, not with cold, but with uncertainty; timidness.

She broke my gaze only long enough to look down at her body, obviously worried about my reaction or there lack of. I was frozen, unsure what to make of this.

I opened my mouth to speak, but only a grunt-like sound of astonishment escaped my lips.

Just then Erika threw up her hands apologetically and began rambling.

"I shouldn't have done this, I'm sorry, I've been waiting forever to tell you, and when I saw you on the floor that day beaten to a pulp like that, I just can't hold it in any longer. I love you, Naomi! I have for years. I've watched you be with these men that don't deserve you. Yes, you have three wonderful kids and that's something I couldn't give you; and I know you're kind of with Dustin now, but I just had to tell you. I had to give it a shot. You've been my best friend for forever, but I want something more. I know you likely don't and I don't want it to ruin our friendship. That's why I've held it in so long. I just thought that night with Dustin, it was my opportunity to actually be with you, and I loved it so much. Yes, I was jealous that you seemed to like him more after, and I'm sorry for that. I just had my hopes all up that it meant the same to you as it did for me!"

She was panting at this point trying to get it all out.

"I just want to take care of you, be with you."

Her arms dropped almost in defeat and her eyes fell downcast.

I was stunned. This was a whole lot of truth, and I wasn't prepared to wrap my head around all this. She turned as if to walk out. I didn't want her to feel like I was rejecting her. I was just in shock!

"Wait!" I exclaimed.

She paused, holding the door's edge, and looked at me somberly, eyes dewy with tears.

My heart caught in my throat. I wanted to give her what she wanted. I didn't want to hurt her, but at this moment, I didn't even know how I felt.

I had no time to process. I once again locked eyes with her.

She took another chance and without hesitation burst forth at me, planting her lips on mine, holding my face so gently and passionately. I closed my eyes and let her kiss me, my mind rewinding to that night at Dustin's condo, letting my inhibitions fade into the abyss.

I returned her kiss, our tongues intertwining, her lips soft and supple against mine, finding my passion. I didn't think anyone would want to kiss my face looking how I looked, but there I was. She tasted like honey and cinnamon, and I couldn't help but savor the flavor. She began working her way down my neck, kissing my skin and gently massaging my shoulders, being mindful of my broken collarbone.

She then eased me forward and slid her thin frame in behind me, making herself my body pillow. She continued massaging and kissing me, stopping to kiss my lips each time before she'd switch sides.

She brushed the hair off my forehead and kissed my blackened eyes, letting me know that my appearance didn't matter to her.

My loofah was hanging on the shampoo rack in the corner of the tub and she grabbed it. I reached for the body-wash that was nearest to me and squeezed some dollops onto its meshy fabric. She proceeded to rub it in circles on my skin, creating a foamy perfumed lather, paying close attention to my breasts in particular. I giggled a bit at this, and she joined in.

"Well, I'm only human."

She followed by locking my lips in a kiss once more. I reached up with my good arm holding the base of her neck.

I was unsure of the feelings I felt, kissing her and being so intimate one on one. I was enjoying the feelings of desire and the sensualness of her touch, but like her, I didn't want to ruin our friendship. That was a lot of years to give up and the risk was so high.

Sensing my sudden indecision, she cupped my chin and whispered.

"Let's just have this one night together, no strings attached, just me and you. We can figure the rest out another day."

I looked at her and nodded, biting my lip a bit in uncertainty. I was worried about Dustin too. I had only just admitted to him being my partner. Now there I was, what only seemed like days later, kissing my best friend.

I felt like a bit of a hussy ... but Erika's sweet kisses consumed me, and I pushed the negative to the back of my mind for the time being. She asked for just one night. I figured I at least owed her that.

I matched her intensity kissing her back, and she took that as a win, her hand sliding down to my breasts, massaging them seductively. I rubbed her thigh. I felt like a clumsy oaf.

Aside from our one night together where I was drunk as fuck and had Dustin present, I had never *been* with a woman. I didn't know what to do. Not to mention the angle at which I sat did not really facilitate reciprocating intimacy well, especially with a broken collarbone.

She laughed again at me and whispered.

"Just relax," then sucked my earlobe.

She pulled my shoulders back into her chest. I must have been tensing up with my awkwardness and leaning forward without even realizing it.

I let my body melt into hers, and she wrapped me in a hug. I reached up hugging her arms with my one capable arm and pecked kisses along her forearms. Then her right hand drifted down, reaching around my waist, up my thigh, and then trickled down my inner thigh, disappearing into the water and bubbles. Without delay her fingers found my clit and she skillfully rubbed. I instantly moaned.

The difference between a man and a woman doing this was phenomenal. A woman knows a woman's body, and what feels good, and where! Plus her smooth, silky hands, as opposed to a man's callused rough ones, made all the difference in my sensitive areas.

She applied pressure right on the button, and rotated it, winding me up. My back was already arching and she'd only just begun. Calmly and expertly she continued kissing my neck and ears, cupping my breasts with her other hand and sliding my ass back into her as I kept squirming down in pleasure.

She meticulously thrummed my clit, making it seem so effortless, then would swipe one finger down my slit parting my labia, doing a small circle around my vulva before sliding it back up my slit again and rubbing. The repetition of this motion was working to arouse me. Even though we were engulfed in bath water, I could feel myself getting wetter, lubricating for entry.

Erika felt the change in texture down there and added a finger dip with each circle. That small bit of penetration was enough. I began shaking in euphoria, my clit swelling.

Wanting to bide her time, Erika eased up. She quite clearly wanted an ample amount of one on one before allowing for climax.

The candle flickered and its amber glow reverberated off the walls along with my moans. Softer and slower she glided her fingertips over my womanhood, barely touching it, nothing more than a whisper; if a whisper was a motion. It was enough. The slight tantalizing touch, stroking me delicately, tenderly, my body quivered. I was so hyper-sensitive with arousal! I felt that if her fingers were to delay their contact with my pussy for even a mere second longer, that I may burst with excitement.

She paused and caressed her hands back up my thighs and whispered in my ear.

"Get up."

"Oh!"

Surprised by this sudden change of events, I did as commanded and leaned forward to get my legs up under me.

She grabbed the fluffy white towel from where I had placed it. Before I stepped out, she wrapped it around my back and motioned for me to sit on the tub's edge.

I followed her directions, my legs still in the bath water. She splayed my legs open wide and I was forced to lean back and place my good hand on the lid of the toilet for added support.

She crawled between my legs, still in the water, resembling an erotic mermaid of sorts, before emerging onto her knees.

Her red hair aflame with the flickering of the candlelight, Erika wrapped her arms around my thighs.

She dived in, lapping at my swollen clit with her tongue. I couldn't help but succumb to her voracity as she consumed all the juices flowing from me as I squealed.

It was like an endless orgasm, without having even fully orgasmed yet. Her tongue devoured my pussy greedily, twisting, and flicking.

She worked her way down, licking up inside me, then sliding back up to my clit, creating a whole new cycle before introducing her finger once more. Stimulating my clam, sliding in and out whilst still working my pearl.

I was once again transported into a euphoric state, quivering and convulsing. She then upgraded me to multiple fingers.

Throwing my head back in ecstasy, I howled, as her two fingers sank deep into me, stretching me out. Thrusting in and out, her other hand reached up and she elongated her body up to reach me, pulling the back of my head forward so our lips met again. Sucking my gloss off her lips, I kissed her deeply, rendering myself a sex driven maniac, insane with pleasure and passion.

The candle continued flickering and casting its dim light, setting Erika's perky breasts aglow. I reciprocated, unleashing on her, pulling her body into me, kissing and sucking her areolas, fondling her breasts. Drawing my hand down and squeezing her firm backside, I didn't know what to do, but at that moment, I wanted her. I wanted it all.

She eased her fingers out of me and stood, water and bubbles trickling off her curves, her skin wet and shimmering. She pulled the plug and grabbed a free hanging towel off the rack, wrapping it around herself.

She opened the door and beckoned me which I jumped at, eager to follow. She skipped down the hallway.

Apparently she had prepared more than I'd thought. My living room was all now cast in candlelight.

She must have gotten this all assembled prior to coming into the bathroom in hopes that things went well.

She picked up the button for the stereo and flicked it on, the bass drowning out the spa music that was still playing on her phone, echoing off the bathroom tile.

She opened the fridge, pulling out a bottle of champagne and began uncorking it.

"To your recovery!" and then in a much softer hopeful tone she added,

"And new beginnings."

It's cork popped and hit the roof. Bubbles frothed from its top and she quickly poured two glasses, then took a swig right from the bottle's mouth. She must be nervous as well, I noted.

Wrapped in our towels still, we walked to the couch. She flicked on the television, and a porn was playing on mute.

"Oh wow! You went above and beyond."

I wasn't sure how I felt exactly about the porn, but I guess it did help to set the mood. I was no stranger to watching porn. I'd used it to spice things up sometimes, competing with the actresses, while servicing Chad. But never had I done this with a woman, nor my best friend!

She handed me my glass, and feeling my nerves again, I tossed it back with one long swallow. I grabbed the bottle and took another long swig.

She laughed, obviously understanding my actions. I took one last huge drink, gulping the carbonated beverage before placing the bottle down. I knew it was my turn and decided to take the bull by the horns.

I lunged at her, pulling open her towel. She let it fall to the floor and let me take a second to take her in.

Her athletic slim build, red hair, a small patch of strawberry pubic hair, tan skin and freckles. She really was attractive, I'd always known that.

I guess I'd never wondered throughout the years why she'd never really settled down herself. I'd known she dabbled with bisexuality in our late high school and college years.

She'd had a few boyfriends and girlfriends over the years, but nothing was ever super serious. Maybe this was why, maybe I was the reason.

I felt guilty, to think maybe I had been preventing my friend from being truly happy, prolonging her torture by never reading between the lines or asking questions. I grabbed her, my one arm still hung, but I used the good one to wrap my fingers into the nape of her neck and coil them within her loose strands of hair. Kissing her passionately, I let my own towel drop as well.

We stood kissing and groping one another's bodies, learning each other's curves and tracing them with our fingers as if we read braille, not wanting to misread a single bump. I opened my eyes, my peripherals catching what was going on, on the television. I re-enacted pushing Erika down on the couch making her bounce on impact. I startled her with my sudden forthrightness, she both giggled and gasped.

I leaned in on her kissing her once more, then her neck, sucking her earlobe, kissing her throat, collarbone, chest and sides, holding her wrist down with my good hand while she clutched her one breast.

I worked my way down sensually, reaching her pubic patch, I kissed around licking her loins and blowing on it, watching goosebumps rise on her skin, then proceeding to kiss and lick her inner thighs working my way in. I could delay no longer, it had come to the point, and I made my move.

Licking her snatch, the smell and taste of vanilla, cinnamon and salt. Having done it, I decided this was no time to hold back.

I let my sexual hunger take over, sucking her clit and lulling her labia with my tongue rolling it over, in and around. Slathering her area with my saliva, flicking her pearl with the tip of my tongue, torturing her with pleasure.

She clawed my hair, her back arching and her crotch thrusting up in my face, as she moaned and hollered. When her hands weren't busy clawing my hair I could hear her nails digging into the couch cushion ferociously. I swore I'd be surprised if the material didn't have holes by the morning.

Her actions fueled me, knowing I was doing a good job, encouraged me and challenged me to do even better. Using my capable hand I slid my middle finger up and down her slit, lubing it up with my saliva. I then plunged in, easing it up and into her.

She was warm and moist. She tightened around me with each push in. I pulsated my finger in and out, continuing to suck on her clit while searching for the spot, then, there it was!

Her g-spot lay up and in. Curving my finger to hit it, I went to work, hastily rubbing and penetrating all the while still licking and sucking. I continued to work away but paused with my hand in order to reach for the champagne bottle.

Tipping the bottle I poured the fizzy liquid over her labia, startling her. But the combination of sudden cool, and bubbling carbonation on her cunt must have felt amazing. Just as I imagined it would.

I sucked and tongued it off her, gargling it over her swollen bean before swallowing. Letting the bubbles fizz and pop on her most sensitive parts.

Her moans echoed in my ears, and her body shook with pleasure. I wanted her to cum!

I slipped my tongue deep within her still fingering her, and her juices began dribbling out around my finger and on my tongue. I lapped them up, thirsty for more. Loving how crazy I was driving her.

I blew a soft cool stream of breath on her clit and watched the hairs on her legs raise. She was swelling, ready to burst. I rubbed her g-spot, circling it, pulling all the way out then pushing deep in, and rubbing.

Her body tensed and her pussy clamped around my finger. I knew it was coming...I licked wildly.

She began to scream in ecstasy. Juices spraying into my mouth around my finger. Her head hung, her hand clutched her breast and squeezed it so hard I could see the indents of her nails. The other hand still scratching the couch's upholstery.

I wiped my lips smiling. Looking at her from down on my knees satisfied with myself as she lay there panting and attempting to recover.

She started laughing amidst her panting.

"And you were worried!"

I couldn't help but join in, and we both hunched over in a frenzy of laughter. We carried on for a few moments until silence finally befell us. Erika rolled to her side looking at me.

"Your turn." She said it quite seriously, as if she'd accepted a challenge.

"I thought we were done?"

"Not even close." She jumped up with a devilish grin on her lips. She tossed back a drink of the champagne laying open beside me and trotted away still naked.

I was curious, I had really thought we were finished. Seconds later she returned with a little black silken handbag with drawstrings. Pulling at the opening and dumping out its contents onto the couch. A fair-sized veiny strap-on plunked out onto the upholstery as well as a small bottle of lube. Her grin grew seeing my expression,

"I know you like your vitamin D...so I thought I'd do what I could to appease you!"

I laughed at her joke as she pushed a few buttons on the remote and a new scene came onto the TV. The star of the porn having a man heaving his manhood into her and her theatrically moaning.

Erika busied herself with doing up her mechanism buckles.

"This seems rather intimidating." I commented, observing her wearing this crazy garment.

"You'll love it." She said hushing my squeamish protests. I took another long drink.

"Come here." She patted the armrest of the couch. I obliged. She hadn't been wrong yet.

She instructed me to kneel, legs spread bent over the armrest. A position I was only too familiar with from my more adventurous days when I didn't have to worry about kids entering the living room unexpectedly.

Erika squeezed some lube onto her contraption and slipped it between my legs. She started by rubbing some of it off onto my vagina, slathering it for ease. She then dragged it back retracing her trail back through the wet entrails before gently prodding at my entrance.

Slowly she pushed in and out, with small upward thrusts, easing me open before finally submerging her silicone cock deep into me.

I had expected it to feel abnormal. Hard and cold. But the soft silicone, although slightly more rigid than a man, still felt very much real; especially with both our bodies to warm it. I also didn't expect Erika to know how to work it so well.

Wrong again. Again, I guess women just know what other women like.

She worked it in and out of me, then I heard a small *click* followed by a constant humming. Her hand came into a reach around and her fingers landed on my pearl once again. A vibrating pad secured to them.

The combination of vibration and penetration was exactly what I needed. I lost myself in the ecstasy of it.

Competing with the erotic scenes being performed on the television. Erika grabbed my one hip with her free hand pulling my rear end back into her so she could get in as deep as she could. Fucking me intensely and vigorously.

I howled in pleasure, being throttled so. In my mind though, it was Dustin fucking me hard, drilling me in such a manner, making me gush more of my nectar. His muscular hips pumping into my backside, driving his dick up into me.

I tried to shake the thoughts from my mind, tried to stay in the moment with Erika, but the closer I got to climax, the more I couldn't escape my fantasies. I could feel the cusp of the shroom catching up inside me, just how Dustin's did. Each time it caught, to unhook it would push forward rubbing my g-spot before sliding back out.

The steady vibration on my clit humming upwards added to all the sensation I was already feeling inside me. I squirted with each deep thrust in, beads of lady-dew dribbling down my thighs.

Erika felt how engorged my pussy was at this point through her vibrating glove, and she pushed my body further forward. My ass raised into the air and caused my back to arc down. Doggy...my finishing move.

Her thrusts quickened, plunging into me deep, then shallow and fast, again and again. With each big heave I gasped feeling the onslaught of that familiar tingling numbness creeping up my toes.

Wave after wave, pump after pump, the heat rushing over my snatch. I felt my pussy clench tight grabbing that silicone cock and trapping it in me while I screamed in elation.

I tried biting the upholstery to stifle myself. The last few dribbles of juice flowing down my legs and Erika's fake dick.

My heartbeat could be felt pounding through my clit and I remained hunched there, allowing myself to lull in the bliss. Erika pulled out slowly, satisfied with her job well done. Unaware that I had shamefully been imagining a man, and not her.

Guilt sat in my gut, and I immediately felt remorse now that the buzz was wearing off. Erika unbuckled herself and tossed me a wet cloth to wipe up with. I did so eagerly, mopping the couch cushions as well that were sopping.

Turning off the TV and throwing the now near empty bottle in the fridge, Erika summoned me to bed. I needed no encouragement, my pain meds were beginning to wear off and I hastily popped another. Sticking my head under the faucet to wash it down before ambling to bed.

She had grabbed my sling for me and helped wrap my arm up once again. I then collapsed into bed, completely drained. Erika switched off the light climbing in beside me, her naked body pressing into mine. My eyes fluttered once or twice before dozing off.

| Chapter 18 |

S oft seductive fingertips caressing my legs aroused me. The hard bulge pressing into my backside alerted me that I was in for a treat.

Hot breath blowing on my neck, followed between slow sensual kisses behind my ears, down my neck and shoulders. A large hand cupped my breasts, massaging them. Tantalizing my areolas, causing them to perk up eager for more attention. I reached behind me, wishing to touch back, reciprocate.

Bulging muscles met my hands, firm taut buttocks, and those sexy lower back dimples that drove me crazy. I rubbed my hands up and down every surface I could reach. Painting a picture with my hands so my eyes could see. I liked what I saw!

I circled my hand down, reaching further behind myself. Feeling my hand hit the rock-hard rod prodding my backside. I groped it. Feeling the warmth. The blood pulsing through every plump vein. Sliding my hand up its shaft, stroking so lightly as I embraced his hefty cock.

I could hear a finger being sucked, then felt the hand slip between my legs. The saliva lubricated me, allowing his fingers to rub me smoothly and tenderly. I tightened my grip and pumped his dick skin up and down. I paid extra attention to his shroom with every stroke, until beads of pre-cum formed at the tip. The added moisture allowed his limited foreskin to glide back with ease.

I envisioned the whole thing. Getting increasingly turned on imagining seeing the salty fluid building up more and more with each pump.

Soft gruff moans stifled in my neck. The sounds of his arousal made me wetter as his fingers rubbed and stimulated me.

Up on his knees he rose. Eager for more. I opened my mouth ready to receive him. His excitement showed as he shoved his meat into the depth of my throat tenaciously. Wanting me to choke on it.

To feel my throat tighten and squeeze around his shaft as he plunged it again and again down my overly zealous passage.

I clutched his curvaceous butt and heaved him into me, his balls hitting my chin.

I graciously gave him what he craved. I choked on that cock. Salivating up and down his girth, slathering it with my tongue. His erection flexed in my mouth each time my throat closed around him, tightening.

My arousal grew as he fingered my pussy. My juices flowing abundantly, readying for entry. I sucked him with such ferocity, spittle dribbled down my chin, inspiring an idea in my head.

I wiped the spittle with my index finger and inserted it into my mouth for a little added lubrication. As I plunged his dick down my throat again, I simultaneously slid my finger into his ass.

He jerked forward, quite obviously shaken with my actions. I laughed, sending a stream of vibrating sensations up his shaft.

I continued to probe his asshole. I figured; guys always have all the fun. This time I'd show a man how it feels to be taken by surprise in the *no-no square*.

Surprising me, he didn't fight it. He submitted, probably smitten with pleasure. Tremendous moans emitting from his mouth.

I loved the control I had. I went hard, slobbering all over his member. Massaging his sack with my free hand. I took a few seconds after every few plunges on his shaft to tongue his balls in order to spread the love to all his parts.

His body now the one quaking in sexual elation. I knew it was time to move up to the head, aka the *man-clit*.

Licking up his shaft, right up to his tip. I commenced sucking on his shroom like a tootsie pop. Swirling my tongue around his knob, submerging it in saliva. It didn't take long for it to plump right up, hot and moist. Pre-cum continuously beading from his tip.

His fingers faltered in their pussy probing as he became so absorbed in his own erotic delight. He struggled to focus.

I fed off this rush. Being the dominant one for once instead of the submissive. Serving his needs ahead of my own.

My finger was getting dry from the friction in his back door. I was about to pull out and spit on it (yes, a total man move), but he beat me to it.

Leaning forward, he grabbed a bottle of lube that I wasn't even aware was there off my bedside table. Uncapping it, he poured some of the cold silky contents onto my finger for me.

He loved what I was doing to him. I pushed in, my finger once again gliding up his arse. Smoother this time.

He groaned in appreciation as I slid my mouth down around him while simultaneously pushing up in him.

Again and again, I sucked and probed, until I found it. His sweet spot. He lurched in ecstasy the second I hit it, and I repeated the motion, encouraged by his reaction.

His scrotum firming up, and the base of his cock bulging with pressure was my signal. I pushed that button again and stroked it, whilst gobbling his dick as deep as I could take it. His well-manicured pubes tickled my nose. That's when I felt that swelling knot rising up his shaft, ready to burst!

Out of nowhere, I'm not even sure where he found the strength or the control while being on the cusp of orgasm.

He grabbed my waist with his strong hands, lifted me clear up off the bed and flipped me over doggy, pushing my head into the mattress. His cum shot all over my ass. He breathed heavily for a moment, and I crouched there in the position he'd laid me, allowing him to enjoy his moment. He kneeled there for a few moments, savoring it. I thought he was done. I was waiting for him to get up and head to clean up, but he didn't. He wasn't moving.

I cocked my head backwards at him, to see what was expected of me.

He looked down at me, his shadowy form not hiding his mischievous grin that was glinting in the dark down on me.

"I am *NOT* the submissive." He said bluntly.

Before I had a chance to let the meaning of his words dawn on me, he took back the control I had so excitedly owned for the past half hour. I felt his still hard erection rub in the jizz that was splattered all over my backside. The now even wetter head of his cock then teasingly rubbed against my ass hole.

"Oh you wouldn't dare!" I started, as the cold lube dribbled on my hole.

It was still in his fist, and without another second passing, he pushed in.

I hollered, both in pain and surprise! He went in as far as he could, his nuts hitting the bottom of my vulva.

My body tensed in pain, and he moaned again, and spanked me hard! He followed with a few light pulses in and out. Letting the lube drip in around his shaft more, surrounding my hole, before pushing in again.

I felt paralyzed. All I could do was kneel there stunned as his dick pile drove into me again and again.

The lubrication was my saving grace. Every few thrusts, he'd dribble more of it into my hole and on his dick until I was so slick his beef slid in and out of me with ease.

The pain ebbed away and he reached around and started rubbing my clit. All the while throttling his dick in my ass.

The combination of the frontal stimulation and the back door initiated a new kind of pleasure, one I was not familiar with.

I realized he was giving me exactly what I gave him. He wasn't doing this to be cruel. He was teaching me a lesson and also sharing his euphoria.

His rhythmic short pulses, then big heave in was easing me into a state of erotic meditation. A heavily building orgasm growing behind each thrust. His fingers thrumming on my clit and then slipping inside my clam, double penetrated me.

I was still completely paralyzed, but now with pleasure and a faint dull ache. In and out, in and out. The wetness growing, juices and lube dribbling down my thighs. His fingers soaked, and his damp nut sack smacked against me again and again each time he pushed in.

He spanked me again. I couldn't hold back an erotic shriek and he quickened his pace. Faster and harder. He throttled his meat into me. His fingers repeated their cycle.

His position changed. He slung his leg up and around onto my back. His other leg mounted on the bed, tee-peeing overtop of me. He was jack hammering his hog into me, pounding it hard! I relished the depth he was attaining with this new position.

Without warning he began rotating his cock. Butter churning me like a frantic milkmaid at an Amish dairy. His shroom was beating some weird new g-spot I'd never experienced before.

I knew I wasn't far off.

I started panting, and moaning, I couldn't hold back. He shoved his dick in further, harder. Pushing that button again and again.

My toes were growing numb and tingly, and it was quickly spreading up my legs. My eyes went black. I could feel my pussy clench as it always does when I orgasm unknowingly. I guess my ass clamped down simultaneously, and he let out a loud enthusiastic grunt of satisfaction.

I felt his fingers fist my hair. He pulled back, causing my back end to arc up further and my head to arch backwards, and that's when I saw the stars.

| Chapter 19 |

W ell...didn't take long for this to go to shit," a throaty voice growled, startling me from my sleep. I jolted up as I saw Dustin's hard steely blue eyes looking down at me with anger and disgust. The sudden realization of what situation he was walking in on, dawned on me. I was no longer slathered in jizz and lube. Instead of a man, Erika's naked body was the one lying next to me in the bed, and quite visible.

Part of last night's experience must have been a crazy erotic dream, while the first half had been quite real. The dampness between my legs was confirmation enough.

I groaned; this was not the reality I wanted, and I knew it was about to get much worse. Erika made no attempts to cover herself, whilst I hurriedly drew the sheets around my body.

"Dustin! What are you doing here?" I managed to choke out.

"Well, I thought I was coming to welcome my girlfriend home and help nurse her for her first few days home, but I guess someone's already doing that."

He snarled, jerking his head in Erika's direction. He tossed his bouquet of fresh cut flowers down on the ground and turned on his heels to walk out.

"I'm sorry." I squeaked.

I was mortified, waking mid orgasm like that, only to then be thrown into a fight. Tears welled up in my eyes. I should have known this would happen, that something awful would come of all this.

Yet, I did it anyway, screwing up potentially two good things in my life. My long-standing friendship with Erika, as well as my new relationship. I'm such an idiot.

Erika was now meddling in one of her pockets, finding her pants on the floor. I ignored her as she was obviously impartial to the conversation at hand. She was better off if Dustin was mad and bailed on me, so of course she wouldn't be apologizing or sticking up for me.

I ripped the sheet from my bed, keeping it wrapped around my body. Tripping on one of the loose ends, I stumbled but managed to stay afoot.

Dustin must have heard me rooting around behind him like a clumsy oaf and turned once again to raise his voice at me,

"You know, I thought for once, things were going my way. I had you in my life, things were going well, aside from this business with Chad of course, but I honestly thought we were going somewhere. There's always another though, always. Someone is always lurking, cutting in front of me when I get close. I didn't see this one coming though."

His hands were motioning with purpose as he spoke, his aggravation obvious. His hands shook in fury, his jaw set.

"I didn't mean to hurt you, there's so many circumstances, please just let me explain. I know it doesn't change anything, but I just want you to know."

I pleaded remorsefully. If only I could tell him. All the while I was sleeping, it was him I was fucking. Letting him do the unspeakable to me, and I to him.

"You're damn right it doesn't change anything, Naomi! I drove all the way up here to be with you, only to find you naked in bed with a woman!"

He was yelling, and I shrunk back as flashbacks of Chad's attack floated back into my mind. Noticing my recoil, I saw him search to find his composure.

"Sorry, I didn't mean to yell, but I am furious. You've been through a lot this last while, and I'm sure, seeing who it is you're sleeping with, that there's obviously a lot more snake-like shit going down, but that doesn't excuse it. If you didn't want to be with me, then you should have spoken up. Been open and honest with me."

His brows now sank in despair, his hands lowering until they hung at his sides.

"I DO want to be with you. I didn't plan for this at all. It just happened. I know it's not fair. I'm horrible for having put you through this, but I can't change it now. Please. I'm sorry!"

Tears were falling down my cheeks relentlessly, and my body shook with sobs. I clung to the sheet and used a corner of it to attempt to wipe up some of my tears.

"So... guess last night meant nothing to you then." Both mine and Dustin's heads snapped in the direction of the hall.

Erika stood, stark naked still, puffing on her vape pen, leaning on the corner of the wall, arms folded, seeming very nonchalant; but her eyes shot daggers.

"That's not what I said." I replied meekly.

"No, that's basically exactly what you said. In less words, but it was said. If you want to be with him, then why were you with me? Do you just enjoy hurting people?"

Her words cut, and I felt their sting ten-fold.

"But, you said..." I began, but Dustin cut me off.

"I didn't ask for any of this. This is too much drama. You guys deserve each other."

He once again turned to exit, but this time I just stood there. I felt completely betrayed and hung to dry. I deserved it, I reminded myself. He had every right to be mad. I definitely couldn't argue that. But Erika. This I couldn't comprehend.

Dustin slammed the door, and within seconds I heard his truck rumble and his tires spinning out on the gravel. I stood there, dumbfounded and filled with sorrow; an empty vessel.

"Guess you shouldn't fuck with people's emotions."

Erika hissed as she coolly puffed another cloud of smoke.

"You!"

My anger rose, and I spit the word at her, wielding around to face her.

"You said *NO STRINGS ATTACHED!*"

She drew in another long puff, blowing it out in my direction with intent.

"Yeah, there weren't. You had no obligation to be with me after. You had a choice to be with me last night, and you chose to. You made the choice to be with me, not with him. Now you're back-pedaling and playing the damn victim instead of accepting responsibility. No one forced you! But clearly, you don't want to be with me now. You want him back, you were just having a one night whore-fest, trampling on everyone else's feelings!"

Her voice was rising, and cheeks reddening. Her eyes glaring with their intense green glint.

Her words fell heavy on my heart. It was true, as much as I hated to admit it. I did have a choice last night. I could have refused on the grounds that I was with Dustin and that should have been enough to suffice Erika. It would have been the noble thing to do, but instead I was so worried about hurting her in the moment, I went along. Ignoring my gut and inner desires to be with a man.

I had no real interest in being with a woman. Yes, it was enjoyable, I couldn't deny that. But my sole interest was men. I knew it before we'd even begun last night, and I definitely knew it after that dream and argument with Dustin.

My gut wrenched, she put it all so harshly. It wasn't my intention to hurt anyone. In fact it was quite the latter. I was trying to spare her feelings, and our friendship. But now I saw, I had only put more strain on it. Perhaps even destroyed it.

"You're right. I'm sorry. That wasn't what I was trying to do. I just... didn't want to lose you. And I know how stupid that seems now, but it made sense then."

I hung my head in shame, blotting my slow rolling tears once again on the now dampened sheet. She was still seething, but she obviously wasn't expecting me to apologize, her expression taken aback.

"You can't just keep jumping around like this. Make up your mind! I've been stuck on you for years! I've made up my mind, I want you! But clearly you don't, even now that you know how much I care."

She spoke more softly now but pointedly. Each word spoken had edge.

"I know, and I honestly didn't realize that was what I was doing. I'm sorry, I really am. It's not my fault I don't feel that way. I love you, but I'm just not *in* love with you. I feel awful. I'd say if I could take it back I would, but I feel like that would hurt you too."

A hint of anger flashed back in her eyes.

"You're damn right!"

She stormed away back into the room, clothing herself in a raged frenzy.

I didn't bother to attempt to calm her. I only seemed to make things worse no matter what I said. Defeated, I walked around to the couch and flopped into it, extremely forlorn.

Erika took only seconds to gather everything into her bag again, stuffing it all in her fury. She stomped by me dismissively.

"Come get your kids when you're done feeling sorry for yourself!" She slammed the door.

On that note, I began to bawl. I had ruined everything. I allowed myself to cry, trying to get it all out before I went to get the kids, but knew I'd likely be picking them up with red swollen eyes.

A few emotional minutes passed before I dragged myself up to go get dressed. Splashing water on my face in an attempt to decrease the evidence of my tears. I dressed again with difficulty, doing much of it one handed.

I managed to get my sling on by myself and took a few more analgesics before tying my hair back as best I could with my good hand, then rushed out the door.

Pulling up to Erika's place minutes later, I sucked in a big breath and checked my appearance in the rear view mirror. Pale, my blackened eyes remained, but the bruises were faded more so than yesterday and the swelling almost reduced completely. My corneas were a pale pink from my recent tears. I blinked a few times in meager hopes that it would deplete the evidence of my crying session.

A complete failure. I sighed and opened my door. Without a second's delay, my kids were already running out to me at full speed, bags in hand.

I hugged them all eagerly and tried not to look them straight in the eyes for fear they'd see my veiled emotions. It was working, until Aeda asked me somberley,

"Mom, why was Auntie Erika so upset? She came home and dismissed Terry and then roared at us to pack our bags. I've never seen her like that before!"

They all nodded in unison, obviously rattled by the display they witnessed.

I was a bit annoyed that Erika hadn't any sense to attempt to hide her outrage from my children, and even went as far as to take some of it out on them. They had nothing to do with any of this. I get that she was upset, but there were limits.

"She just got some really bad news this morning, that's all." I said in an attempt to brush it off.

"I'm sure she didn't mean to treat you like that. She just has a hard time controlling herself when she gets worked up."

They seemed to buy it, and that was enough. I ushered them into the car, and we drove home.

Two days later, I heard Chad was still being detained at the local prison. I was surprised; I thought they only usually held people overnight. No one had bothered to mention it to me, not even

Sergeant Webb. I received a call from the police department explaining the legalities to me that morning.

I guess Chad hadn't had enough money for bail and didn't have anyone near enough to come post bail or vouch for him.

He'd been sitting behind bars this whole time due to the extreme nature of the charges against him. I suppose that's why no one had been being harassed for his custody time in my absence.

The clerk at the station's front desk apologized for the delay and informed me that I'd likely have to appear in court in the near future, so to expect a letter informing me of the date and time.

She also let me know that Chad had requested a supervised conversation with me before he was let go. Once he was released he'd be under a temporary restraining order. I agreed to the meeting, as long as it was supervised.

I figured it couldn't hurt to hear what he had to say. Who knows, maybe he'd want to settle out of court? I had no idea, or perhaps he wanted to discuss the children? I could only guess.

They had arranged for me to meet him that afternoon at three. It was quarter to, and I was enroute. Pulling into the station parking lot, I began self-coaching, preparing myself to confront him. I didn't even know what I would say, how I would react.

I had been dealing with my grief in silence the past two days over Erika and Dustin. Now to add a conversation with a suddenly abusive ex-husband, I felt emotionally stunted. There was too much to handle, so I'd just have to put on my mask, and face it head on and solo. Fight or flight, right?

I opened the door to the brick building and walked into the front desk located behind bullet proof windows.

The kind clerk seated behind it gave me a compassionate smile while requesting my ID in order to sign me in for my appointment. She guided me to the doors on the side and buzzed me in.

I received a quick pat down by another male cop whose name tag I couldn't read under his bulky arms that he mostly kept folded on his chest. I was then allowed entrance, and another cop, whom I nicknamed Blaze, guided me to their holding cells.

Blaze quickly gave me an overrun of the rules and gave caution as is their duty upon letting the public into their celled area. He had set a chair up for me several feet away from the bars.

Their facility wasn't big enough to have a private room with a two-way mirror like we see on television sitcoms, he told me.

I think it was his attempt at a joke, but he seemed so serious I couldn't muster a laugh. He took his place near me, but allowed me space to talk.

I slowly sat on the chair placed for me, and saw Chad sitting directly across from me but several feet away behind his bars. I shivered at the sight of him. Sitting there in that chilly holding cell. I couldn't read his expression as he watched me, and I felt my nerves rise on end. His appearance scruffy and disheveled.

"I wanted to tell you I'm sorry." His deep voice mumbled but still echoed off the walls.

"I shouldn't have done what I did. I'm ashamed. But Dustin Trail... you have to understand why that was so infuriating for me?"

I was aghast. Was he really using Dustin as a valid excuse for beating me to a pulp?

"I don't think there's anything to understand here. You never have an excuse to lay a hand on any woman. And what difference does it make WHO it was? We're not together and haven't been for a while now. You also cheated on me numerous times."

I was trying to maintain an even tone so as to not get officer Blaze feeling like he needed to intervene. But I admit I was struggling a bit.

The inflection in my voice rang true. Officer Blaze permitted me to use some emotion and left us to our conversation.

"Let's try not to focus on me here. I'm just saying, Dustin was my friend in high school, and he was all goo-goo eyed for you then too, creepily so. Now he just mysteriously swoops in once I'm out of the picture? Did you know he's also a cop? Erika told me he was moving in on you fast, and the kids, and yeah it pissed me off! That's what ended our friendship all those years ago. He wanted you for himself. I wasn't about to let him move in on my girl. Now here he is again!"

I was listening, but it was hard not to get my defenses up.

"Yes, I know he's a cop. Actually, he's a sergeant, not that that has any relevance to the situation at hand. And no he didn't, you guys were friends, we all were. If he had a thing for me then, whatever! Still didn't make you keep it in your pants! Maybe he knew about you cheating on me even in high school and didn't figure you deserved me! Which he was correct! But that all aside... Erika seriously told you that? When?"

I was starting to be suspicious of a few factors coming to fruition.

"I don't know. Probably a day or so before I came to pick up the kids. She bumped into me outside of my gym. Then the kids told me he'd been there with you all and I lost my shit. Fucking loser starts moving in on my family."

He slumped into his chair, clearly pissed.

Interesting that Erika happened to conveniently *bump* into Chad outside his gym, when she had no real reason to be anywhere near that building. I knew her gym was on the other end of town, and there were no other businesses worth frequenting around Chad's gym.

Realizing I wasn't going to respond to his last comment, he moved on.

"Anyways, I just want you to know I won't be a bother to you again once I'm out. They said my mom is on her way down to post bail for me finally, and then we go to court. But I wanted to apologize, not that I'm sure it means anything after what I did to you, but I am sorry. I still want to be able to see the kids. I promise I'll be kinder, and I'll stay out of your business from now on, but please, look into this guy."

"I won't say I forgive you, but I will do my best to put it behind us. I have no wish to keep the kids from you as long as you abide by the court's ruling and be pleasant. I will be insisting on someone else doing the pickups and drop offs as well. As for Dustin, he's a cop for craps sake, Chad. Give him some credit. It's only an issue to you because you're so damn territorial, even when we've been separated for this length of time."

I ended with a firm tone, in hopes he'd read into it and see I was finished speaking on the matter. My life was no longer his concern, and he'd lost the right to be upset about what I did on my own personal time long before we even separated. About the same time he started sleeping around on me again.

"I know that! And yeah ok, I have no right to be jealous, but Naomi, can't you see? There's more to this than meets the eye, I can feel it!"

"You're delusional. Yes, there's something to a small portion of what you said, and I'm going to look into it. But what you're saying about Dustin is completely offhanded. Doesn't matter anymore now anyway." I grumbled miserably.

"Huh? Why's that?" Chad inquired, his curiosity peaking.

I sighed, not wanting to get into it, especially not with my ex.

"Never mind. Is that all you wanted to discuss with me?" I asked, deflecting his question as quickly as he had sprung it on me.

"Uh, yeah, that's about it. You accept my apology then? And agree to still be fair in matters regarding the kids?"

"Again, I can't say I forgive you. Like I said, I'm willing to work with you. I don't wish to deprive the kids. They've suffered enough and have to live with the fact that their father did this to their mother. I'd like to try to stay as amicable as possible. I will give you a bit more time to get your life back in order though before I return the children to their custody time with you. I'm sure you're still needing to catch up on work once you get out of here. I'm still surprised your mother didn't come to your rescue sooner?"

"Yeah well... I didn't use my phone call, didn't exactly want to tell anyone I was in here, or for what reason."

His eyes fell downcast and I could read the regret in his expression. He went on,

"Better off in here than out there for the time being, let myself alone to my thoughts. I am really sorry, Naomi."

His eyes gazed up at me, dewy with tears.

I nodded my acknowledgement at him for his apology, then stood to leave. Officer Blaze grabbed my chair and escorted me back out.

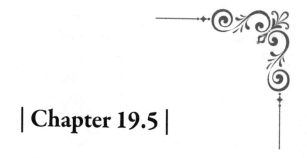

| Chapter 19.5 |

The hurt was undeniable. It felt a little like my soul had been crushed. I never thought her capable of such actions. Maybe I had her up on too much of a pedestal.

I had gotten a text early that morning from an anonymous number telling me Naomi was home and could use some nursing care. I had thought it weird, especially from a number I didn't recall at all. Perhaps it was one of her nursing friends letting me know on her behalf or out of concern for her? But at the thought of Naomi home alone after her stay at the hospital, I couldn't get there quick enough. Only to arrive and find her naked in bed with none other than Erika Crane.

The ache in my gut made me want to hurl, and I wasn't usually one to wretch. *Why? We had just become an item, and now this? Had this been going on the whole time behind my back? Was I that big a fool?*

I felt crushed. All the high hopes I'd had for us, shattered. Her pleading only made it worse. The remorse on her face just made it hurt all the more.

There is nothing more insulting to a guy than being cheated on, especially when the person your girl is sleeping with is a chick!

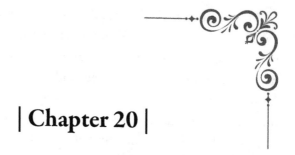

| Chapter 20 |

Once I had tucked Aeda, Austin and Everley in that night for bed, I was alone and had time to ponder. Chad's words had been lingering in my head all afternoon and evening since my departure from the station. He said that Erika told him about Dustin. She clearly went out of her way to tell him. Why? What possible reason could she have to try to trigger Chad like that?

I raked my brain, but none of it made any sense to me. I was however flooded with relief that Chad and I had been able to have an honest and open conversation without conflict, and any differences of opinion we had didn't lead us to a screaming match or worse. Perhaps that was due to Officer Blaze's presence though.

I had a follow up appointment the next day with my doctor to see how my collarbone was mending. It was feeling much better, although like all broken collarbones, it would never look quite the same again, I'd say I was making a quick recovery.

I had been able to move more and more and was requiring less medication. In fact, I was only taking one every other day now, and only because I'd over-do it.

I was daily doing the rehabilitation exercises that I was provided with prior to discharge and they were helping immensely.

I had no further issues with walking, and my face, aside from one small swollen lump above the one eye, was almost completely normal again. A faint yellow tint remained of the bruising on my face which I was able to fade with makeup easily.

All in all, I'd say I was completely recovered or on the verge of it. I was eager to see if my doctor agreed.

I had stopped using the sling the past few days. For that I thought I'd likely get in shit, but it was hindering my movement so much that it was no longer beneficial for me to continue wearing it, if I were ever going to build strength and mobility back up in my arm.

Work had been paying for me to attend further professional physio appointments as well, but as demand was so high, I'd only had one appointment thus far. I'm sure once my doctor was satisfied, she'd set a return-to-work date for me and I'd be starting off with short shifts, building up to a full return. I had managed to get employment insurance while off work so money wasn't such a huge concern anymore, thank goodness.

I missed talking with Erika and Dustin as well. I hated thinking I had caused all this and hurt them both. I wished to make amends but wasn't sure either one would receive me. I knew things would take time but hated the wait.

I decided to take my chances, and at least make a gesture, in hopes they'd see I was making some efforts and still wanted them in my life.

Erika was tricky because she wasn't like most girls. Flowers would not cut it.

I opted to pull a trick from a movie we had enjoyed in our youth together and sent her a pizza with the word *Sorry* spelt on it in M&Ms chocolates.

The pizza place was a little baffled by my request, but I dropped off the bag of M&Ms in order to make their job easier, and in doing so they were more than willing to oblige. I figured I probably wouldn't hear from her, but at least I did something.

Next, Dustin. I honestly had no idea. I debated texting or calling him, but again, I thought he'd likely just reject the calls and leave me in silence with the texts. I decided to go with a similar approach as I did with Erika and called around in Kelowna to find a place that delivered *man bouquets*. It ended up being easy to find a place. I had them write me a note to attach to the 12-pack of beer that simply said,

"*I'm sorry- Naomi*" and requested they deliver to the station where he worked as opposed to his condo, just so there was that peer pressure to accept and not just trash the beer. Wanting to serve his comrades one of the cold beverages after shift would surely melt a soft spot in his heart, perhaps cause him to feign some forgiveness, or so I hoped.

There! My deeds were done. All I could do was wait.

I was still waiting even a few weeks later, with no contact. Chad had finally started taking the kids again with supervised pickups and drop offs, so I had days to myself when they were gone.

With my mobility improving and all this extra time on my hands with not working yet and kids gone, I had made the decision to use the time to really focus on my health. I had been clean eating, meal prepping, going to the gym daily, as well as running.

I'd never been much of a runner, but I suppose I was so grateful to be alive and functioning I was seeing things through a new light and decided to embrace a new hobby.

I was still building up my stamina, but each day I improved a little and made it a bit further before needing to stop, breathless. It had only been two weeks, but I could feel that my efforts were having some benefit.

My clothes were fitting looser, and my muscles were more well defined. I felt better, no bloating, and less fatigue.

The kids were supportive when they were home, although they weren't fans of a lot of the meals I served up nowadays. But they could see it was offering me clarity and I was happier for it, so they didn't hassle me too much about it.

I had started hanging out with a few of the women I met at the gym as well. It was nice branching out and finding new social circles. Intimidating at first, but I was adjusting and enjoying the increased socialization. I wasn't so lonely anymore and had people to talk to.

I had just gotten back from my evening run and was untying my shoes when I heard my phone ring. Pausing my un-tying I reached for it. It had been stashed in my shorts as I'd been using it as both a pedometer as well as a music player to fuel my runs.

I struggled fishing it out from the sweaty material but managed to answer it on the last ring, not bothering to read the name on the screen before swiping right.

"Hello?" I prompted, wondering if perhaps they'd hung up due to my delay. The silence went on.

"Helloooo?" I prompted again.

Still nothing. I hung up. That was weird, I thought, maybe just spam callers. Not thinking much of it, I put my phone down and finished un-lacing my shoes, kicking them off.

The cool air rushing through my socks provided relief for their excessive damp heat that consumed them when I ran. I wriggled my toes, allowing more air to flow between them. It felt deliciously good and refreshing!

I didn't get much time to enjoy it before my phone rang once again. This time I was able to pick it up faster, but hesitated, seeing the name come up on the caller ID.

Dustin Trail... My heart stopped. Was this a pocket dial? Was it him that just called? I was so nervous I almost forgot to answer it.

"He..hello?" I stammered, my nerves getting the better of me. This time I could hear his breathing on the line and waited for him to reply.

"Hey Naomi... this is Dustin. It took me a while to build up the grit to call you, but I figured I had to."

"Oh ok. Did you get my man bouquet a while back?" I asked.

"Yes, I got it. Bold move sending it to the station. Guess you knew I was less likely to trash it there hey?"

My gut lurched, a bit saddened that that was indeed what he had thought of doing.

"Yeah well, I owed you an apology and that always goes down better with beer and friends, so I figured it would be a good bet to send it there."

He *hmmphed* through the line.

"I really am truly sorry though. Please believe that. I know it probably doesn't seem like it, but I truly never intended on hurting you. It just all got so complicated so fast. I have no excuse for my actions. You were great to me and my kids and I fucked up."

I tried to keep my voice from wavering, but by the end of my sentence I was borderline in tears, pleading for forgiveness.

I didn't expect him to want to be friends or anything, I just wanted him to accept my apology, to know how sorry I was.

"Yeah, you fucked up big time. I just can't trust you. I thought with how Chad treated you, that you'd be above all the cheating bullshit. I was so wrong."

Ouch, I thought. Another cut, but I deserved it.

"I guess I just want to know why? And why Erika of all people? Is this why you guys are best friends? Because you have some weird, twisted love affair?"

I sucked in my hurt from his accusations, again. He was asking and now was my chance to tell him.

"No, not at all. We've been best friends forever, with no romantic involvement whatsoever. I was caught completely off guard. She showed up at my place when I got home from the hospital and said she was going to take care of me. She poured me a bath and everything. I went in the bath alone, and then minutes later she was naked in the bathroom confessing her love to me. I had no idea. But I also felt awful. It felt like she'd been in love with me for forever and then was giving me shit almost for never realizing it and moving on to you."

"I didn't want to hurt her, but I also didn't want to hurt you. She asked for me to give her just one night together with no strings attached, and I felt obligated. It wasn't fair to you, I know. You've been so good to me, and I was so happy being with you. But it felt like my friendship was on the line, and yes looking back I see how stupid that rationale is now; but at the time, I felt like I had to."

I sucked in a long breath after finishing my ramble and waited to hear his reaction.

"Wait, so Erika came on to you? Not the other way around?" He seemed very puzzled.

"Nooo! Like I said, she poured a bath for me and when I went in, a few minutes later she walked in stark naked and said she was in love with me. I was completely baffled. But wait, why did you think it was the other way around?"

Suddenly my own curiosity was piqued by his comment. *Not the other way around.*

"Have you guys talked? What exactly did you mean by that comment? Because it seems to me that you're inferring that you heard otherwise?"

I could hear shuffling going on in the background, clearly he was uncomfortable.

"This isn't the point. I just wanted to tell you that it wasn't cool what you did, and that I don't know if I can forgive you."

I swallowed hard letting his words sink in, but then he went on.

"But I'm also not ready to lose you. I needed time to process. But even if it was for a short time, my life was better with you in it. I'm not ready to give that up just yet."

I gasped, and felt my chest swell, I was not expecting this!

"So, I guess what I'm saying is, even though I'm unable to forgive you just yet, I'd like to still try to be with you. I mean if you're still willing? We don't have to be a couple yet, I just was hoping to reserve a spot in your life at the very least."

I covered my mouth to stifle my sheer joy.

"Yes!"

Whoops, I may have shouted that a little louder than intended.

"I mean, I'd really like that."

I could hear him chuckle.

"Well alright then, I'll text you, and you can let me know when you can join me for dinner one evening."

I didn't even know how to respond at this moment. I was so overjoyed and stunned in disbelief at my good fortune.

"Ok!" Was all I could make out.

He laughed again.

"Ok, well enjoy your evening, Naomi, and I'll talk to you later."

I smiled a big shit eating grin.

"Bye!"

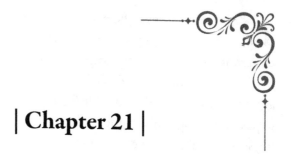

| Chapter 21 |

Days and weeks floated by under increasingly blissful circumstances. Dustin and I were once again talking regularly, even more than prior to my hospitalization.

We'd gone on a few dates but had been keeping the physical aspect of things mostly out of it for now. I think we were both in hopes of creating a solid emotional foundation before bringing in the physical this time around, although on a few occasions, lust got away with us.

The kids were enjoying floating back and forth between Chad and I again and our court date was coming up. I was still going forth with the charges, with much encouragement from my friends and family, although I had almost let up for the sake of the children. However, they convinced me that he had to learn and pay his debt as his actions had taken it too far to be swept under the rug. That I could agree with.

We'd been managing to keep things amicable between us as there'd been little contact which was still preferred.

I had returned to work and had been tolerating the workload. My collarbone gave the occasional *click,* when turning or supporting heavier patients, but it wasn't giving me any pain.

I continued with my daily gym and runs and had been making great strides in my endurance and strength as a result. I really had never felt better! Dustin on occasion would join me on my runs or gym escapes, and it was fun to have a companion.

On the downside of things, I still hadn't heard from Erika. I swear I had seen her drive by my place a few times, but each time Dustin's truck had been in the driveway and her car would suddenly increase its speed until it had passed.

This was hard for me, I knew she must be still struggling and wished to comfort her. I'm sure I was the one person she did not want comfort from at this point though, and that's why I had kept to myself as of recently.

However, I was feeling the urge to reach out to her again. I wanted to clear the air, see if there was any chance we could be friends again.

As I had no response to my pizza idea, I thought I'd try a more personal approach this time. I had gotten off my set the day before and had slept in to recuperate. I was now ready to take on the challenge of confronting Erika in person.

I showered and dressed, donning my cargo shorts and an old band tee. Brushed my teeth and walked out the door. I didn't want to risk losing my *gumph* if I took too long getting ready. I had to just do it. Before I lost the nerve. I stomped out my front door with an air of confidence. I was really hoping to make changes today.

I pulled up to Erika's house, I could see she was home. Her car was parked in the driveway still. I had specifically planned to take action being that it was a Saturday and I assumed she'd be home. I parked along the street and clicked my lock button as I got out.

I strode forward, my confidence fading as I reached her doorstep. Why did I think I could do this? Face her? I stood there, staring at her door. My fist raised ready to knock but unable to bring myself to make contact with the white paneled wood.

I don't know how long I stood there, it probably felt longer than it was. I was about ready to just turn and leave accepting defeat, when the door swung open.

Erika stood there glaring at me. Her face was paler than usual, her cheeks gaunter. She looked almost sickly. Her morning coffee in hand, wearing panties and an oversized men's striped pajama top. Her hair was still bedraggled.

"What?" She demanded.

"I, I just came to see how you were? And to tell you again that I'm sorry."

She looked me up and down. Her eyes were hard and cold. She sneered a bit when she spoke.

"I'm fine. I still don't accept. No way I'm letting you off, making you feel better about yourself for getting forgiveness. You don't deserve it. Are we done here?"

I gulped. She was still really pissed.

"That's not what I want. I don't want it so I feel better. I want it because I don't want you to still hurt. I want to be able to do whatever it takes to make you feel better. That's all."

Figuring our conversation was now over, I let my eyes fall downcast and waited for the door to slam in my face. But it didn't.

"How are you so smart and still so clueless?"

Oh great, now she was going to insult me. I made no effort to defend myself. There was no point. She'd just keep drilling away at me regardless.

Instead, I just shrugged and turned to descend the walkway back to my van.

"Just giving up and walking away now huh? That's so like you! Guess I'm not worth your time!"

She continued to cat-call me, but I couldn't take it. I had to respond to that last comment.

"You were worth my time, that's why I made the effort to come here today. You asked if we were done here, and I guess we are. If you can't stop shit talking me long enough to see that I just want my friend back! All of a sudden I'm only worth your time if I'm willing to eat your pussy!"

I was horrified at my own words, but I also wanted to savor the look on her face. The utter shock at being called out and me finally giving her a dose of her own medicine. I flung her a peace sign over my head, and strutted back to my van. My confidence returned. Fuck her.

I picked up the kids from Chad's appointed "kid-exchanger" as I deemed her, Maggie. An old family friend. And we headed to the beach, eager for some time in the sand and sun.

Being as it was the weekend, I had invited Dustin to join us at his leisure if he felt up to the drive but didn't have much expectation that he'd show.

Austin and Everley wrestled each other out of the van in order to be the first one at the beach. Although I did point out that there were already tons of people at the beach so it really didn't matter who was "first." I was ignored, but at least they were having fun.

Aeda helped me to load our folding wagon and haul stuff down. With their assistance we located the perfect spot to unload and set up. Close to the park, near the water but also near the washrooms and with some shade from a nearby bush as well.

Plumping our towels and stretching them out over our sandmat while the kids undressed and changed into their bathing suits in the changeroom, I then dug my own suit out and headed to the changeroom.

The girls passed by me as I went in and they ran out. I yelled at their backs not to go into the water fully until I was out to supervise, then disappeared through the door to change.

It was a quick change, and I discovered that I needed a new suit as I had been losing so much weight recently that my previous one was now very loose! I threw on some shorts over it for fear my bits would end up being exposed by accident.

Satisfied with my temporary band aid fix, I made my way down to the sloped beach and plopped my clothes in the beach bag before heading to the water to join my kids.

They were only up to their calves and splashing one another, Everley had already busted out her sand pails and shovels as well.

Once they saw that I was now present they threw themselves into the water, splashing me. Not to be outdone, I splashed back and it turned into a huge water fight! Austin ran up grabbing the water guns and the pool noodles with holes so we could blow water at each other through them.

Up until this point I had been completely unaware of the other beach goers as we had all been so swept up in our water fight, but as the fun started to die down, the kids all began immersing themselves in their own solo activities.

Everley, sand castle building, Austin swimming to the floating dock, and Aeda skipping rocks and talking with a girl friend who had recognized her and came down to socialize.

I started walking back up onto the shore soaking wet when I saw a figure standing alongside our towels and wagon.

The glaring sun blocking my vision, I had to shield my eyes in order to see the face.

Erika! Well now what the hell was she doing here? We had only just finished fighting this morning, and better yet, how did she know we'd be here?

I let out an exasperated sigh, and tried to conceal my expression as I continued my trek towards her looming stature.

"What are you doing here?" I muttered bitterly.

"I thought about what you said this morning, figured you had a point."

She scuffed her toes in the sand shrugging.

"What do you mean?"

I inquired furtively, thinking there must be some angle she's playing here because Erika NEVER apologizes or admits anyone else besides herself is correct.

"The part about you only being worth my time if you're eating my uhh....me."

I stifled a smile at the fact that she couldn't bring herself to finish my words.

"You're...right."

She sighed obviously struggling to bring herself to admit it to my face.

"I said no strings attached, and then I turned on you when you didn't choose me. Then I didn't even allow you to apologize despite your many attempts. I fucked up, so did you, but I shouldn't have carried it on like I did. You clearly aren't interested in being with a female, and I have to come to terms with that and move on. I think I was just trying to protect myself from the truth, I didn't want to face it. I think I knew all along but was in denial. I've been in love with you for so long, I just couldn't give it up. So for that I'm sorry. I don't want it to ruin our friendship, but I'm not certain I can JUST be friends with you now, it will hurt too much. Even standing here in front of you now is gut wrenching for me. I thank you for giving me the chance to at least try to change your mind even though you clearly weren't completely comfortable with the idea from the get go. I wish it had worked out in my favor, but it didn't. I have to live with that. But I don't want us hating each other."

She finally lifted her eyes to look at me, and I could see the welled up tears, the tears that Erika almost never shed, in her eyes. She feverishly blinked them away.

"I appreciate your apology and extend mine once again too. I didn't mean to hurt you, but the heart wants what the heart wants as you know. You're my best friend, and that's all I've ever wanted for us. I understand that too, I felt like I ruined it too."

We exchanged somber but loving looks before Erika was tackled with a surplus of hugs from kids having finally noticed her presence. She giggled and held them all, and that was enough to make my heart happy again.

They harassed her to come swimming with them and toss around the volleyball, she looked at me unsure; but I gave her an approving nod that she was welcome to crash our day at the beach and partake. With a small smile she ripped off her wrap around dress revealing her newly emaciated frame and ran into the water, tossing Everley over her shoulder as she ran.

Their squeals of delight echoed across the beach. And so, she spent the afternoon with us. We didn't overly spend a ton of time together per say, but kind of bounced back and forth between the kids and doing stuff to keep busy. It was relaxed and although awkward at times, a very pleasant afternoon.

I had forgotten about my invitation to Dustin until he plopped down beside me on the sand with his shorts and sandals on, startling me. He noticed me jump and chuckled.

"You forgot about me didn't you?"

He asked knowingly. I swear he could read my mind sometimes. I grinned guiltily.

"I knew it!"

He shook his head laughing.

"We were preoccupied."

I nodded in Erika's direction, she was busy in the sand with her back to us building a mote to Everley's castle and Austin was hauling buckets of water to assist.

Upon seeing and recognizing who was feet away from us, his head cocked jerkily, his expression now serious and hard.

"You invited her here?"

His eyes not hiding their steely look, not that I could say I blamed him for being miffed by it.

"No I didn't, we arrived and had been hanging out and the next thing I knew she was here. She apologized Dustin, we truced."

"I just want my friend back."

I threw in when I could see his expression not melting. His teeth were grinding through his square jawline and he was now glaring in Erika's direction. Caught on my words, he took a deep inhale through his nose and blew it out through his mouth.

"I know you guys have a long history, I can't get in between that. I don't have to like it though. I'll try to put on a good face, but just know it's still not settling well with me, but I'll deal with it, for you."

I hugged his side and kissed his shoulder.

"Thank you." I whispered.

He grunted and quickly kissed the top of my head. We sat there awhile, watching them all play and the waves from passing boats washing up further and further on shore. The water lapped at the sides of their sandcastle, the moat flooded.

Realizing the water was winning, they all communed, calling it quits before turning to walk back up to the towels. The sun cresting behind them on the verge of setting behind the peak of the looming Mt. Baldy.

Erika turned and looked stunned when her eyes settled on Dustin, her smile disappeared off her face in an instant and her face lost its color. *Uh-oh, was this going to be an issue?* I thought to myself.

I hadn't thought how Erika and Dustin would react to me repairing the rifts between each of us, and I had also not thought ahead to think that they had rifts of their own to mend as well.

The kids started toweling off, and Erika finally spoke.

"What's he doing here?" No warmth in her tone.

"I could say the same thing about you." Dustin responded icily.

"I had invited him when we arrived." I cut in.

"I didn't know you'd be here too. But honestly, we all need to learn to get along, if you're both going to be in my life."

I could feel the tension and the daggers being shot back and forth between their eyes, despite my attempts at keeping the peace.

"Shall we get some beers? Or ice cream? Anything?"

I suggested trying to break the ice. Dustin was the first to crack and shift his energy.

"Yeah, sure, either or. I'll help you pack up." Aeda had stopped and was sensing the tension but once again began bustling around packing up the sand toys and dictating to Everley how she should rinse them first, when Dustin joined in rolling up towels.

I stood up, dusting sand off my legs before bending to lift up the sand mat and shake it out. Erika was on her phone texting, when she finished she seemed to have gotten over it and helped me to fold the mat up.

"Many hands make light work!" I sang harmoniously as we finished. More in an effort to start conversation once more, but to no avail. Oh well, I thought, at least they were tolerating each other.

Walking up the beach and onto the cement, the silence among the adults continued. The kids at least rambled on telling us all different stories or ideas they had, providing a great distraction for the uncomfortableness at hand.

I dug the keys to my van out of my wagon pocket as we headed through the tunnel out into the parking lot. Seeing the van, I clicked my key fob unlocking it. The lights lit up letting me know it was successful.

Dustin's truck was just across from mine, and Erika had parked conveniently right beside mine. I thought this a bit of a strange occurrence just considering how busy it was when we had arrived, we had gotten extremely lucky with our parking spot. It could surely be a coincidence, but it irked me still.

My train of thought suddenly ended with the sound of a nearby car door slamming. Snapping my head in the direction of the noise, holy shit, how is this happening?

"Chad?"

My jaw dropped. How was this possible? This bermuda triangle of drama happening all at once, all at this location. He looked livid once again as he stormed towards us.

"Daddy!"

Everley exclaimed upon seeing him, but her excitement died fast when she saw the glint in his eyes and his lack of acknowledgement.

"Get in the van, Aeda. Austin, take Everley, get her in there, *now*!" I commanded.

Fear took over my body with each heavy stride his large legs took in our direction. Dustin stepped in front of me to shield me from whatever may come. Erika took a few steps back watching, probably stunned herself and unsure what to do I speculated.

"I thought you were done with him Naomi? What the shit is this? Why is this scum bucket here again with you and my children!" Chad growled ferociously in his booming voice.

"*Our* children!"

I threw back at him over Dustin's shoulder, wanting to make that point very clear.

"It's none of your business either Chad! This is my time with the kids, and they're not in any form of danger so you have no concern here."

I was stating the facts, trying to make it unarguable. Finally reaching us, his chest puffed, hackles up. I recognized that look in his eyes, and my muscles tensed.

"You have no idea that they're not in danger! You're too infatuated with this cocksucker to see what's right in front of your eyes!"

He screamed at me, gesturing at Dustin.

"Whoa! Back up Chad, I believe you have a temporary restraining order pertaining to Naomi when an exchange of the children isn't occurring."

Dustin said at length, trying to be professional. I could hear his sergeant's tone and hoped it was enough to make Chad realize what he was getting himself into. However, it had no effect.

"Don't talk to me, you fucking shit stain! That's the only way you've had a chance with her you know? It's because she's still getting over me! She won't even look at the bigger picture and see what's really going on! You're still a fucking stalker even now! Nothing's changed, you're still as slimy as you ever were! Take another crazy pill and try to convince yourself otherwise ya' douche!"

Spit was shooting from his lips and his body quaking with fury and disdain.

Dustin was clearly reaching his peak for Chad's aggression and obscenities and took a firm step forward.

Hearing Chad talk about Dustin's "crazy pills" though, struck me again as odd. *Has Dustin been on these meds since high school?* I originally hadn't considered this an option, I just assumed it was a newer development.

I had no time to waste thinking about it though as tensions were rising higher and I knew there was no chance this was going to end well...

"That's enough!" Dustin hissed at Chad.

"You're already on thin ice. What's going to happen when your local authorities get word of this?"

Realizing Dustin had no jurisdiction here was also a bit unnerving to me. He was just an ordinary member of the public here. The most he could do was make a citizen's arrest.

"Don't you threaten me! You're on my turf!"

Chad was advancing forwards again, and I shrunk back further. Dustin however, stood his ground. They were almost nose to nose spewing insults and threats back and forth in an attempt to intimidate the other.

Once again, I began to wonder...*how did Chad know to come here? How did he know where we were and that Dustin was here?* My brow furrowed, thinking, raking my brain trying to connect the dots.

Chad threw the first punch, but Dustin maneuvered and it missed him. Like lightning he counterpunched Chad back in the jaw, his fists raised ready for more. Chad's neck spun on impact, but he caught his jaw and looked back menacingly at Dustin, then lunged.

The brawl began, fists flying, making impact, interlocking holds, grappling. The sound of their grunts and adrenaline packed breathing.

I scrambled looking to make sure my kids were in the van out of harm's way like I had asked of them. Their faces were horrified looking through the glass, tears in Everley's eyes.

I moved, dodging the two men wrestling one another, just escaping a rogue clenched fist. I scraped my hand on the pavement in the process but still had to crawl away as quickly as possible in order to miss further potential hits.

I glanced up and couldn't believe my eyes; Erika stood there by her vehicle, just barely in sight. A wry cruel smile curled on her face, and that's when the dots finally connected!

Building my courage, I screamed at the guys still fighting ruthlessly, Dustin had Chad in a choke hold and Chad attempted to elbow him in the ribs to make him let go.

"STOP! Both of you!"

Of course, I was ignored. I would need to push harder to be either heard or noticed.

Thinking fast, as a crowd was starting to form as people were starting to leave the beach, I sprinted to my van. Aeda, seeing my urgency, unlocked it as fast as she could and I leapt in, simultaneously fishing my keys out of my pocket and jamming them in the ignition.

I turned them, heard the engine rev to life, and began honking like crazy.

In my rear view mirror I could see them pause for a split second, alarmed by the noise, but without seeing any other action they consequently returned to brawling.

"Alright kiddos, buckle up!"

I encouraged my kids, they timidly did so in a hurried manner. Everley whimpered, her little bottom lip quivering.

I punched it into reverse and honked some more before taking my foot off the brake and dropping my foot on the gas.

The tires squealed as my tires peeled backwards across the pavement, my horn still blaring. This time they looked up and saw my van flying at them and jumped in opposing directions.

I stopped in between them and rolled down both mine and my front passenger's window. I stopped honking long enough to yell at them.

"Stop you guys! I have something to say! I know what's going on!"

Puzzled and exhausted they stood there on either side of the vehicle panting.

"Will you listen?" I asked, or more demanded

They looked at one another. Chad being the first to nod, likely recognizing how tired he was and not wishing to have to forfeit on account of not being able to carry on.

The ring of sweat around his neck and pit stains giving away his stance on the physical threshold. Dustin, although breathing hard, was completely dry and still looked ready for combat if provoked.

"Ok, I'm going to park and then we're going to talk!" I yelled at them again.

I pulled ahead back into my space, left my air conditioner running for the kids and pushed play on a movie for them in order to distract and calm them down. I left them with encouraging words before exiting the vehicle.

"I love you guys, everything is ok. I'll be right back, you just sit tight while I take care of this ok?"

I didn't wait for their response as I'm sure it would have led to a stream of protests and tears. I pressed lock as I left so they'd know not to follow me.

Instead of going the direct route, I swung around the front of Erika's vehicle and snuck up behind her. She still stood there watching, likely confused as to why they had stopped fighting, but her crooked smile remained on her.

I tapped her right shoulder, surprising her. She turned around. I pulled back and thrust my own fist solidly into her cheek and eye with all my strength, knocking her to the ground.

I wasted no time, not letting her recover. I grabbed her arm, yanked her back up and locked her arm behind her back then walked, shoving her forward, steering her with my knee and hip.

Chad and Dustin looked fully blown away by my man-handling of Erika and probably wondered how this turn of events managed to take place during the time they were fighting.

"What's this all about now?"

Chad sputtered through his panting and wheezing, wiping a dribble of blood from the corner of his lip.

"Chad, how did you know to come here today?"

He looked flabbergasted.

"I got a random anonymous text, I don't even know who it was from. I almost ignored it, but I was so mad when I read it, I dunno, I just raced down here to see if it was true. It was!"

"Ok."

I said, now turning to Dustin.

"Dustin how did you happen to come across me in Kelowna that day we reconnected again? And don't for a second try to tell me you just happened to pull me over. We both know that's bullshit!"

His expression was taken aback, but I could see a desperate look in his eyes as he glanced at Erika flittingly.

"I..uh..I got a message on Facebook. I wouldn't normally have responded, but she was just being friendly and then she brought you up. Saying you'd be picking her up when she returned."

I reached into Erika's pocket, she fought, trying to stop me, but I twisted her arm unrelenting. I pulled out not one but two cell phones.

One I recognized as her usual phone in its weathered blue case. The other, newer, no case, just a basic flip phone. I threw it to Dustin.

"Open the messages."

I demanded. He obliged and read the first one that popped up.

Flip phone: *That stalker is with your wife and kids at the beach, schmoozing his way into their lives, leaving you in the dust."*

Chad's eyes opened wide.

"That's the message I got!"

Dustin scrolled up and read another.

Flip phone: *Chad, you don't know me, but I know you. Your cunty ex is sleeping with Dustin Trail. You remember Dustin don't you...I believe he always wanted to fuck her, in fact you probably fucked her right after he jizzed in that cess pool of a twat while in high school. Did you know he's with your children right now?*

The contents of my stomach churned and I twisted her arm even more, causing her to squeak in pain. No wonder Chad was so mad when he came to my house the night he attacked me, after reading this kind of smut.

"Open another message, Dustin." I ordered. He once again scrolled up and clicked.

Flip phone: *She's home right now, could probably use some nursing.*

The fearful look in his eyes became more prominent.

"What date and time was that one sent?" I asked. He gulped.

"July 6th at 6:45am."

"Interesting." I said.

"Considering that was the morning you found me in bed with Erika."

I let the weight of that dawn on both men before continuing on.

"Dustin, you had implied that Erika told you that I came on to her that night?"

"Yes, that's what she told me."

I turned to Chad.

"And did Erika not conveniently bump into you at your gym before you blew up at me, telling you Dustin was moving in on me and the kids?"

Chad nodded. I could see both his and Dustin's gears moving in their heads, piecing it all together now too.

"There's only a few things I can't figure out."

I admitted, still holding her in place.

"Where did my missing panties go? How did you really end up showing up at my house after Chad pummeled me? And why? I just don't understand why you'd cause all this trouble for me? I can't honestly see you doing it because you're in love with me. People who love don't do shit like this!"

She bared her teeth, refusing to answer.

In order to persuade her I forcefully kneed her in the ribs, letting her know I'd use as much force as necessary at this point. She curled gasping for breath, and I twisted her arm even more.

"I don't know anything about your panties!"

She howled.

"I knew you were there, not because staffing called me, I knew because I sent Chad there. I never imagined he'd take it as far as he did. But when I didn't hear from you even days later, I went to check and found you in that bloody mess. I felt awful about it. He could've ended you, but I don't regret it! And how can you honestly ask me why? We were supposed to travel abroad together. Instead, I ended up going, trying to escape you! I couldn't stand you being with Chad and not being with you in general. I thought if we traveled together and I got you away from your husband and your kids you'd realize you could do without them. You could be with me! But then you fucking backed out, afraid of leaving your kids and Chad. I wanted Chad gone! He's a prick and doesn't deserve you. He never has. So yeah, I played with him a little, whatever."

I was stupefied hearing this vile confession from her but pressed on trying to get to the very bottom of it.

"Well Chad was already out of the picture, I'd left him! So there was no need for you to trigger him into beating me."

I was crying, filled with rage, my voice cracking.

"No no, the Chad thing was my fuck you to you! You got rid of Chad and turned right around to be with another fucking male! You play games with me constantly, fooling around with me and Dustin, then just me, and still you go back to dick! I can give you more than they can! Commitment! Sex! Love! Everything!! Yet you still chose them over me!"

Chad's, Dustin's and my eyes bulged with the amount of truth just spilt on us. This was far more twisted than I ever thought imaginable.

Obviously some poor mental health at play, but I had never caught on, never guessed. As far as I had ever been concerned she was my best friend, or was she? I grabbed her personal phone and flipped to her texts with Dustin, I didn't have to scroll far to find the messages I wish weren't there. I read:

Erika Crane: *Oh yeah, she was all over me, I didn't know what to think of it. She was hitting on me and asking if she could put her fingers in me. I thought she was drunk, but she hadn't had anything to drink that I saw. Sorry it happened like that, but hey maybe it's for the better, she's realized now she prefers rug to log.*

I was seething, the way she talked about me, so derogatory and malicious.

I switched to the Facebook messages they'd shared and swiped up to the top this time.

Erika Crane: "Hey Dustin, do you remember me? We went to high school together. Anyways, I just saw you pop up in my friend suggestions and figured, why not?"

I noted the date to be back in late May.

Wait, but I thought I re-introduced them when I picked Erika up from the airport? I decided now was the time to read Dustin's half too, my gut clenched, fearing the worst.

Dustin Trail: "Yes, I remember you Erika. How goes things?"

Erika Crane: "Not bad, doesn't seem like all that long ago we were in high school. I'm presently traveling, due back in a few weeks. I'll get Naomi to pick me up. Oh wait you'll remember her too, I think you had a thing for her back in the day actually!"

Dustin Trail: "No time goes by fast that's for sure. Oh that's great that you're traveling, I'd love to hear about where you've been sometime. Yes, I could never forget Naomi, where is she picking you up from?"

Erika Crane: "Kelowna airport. That's where you live now right? Kelowna?"

Dustin Trail: "Yes, I'm in Kelowna. Wow, I'd love to meet up with you both one day. Catch up with old friends, if that's at all possible?"

Erika Crane: "For sure! How about the day I arrive back? Might as well, I mean we'll all be there. Although I get the feeling it's really Naomi you want to see?"

Dustin Trail: "Well, I'd like to see you too but you're correct, I would definitely fancy seeing Naomi again. No secret I used to have a real thing for her. That would be fantastic, I'd definitely be down for that."

Erika Crane: "Well lucky you, she's single now! She separated a little while ago, she was supposed to come traveling with me, but things didn't work out. Bet she'd notice you now. I took a peek at your profile pics. She will definitely approve!"

Dustin Trail: "Oh wow! Yes, I'd love to arrange! Well, thanks, I don't know though, hopefully."

Erika Crane: "Ok well if you want to meet up we can make plans, but I suggest we don't let her know we talked beforehand, if she has any inkling we arranged this she won't go for it."

Dustin Trail: "Deal! Look forward to making further plans with you!"

Ugh! My heart sank. The whole thing was a set up. Every feeling I'd had was based on a lie. I looked at him, let him see my feelings of betrayal plastered all over my face.

I'd read all I needed to, but one more thing still had me itching my head. I exited her messages and began flipping through her apps.

Reaching the last page, I found what I expected. A tracking app.

I opened it and saw my phone's information logged in and the red icon on the map blinking, alerting to my location at Canoe beach. I threw her phone on the ground. This whole thing was sick!

"Why would you set me and Dustin up if you wanted to be with me?" I asked scathingly.

"Because, I wanted to test you! I needed a way in! I knew you wouldn't just make love to me out of nowhere, I had to bait you in with a hot guy! Dustin was perfect, I'd been following him for awhile, before I even made contact with him. Found out how unstable he still is and that he was single. I bet anything he'd be enough to get you in bed. What I didn't bet on was that he was still into stalking! Idiot used his cop stuff to track you down, look up all your information, from your driver's license to your house address. That's how he beat me to you and slept with you the night before I flew in! Fucker tapped your phone too and put a tracker on your van! I bet anything that's where your missing panties went too!"

My eyes darted to him and he looked embarrassed.

"You took them didn't you? This is all true isn't it?" I asked.

He didn't reply. He didn't need to, the look he gave me was enough to confirm.

Now it all made sense...how he pulled me over, how he was able to show up at my house without me having to give him my address.

"Holy shit..."

I let the words escape my lips. I felt so sick, how could I have let this, all of this into my life? My kids lives?

"You're all fucked!" Chad's voice filled with disgust, and for once, I agreed with him.

There was still a small crowd of beach goers lingering nearby us, some had their phones out filming, one was on a call giving details.

Great, they'd called the police or 911. The faint sound of sirens slowly growing louder confirmed this.

Dustin and Chad, realizing they had no real beef with each other, they'd both been set up, we all had, got up off their knees and shuffled awkwardly, awaiting the inevitable.

I was so done. I felt like my entire life was an illusion; or more, a lie. The whole damn thing, right back to my youth when I first met Erika, all those moments, the fun we'd had, the secrets we told. I had no interpretation of what was real or fake. The lines were all blurred, nothing concrete. The only real thing in it was my kids.

I held Erika firmly, still in a shell-shocked state, when the source of the sirens appeared. Two cop cars, their lights flashing, raced towards us. Veering around the corner and barreling down the road flying straight at us. Erika looked up at me.

"Guess this is the end, hey?"

I peered down at her, unsure what exactly she meant? The end of our "friendship", hell yes it was over. The end of our almost romance, yep! The end of the lies, the vicious attack on my life, I sure as hell hoped so. But I couldn't say, I just nodded solemnly.

Her eyes looked sad for a second, and then that weird twinkle came back into them, I didn't recognize her, and she smiled an unnerving, twisted smile. Her cheeks looked increasingly gaunter than ever before and dark circles I'd failed to notice previously shadowed her eyes. I felt my skin crawl, goosebumps rising all up my arms. Then, she bolted.

Wrenching her arms from my grasp, I'm sure tearing the one out from its socket, she leapt in front of the still racing police car.

Thud!

She hit the hood and flipped while rolling up and over the car landing on the pavement, the car behind had no time to react and then...

Crunch!

...as it rolled over her body the sound echoed in my ears. I screamed, mortified!

I ran over as both cars managed to skid to a halt. A fresh puddle of blood formed under the second car's tires. Her limp body lay there, no breaths could be seen rising and falling. Her corpse twisted and mangled, and I'm sure, her skull was crushed.

Her fiery red hair could barely be visualized wedged under the rear tire. The front tire had a smear of blood and brain matter etched in its tread.

I could feel my face go pale and I turned, vomiting regurgitated food all over the road behind me.

The rest was a blur...cops pushing us back, cuffs being strapped on wrists, my kids screaming and crying, yellow tape being flagged up and the cop's fuzzy radio reception calling in an ambulance and coroner.

Sergeant Webb, who had been in the first car, crawled under far enough to check for a pulse, and just as suspected, re-emerged with a dismal expression on his face, his skin tinted a pale green and his lips pursed tight. Likely holding back a surge of vomit like my own.

Chad was able to provide a contact number to the police for our kids to get picked up and stay until statements could be taken.

I was ushered in cuffs into the back of one of the cars once a third showed up, driving up cautiously this time.

Seeing Dustin also in handcuffs being placed in a cruiser, I think I would have normally seen the irony in this particular situation, but in this instance I was numb.

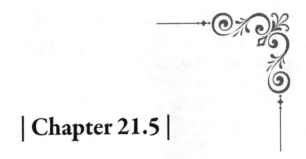

| Chapter 21.5 |

Shit! Sergeant Webb closed the door on me, locking me in the back of his squad car. The sinking feeling in my gut was growing, threatening to swallow me whole.

My life's work, my title and career...gone. Being restrained by men in similar uniforms to your own, is nothing short of ironic. Cuffs and everything, the humiliation was unbearable. And furthermore, I was certain I'd lost Naomi for good too.

Looking through the shatterproof pane, seeing her being loaded into the back of another car, my heart sank. If I could go back and redo this whole fiasco...would I? I wasn't sure. I had been so elated to be with her. Finally, after all those years of waiting and hoping I had gotten a chance. Had I not been thrown under the bus by Erika, things may have worked out...

Sergeant Webb entered the interrogation room several days later. I sat at the gray portable table in my orange jumpsuit like a common criminal. Cuffed and being watched by multiple security cameras in every corner. I had been transported back to my own prison in Kelowna, as the prison in Salmon Arm wasn't made to hold people for lengthy times and they had too many incoming to secure individuals long term. Sergeant Webb had made the trip down here as he was the one in charge of the investigation.

His eyes showed no warmth and not a sliver of empathy for a fellow officer. He held a folder in his left hand and drug his chair across the cement floor, its squeal echoing off the walls.

Swinging his leg around, he sat begrudgingly across from me and slapped the folder on the table before me.

"We have a problem...actually we have a few." I just watched him. There wasn't a lot he could say to me at this point that would perturb me more than I already was.

"I looked into your medical records after we investigated your condominium. We found your medications, Trail. There's no record of you ever reporting your diagnosis or your meds to our facility or your captain. We also obtained a warrant and spoke with your last doctor, Murdoch. He says he warned you that you'd been maxed out on your dosages for some time and it appeared they weren't having their full effect on you any longer. He had recommended you try something else, perhaps even some time off and a cleanse at a ward in order to start you fresh on a new medication. He'd also sent you to see a psychiatrist, who informed us you only came to one session. His findings from that one session were that you had a blurred sense of reality and fantasy, you couldn't tell the difference in some cases at all. Not to mention he noticed your compulsive disorder was amplifying, and you were reverting back to your obsessive behaviors."

He took a long breath and continued.

"Your mental state, which we were unaware of prior to you becoming a cop in the first place, is very troublesome. As it would appear, you lied on the forms getting you into the police academy, making your graduation revocable by law. Given the information provided to me by your GP and psychiatrist, you also would fail your mental examination. We also found evidence of you tampering with and the misuse of police equipment. Tracking people with no warrant issued, not even persons of suspicion, you should know you cannot spy on people Mr. Trail, you've been taught as much. I also took the liberty of checking out your search history, both on your personal computer and work computer. It showed disturbing content to say the least, unfit for an officer of the law."

"I also found these in your glove compartment."

He reached behind him and pulled a small evidence baggy out and tossed it on the table. Its contents a disheveled mess but you could see what they were at first glance. I knew what it was before he even threw it down, and glared at him with disdain. He matched my gaze undeterred.

Naomi's panties. I had kept them as a memento, and stored them in my glove compartment for those long hours at work when I missed her so. Her scent still lingered in the fabric.

"I had the fabric swabbed, the lab sent me the results this morning, hence my trip down here.

Naomi Wilkinson's DNA is on those panties sir, but I'm sure you know that. However, that means worse news for you, as it further incriminates all your other activities in regards to Mrs. Wilkinson."

"It's *FINSTEAD*! Naomi *FINSTEAD*!"

I brazenly corrected him, perhaps raising my voice a little too much.

"Well, by all her records that was her maiden name, yes, but she is still married so her name remains Wilkinson until she decides to change it back. Although I'd say her last name is the least of her concerns at the moment. Or yours."

He stated looking me up and down.

Folding my arms over my chest I leaned back off the table.

"So now what?"

"Like I said, your title and badge will be revoked, charges are being pressed. It appears you will be staying with us for some time, Mr. Trail. I spoke with your lawyer already as well after your initial meeting with him. As the evidence wasn't really arguable, he's looking to try to settle on your behalf. But I'll let the two of you discuss that on your own time. As it stands though, we will need to locate and contact your family to see what can be done about your property and belongings."

I swallowed hard, my cool demeanor now shot.

"We'll be starting you on new medications and therapy as per your prison residence demands it."

Outrage overflowed my body at his words and I lashed at him from across the table. My cuffs held me back to where they were strapped in the iron loop of the floor. A rookie mistake.

"I'm *NOT CRAZY!*"

Feeling my body shake with fury, Sergeant Webb just sat there idle, unbothered by my outburst, like any seasoned officer.

His lack of reaction was enough to make me recoup myself and simmer back into my seat.

"Is it crazy to love someone so much you'd do anything to be with them?"

I asked him directly, as if his answer would validate my actions and he'd dismiss the charges on empathy.

"It is when you've known the individual for as little time as you have known Mrs. Wilkinson. You may have attended secondary school together, but that was years ago. You're not much more than acquaintances at this point. And Mrs. Wilkinson doesn't seem to feel quite as strongly as you...either way, your actions aren't what any sane citizen would have done to sleep with a woman." He responded dismissively.

"She's not just *ANY* woman!" I spat.

"I wish you luck, Mr. Trail, I hope you get the help you need."

With that, he stood up to take his leave. Gathering his folder, papers and evidence baggy off the table before walking out.

I slumped my forehead on the table, a quote I vaguely recalled reading in a novel at some point now resonating within me:

Desire is the kind of thing that eats you and leaves you starving.

Repeating it again and again, I allowed the grief and anguish I felt to swallow me whole, immersing me. Retreating into my mind, my only sanctuary.

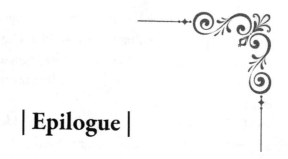

| Epilogue |

The trees whipped by, once again a perpetual blur. The only end being the stretching lengths of blue choppy salt waters when there was a break in the tree-scape. I had rolled the top down on the convertible, and we were enjoying feeling the wind blowing through our hair.

I lifted my left arm, holding it out the side of the car and doing a wave-like motion. The air caught and lifted it as I dipped my hand with its current. Everley seeing me do this, imitated me. A look of astonishment and a large smile crossed her face as her hand soared through the air.

Austin took in the view in his quiet observing way. His sandy hair ruffled as he squinted his eyes against the sun, a faint smile tracing his lips. Aeda sat next to me, DJ-ing for us. She grinned at me as well, pointing out the old stone buildings in the distance. I peeked over my shades to see them better and took the time to really appreciate their beauty.

We had spun a globe, Austin had planted his finger on Greece, and now here we were. At long last, we were traveling, and free.

It had taken us a while. After Erika's death, we all needed time to mourn. I didn't know what I was mourning exactly until I heard the whole truth. But the kids grieved for their "aunt" and I too, felt their pain.

My thoughts wandered as I drove, weaving around the rocky hillside corners alongside the sea line. When Sergeant Webb took my statement and delved into his investigation after my testimony, he came across some very interesting information that connected the dots together. He had collected Erika's phones from the scene where I had thrown them on the ground. With everyone's testimonies including the on-lookers at the beach, her death was deemed a suicide.

On further investigation however, Sergeant Webb also uncovered Erika's medical files. Apparently, she had been diagnosed with cancer two years prior. It was terminal.

She had a large tumor growing in her skull and as it grew the forensic pathologist who performed Erika's autopsy considered all her strange behaviors over the course of the past year and investigated even further. He came to the conclusion that the tumor, being as large as it was, had been pressing on her frontal lobe, causing her to have no control over her behaviors and emotions. Her logical thinking was compromised. As a result, her affection for me took a very volatile turn. She ran on impulse and unhinged emotion. That led to her end sooner than even her doctor had predicted.

This news made my heart ache. To know she had kept her diagnosis hidden from me. I maybe could have recognized the signs, if only I had known... It at least made more sense now, and also her desperation for us to travel together. She must have been doing her bucket list and wanted me to be a part of it, I concluded.

Thinking this was the worst to endure. How I had let her down in her time of need. She had been there for me through all my hardest times and helped me through my pain, and I was unable to return the favor.

Her parents requested she be cremated as per her wishes, and we held a celebration of life for her instead of a formal service. I know she would have preferred that. Her ashes were placed in a gorgeous oak box with a tiny glass ornamental clasp that held some dried flowers. Engraved on the box was her epitaph:

Although your smile is gone forever and your hands we cannot touch, We still have so many memories of the one we loved so much. Your memory is our keepsake with which we'll never part. Heaven has you in its keeping, We have you in our hearts.
Erika L. Crane 1987-2019

Ever since her death I couldn't shake a constant nauseous feeling, sometimes to the point of actually throwing up. I summed it up to all the stress and my own form of PTSD after watching my best friend jump to her death in front of me. I had hoped with time it would eventually fade.

Sergeant Webb called me a few days after taking Dustin in. He wanted to let me know he had looked into Dustin's records and search history. Found his active wire taps and various other misuses of his police equipment. He was stripped of his badge and employment. He was ordered to receive counseling and six months behind bars.

I felt bad for him as well, having dealt with many patients suffering from mental health issues. It's hard when their medications stop working, as they don't usually recognize the changes, and they think they're still taking their medicine so it *should* be working. It was deeper than his pills stopping working though. I guess he had somehow managed to hide his mental status from the police academy and got through all the screenings because his meds were working at that time.

He had very much earned his title. Regrettably though, his deception of not exposing the truth inevitably led to the loss of the job he was so passionate about. We all have skeletons in our closet.

Unfortunately, Dustin's came out and ruined what he'd worked so hard for. Had he done things differently. Been honest and open, who knows, things may have worked out between us. But I'd already done dishonest and I couldn't do it again.

As for Chad, the charges against him were even more severe than I imagined. Due to him showing up at the beach that day he was also given an additional charge of breaching his restraining order. He was charged with assault and battery, as well as attempted murder against me. He was found guilty on all charges and would remain in prison for some time now.

So much devastation all at once. I wanted to escape it all. So with no restrictions, I let the kids pick a place.

We had gotten the money from selling the old family house as per our separation agreement, and I used a small portion of my half to fund our trip.

We had sold my van, and I gave notice for my rental. We sold everything we didn't need, only keeping the necessities, and we left.

As much as we loved Salmon Arm, there was too much sadness there for us now.

I quit my position and applied for travel nursing. When Austin picked Greece, I informed the agency that is where I was looking to work. Low and behold they found a posting for me.

Now here we were a few months later, in early October. My ever-daunting nausea had finally disappeared, and we were in our new convertible cruising the coast line of Greece.

The strength it took to leave everything behind was abundant. Leaving my home, my kid's home, all our memories. Some we wanted to leave behind, however some we would always cherish.

Wanting to stay optimistic, I focused on the biggest change. This new feeling of empowerment I possessed.

All that I'd overcome this past year; finding out my husband was cheating, my divorce, the destructive trifecta, being beaten to a pulp, the loss of my life-long friend, and the end of all the relationships I held dear. I could now fully appreciate that old saying,

It takes the rainiest of days to make us truly appreciate the sunny ones.

I had come out stronger, of that I was sure. I was fitter, felt healthier, finally saw value in myself, and above all I finally appreciated the body I was given.

It may not be perfect. Yes, it had faults, but it was mine. It had endured childbirth three times over and it had recovered. It had carried me through all the days of my life thus far, tolerating all my harsh ridicules of it and my shame without ever failing me, despite my insensitivities to it. It had also recovered from all those injuries I was subjected to and came back fighting harder than ever before. And it was sexy, whether I thought so or not. It was.

Every scar was a symbol of what I'd been through, a badge of honor. Every stretch mark, every laugh line, every roll.

I wished more women could feel this new found confidence as I felt now. I saw beautiful women everywhere, every shape, every size, every age, every color. I knew most of them felt the way I had once felt, not attractive, not up to someone somewhere's standards. But I saw more.

I now knew beauty was more than skin deep. It was the whole package and every woman's package is different, but no less glorious. We each had different priorities, wants, desires, goals. None of it made us any less than what we are.

Sometimes others saw it, sometimes they didn't, but we're all beautiful to someone. When people take the time to see the whole person, they'll discover their true attractiveness.

Dustin and Erika had both seen mine and I had seen theirs.

Regrettably, they both went about getting my affection in the wrong way, and it led to disaster. But I was learning to forgive. Not just them but myself as well and not forget. I wanted to learn from the past and not let it wreak havoc on my future.

I had my children by my side and they were now happy. I may not have found a man, but I had true love all along, Aeda, Austin and Everley.

We were starting a new life, one where we could travel and explore, no limits, no restrictions, no fears. It was a wonderful feeling! Things had been bleak for a time, but good had prevailed. Rewarding us with a new start, and I hoped to make the very most of it.

My kids would study abroad and learn more than they ever would being limited to our public school systems, and their life experiences would be an asset to their futures. I could now give them a life I could have only dreamed of.

I looked over at my eldest Aeda, her hair flying in the wind and we exchanged big smiles.

"You're beautiful, never forget that, hun." I told her, instilling confidence in her.

"You're beautiful too, Momma."

I felt tears of joy brim in my eyes, because for once...I felt it.

Z.M. ALCOCK

| **About The Author** |

Z.M. ALCOCK

Z.M Alcock is a first time author born and raised in British Columbia, CA. She is presently developing a series in erotic romance mystery for adults and is currently in progress writing the second book in the compilation. Current prediction for the world is at least 3 novels but may be more. She spends her days homeschooling her little ones, cooking, and writing. If you get to know her for any length of time, you will figure out what a humorous person she is, and that she thoroughly has a passion for caring for people as well as getting them talking about topics often shamed in society, in an open and casual forum.

If you would love to help her get word out about these stories and you enjoyed them, consider leaving a review on any of the sites you can purchase the book from. Reviews help other readers find work they may enjoy.

The font used in this book is EB Garamond.
http://www.georgduffner.at/ebgaramond/index.html
This book was edited by Creech Enterprises.

Don't miss out!

Visit the website below and you can sign up to receive emails whenever Z.M. Alcock publishes a new book. There's no charge and no obligation.

https://books2read.com/r/B-A-UCVX-LWRHC

BOOKS 2 READ

Connecting independent readers to independent writers.